THE
GRAND

**Get the Water Street Crime Starter Library
FOR FREE**

Sign up for the no-spam newsletter and get *four* full-length ebooks—the thrillers **BLOODY PARADISE**, **FROM ICE TO ASHES**, **TROPICAL ICE**, and **SING FOR THE DEAD**—plus two introductory short stories by the author of **THE GRAND** and lots more exclusive content, all for *free*.

**Details can be found at
the end of *THE GRAND*,
or go here now:
mailchi.mp/waterstreetpressbooks.com/
waterstreetcrimemailinglist**

THE
GRAND

DENNIS D. WILSON

Water Street Press
Healdsburg, California

All the characters in this book are fictitious, and any
resemblance to actual persons living or dead is purely
coincidental.

Published by Water Street Press
Healdsburg, California

Water Street Press paperback edition published 2016

Produced in the USA

Print 978-1-62134-330-1
E-Pub 978-1-62134-331-8
Mobi 978-1-62134-332-5

Cover design by **thecovercollection.com**

Typesetting services by **bookow.com**

For Paula, my muse.

Acknowledgments

It probably seems odd to many people to refer to a political crime thriller as a love letter, but that's how I look at it. This book is the culmination of my life-long love affair with the Tetons, and without the support and faith of many, this story would never have made it from my imagination to the published page.

My agent Elizabeth Trupin-Pulli took a chance on a middle-aged, first-time author when she found something in the story of a Chicago cop who can't let go of the love of his life that touched her heart.

My editor and publisher Lynn Vannucci opened her editor's toolbox and skillfully helped refine my manuscript into a political crime thriller so intriguing that she made it one of the inaugural books of Water Street Crime.

The feedback and encouragement of my Corp of Readers—Paula Carson, Gina Cochran, Dan Kotynski, Katharyn Wheeler, and Mark Wilson—on the early drafts of the book were invaluable.

My wife, Paula Carson, insisted I get off my ass and write the book I had been talking about since I met her, then sent me off to Wyoming on a writing sabbatical that kick started the story. When I returned, on my desk I found a thank you card signed by all of the characters in The Grand—then she endured the months of suffering as the novel wound its way through the publishing gauntlet.

My children Katie, Mark and Megan's embrace of the magic of the Tetons have created mountains of memories that every day add fuel to my literary fire.

A final thank you to Leslie, who first opened my eyes to the Tetons, all those years ago.

"The mountains are calling and I must go."

John Muir

Chapter 1

Senator Thomas McGraw sat back in the hand-distressed, buffalo-hide easy chair and contemplated the room around him. This was his first visit to the brand new, custom-designed mountain home of his lover. When their affair started a little over a year ago, what a sweet and savory surprise it had been to both of them. A business relationship grew into friendship, and then suddenly and unexpectedly exploded into something else—a red-hot, cross-country, obsessive romance fueled by shared erotic tastes. The senator felt sexually liberated under the spell of his exotic lover, and he was pretty sure those feelings were mutual. True, they needed to be discreet for a variety of reasons—indiscretion had nearly cost them everything—but they had worked it out. Although hectic schedules limited their rendezvous to only a couple of weekends a month, the deprivation and anxiety of anticipation made these weekends that much more satisfying. He was generally in a frenzy by the time he could get to her.

The room was the den of a typical ten-thousand-square-foot vacation home of the rich and powerful in Jackson Hole, Wyoming. Decked out in nouveau western, its reclaimed timbers, Wyoming sandstone, and river rock were either complemented by—or detracted from, depending on your esthetic point of view—the original modern paintings depicting bold and most definitely non-earth-toned western landscapes and various forms of neon-colored wildlife. As Tom sipped his twenty-three-year-old Pappy Van Winkle, he studied the visage of a purple and orange moose head sculpted from California mahogany hanging dispiritedly over the fireplace. Damn, any self-respecting Wyoming moose would be embarrassed to know that this is some guy's idea of what a trophy moose should look like. His personal style was more traditional Western—big wooden beams and a glut of real dead animal heads on the walls. But, the sex was still new and novel, unlike anything he had felt before, and he was willing to overlook these stylistic differences for the time being or, who knew, maybe for a long time. As his mentor had told him a long time ago: "Pussy is a powerful motivator."

"I am soooo happy we were able to start our weekend a day early," his lover called from the other room. "I've been so horny this week that I've been bouncing off the walls. I brought back something special for you from Chicago. Just give me another minute, sweetie." Charlotte Kidwell dressed, and undressed, to accentuate her best features: her big green eyes, her long, toned legs, and her perfect bubble butt. Her regular head-to-toe salon appointments, personal trainer, and strict dietary regimen were essentials to the healthy, put-together appearance that women of her age and social status often have, if they have the money and motivation to work at it. In her younger days, her insecure attempts to add sex appeal fell short, and she'd ended up with an oddly unfeminine look with her clumsy and unsuccessful experiments with cosmetics. But middle age had actually softened her features, and as she became more adept at the finer points of female grooming, she began to realize how much she resembled her sister. During what she referred to as "The Sexual Awakening," she had finally developed the confidence in her sexuality to consciously emulate her sister's makeup and dress. Her older sibling had always exuded effortless sexuality, and throughout high school and college had gone through more boys in most years than Charlotte had dated for her entire youth.

The senator had certainly surprised her. Although his belly professed his lust for food and drink and a disinclination for exercise, his face was the opposite, exuding an irresistible cowboy masculinity. At middle age, most people have to choose between a wrinkle-free face and a toned and youthful body. What was it her friend in Chicago called fat? "Nature's botox."

He had chosen his beautiful face at the expense of his body, but that was fine with her, because he was a sexual artiste. Certainly no one who knew him could possibly conceive of the hot spring of sexuality that was percolating beneath his surface. In spite of their distinctly different personalities, she considered him her soul mate. The first man in her forty-four years who had ever laid claim to that title. The thought made her giggle.

"Hurry up, baby, and get your pretty little ass out here."

Appearing in the doorway, she framed herself with the hand-on-the-hip pose so popular with women much younger than herself. "You like? I know this little specialty boutique in Chicago, and it ain't Macy's Intimate Apparel."

He liked the look very much. The red lace push-up bra, matching thong panties, silk kimono, and six-inch stilettos appealed to the man who'd had a weakness for strippers in his younger days. Though the untied robe looked more like a cape than boudoir attire, and the entire outfit reminded him of a porn movie he once saw—*Superslut*, a parody of Superwoman, he had to give her an "A" for effort. "Wow, you look like a very sexy Little Red Riding Hood. And where in the world did you find a bra that makes those pretty little A cups of yours look like Cs? Now turn around and let me admire your world-class bootie."

She did a little twirl for him, grinned, and pushed together her bra cups to emphasize her cleavage. "It's called a miracle bra, and see, it does work miracles. Now you just sit there and sip your whiskey. I have another surprise for you." She strutted over to the bookcase, flipped a switch, and AC/DC's "Shook Me All Night Long" filled the room. And she began to dance.

"Oh my." Tom took a big swallow and relished the burn. "You are just full of surprises tonight."

"Just sit back and enjoy, Senator. I've got a few more surprises coming your way."

Watching her rehearsed moves, the familiar hunger began to stir below his opulent belly. And then, in a maneuver that would have been impressive for a woman of any age, she turned away from him, spread her legs, touched her toes, looked straight up at him from her bare inverted V, and twerked. She had been practicing all afternoon, and when she saw the image of her quivering butt in the mirror she couldn't wait to see his reaction.

"Oh, my god, where did you learn that?" The stirring rising now to a different level. And he was also wondering... her dance routine looked really professional.

"I have a very good friend in Chicago who does this for a living, and she's been giving me some lessons."

"Judging from that pose, sweetie, your friend must be an instructor in 'stripper yoga'." The senator, feeling the fire down there, leaned forward and reached for that perfect ass. "Get over here and let me take you the way I like, the way I know you like." Putting his hands on her bare cheeks and grabbing two hands full, he left his chubby fingerprints as indentations on her flesh. Crazed now, pulling off his pants and underwear but not bothering with his shirt and tie, he pulled her thong aside, mounted her, grunting, sighing. Both of them grunting, sighing, grunting some more. And now just the sounds of flesh slapping flesh. And AC/DC, urging them on...

Hayden Smith was running late. He was always running late. It was common knowledge in town that you had to book every appointment with Hayden an hour early to get him to show up on time. Attorney, county commissioner, real estate broker and developer, owner of a property management company—all that, plus trying to live up to the moniker of Teton County's most eligible bachelor as determined by *Mountain Woman* magazine, well, that could take a toll on a man, even a man as fit and athletic as Hayden. And it was taking its toll on Hayden today. Sometimes he thought there was little point in taking any time off because you had to work twice as hard just to clear your schedule.

The last item of the day on his long list was to make sure all was in order in the home of his newest property management client before their arrival the next morning. But what he really was thinking about, as he put the key in the door, was that he was already an hour late for a dinner date at the home of one of Teton County's richest and most beautiful socialites. And so if he hadn't been fantasizing about the evening's upcoming sensual activities, and if he hadn't assumed that it was his cleaning crew that had left that open bourbon bottle on the counter, and if he hadn't been formulating the words he was going to use to chew Pablo's ass about getting control of his maintenance team, and if he had checked his voicemail after his last two meetings instead of engaging in licentious banter on the phone with the young socialite, then he might have reacted differently to the pounding bass of one of the most iconic rock anthems of the 1980s. He might not have followed the mesmerizing sound of Brian Johnson's sandpaper voice into the den, assuming that he would find some of his employees having an unauthorized party; and he might not have witnessed the sight in front of him that would not only drastically change his life but would also set in motion a chain of events that had the potential to change the course of American history.

If he had looked directly at the man's face, he almost certainly would have recognized one of the most well-known faces in Wyoming, soon to be equally famous throughout America. However, Hayden looked everywhere *but* into his face. The man, still dressed for business on top but naked from the waist down, was humping a pretty redhead doggie style, and Hayden was fascinated that with each thrust, her red stilettos would come off the ground about twelve inches, and then at the end of the thrust, the tips of her heels would bang down on the pine floor. Thrust, bang, thrust, bang, thrust, bang. Later when he played that video clip back in his mind, he captioned it "porn star tap dancing."

He looked all around the room, but his eyes kept coming back to those red shoes, maybe because he didn't really want to look at the man's jiggling ass, or maybe because when his eyes followed those shoes north he was treated to a pair of the finest legs and most delicious bootie that he had ever seen. If he had been thinking clearly, he would have just turned around and walked right out of the house and he would have been able to go back to his great life as Teton County's busiest and most eligible bachelor. But for whatever reason—the shock of the scene, or his own perverse voyeurism—he did not turn back around. He knocked on the door jamb with his clipboard and stammered loudly enough to be heard over AC/DC. "Ah, ah, ah, I thought you weren't coming in until tomorrow. I just came to check on the house. Is everything OK? I mean, just call me if anything isn't OK. Sorry to interrupt. I'll just let myself out..." And then he backed out of the room and nearly sprinted out the door.

Tom jumped up with impressive agility considering his exertion and girth, partly hopping, definitely bobbing. "Oh shit, oh shit, oh shit."

Charlotte rolled over onto her side. "What the fuck, I left him a message that I was coming in today. What was he thinking?"

And the senator just kept repeating, "Oh, shit, oh, shit, oh, shit." Then, catching his breath, added to his mantra, "I'm sure he saw me, I'm sure he saw me, I'm sure he saw me."

His lover, handing him the rest of his twenty-three-year-old Pappy, said, "Here, drink this," trying not to let the panic sound in her voice. She thought for a moment. "We'll call Mario. He'll know what to do. If that asshole tells anyone it'll hurt Mario as much as us. Well, maybe not quite as much as us, but you know what I mean."

Tom sat down for a minute, his white dress shirt soaked through, wheezing from the exertion, from the excitement, from the fear, his heart a thumping kettle drum in his chest. Neither of them said a word for a minute, then two. Finally realizing the heart attack wasn't coming, he took a huge breath and said, "OK, call him."

Charlotte punched the number into her mobile phone. "Mario? Sorry to bother you, but we have a problem. Some asshole just walked in on the two of us. Walked in on us... you know. What do you think we were doing? How could he not recognize him? Yeah, he's my property manager. Hold on. Honey, would you hand me that business card on the table?"

Chapter 2

THE first time Dean Wister had visited the Tetons was twelve years ago, the summer before his senior year in college. Although he said it was adventure he was looking for, it was escape that he was really seeking when he answered an ad to guide for one of the rafting companies that run whitewater trips down the Snake River, just south of Teton National Park. It was a grueling twenty-four-hour drive from his home in Chicago to Jackson Hole, the mountain town at the foot of the spectacular Teton Range, and the route that he was taking, I-90 across Illinois, Wisconsin, and South Dakota, was one of the most monotonous and boring stretches of highway across America. Hour after hour he would stare at the road between truck stops, trying to keep alert for the highway patrol and the erratic driving of drowsy long-distance truckers. He tried listening to music and audio books, but his mind wouldn't let him focus. Lately, he had a lot of trouble focusing. He'd once tried meditation, taking a Transcendental Meditation workshop with his wife, Sara, but meditation wasn't for him. His mind would inevitably wander from the rhythm of his breathing to some problem from work that he was trying to solve. Dean had always been more of a ruminator than a meditator. And so he ruminated for hour after hour. He ruminated about all that had happened over the last twelve years. He ruminated about the horror of the last year. And he ruminated about what the future might, or more importantly, might not, hold.

That first trip had also been a time of transition for him. His mother died after his freshman year in high school, and his dad was killed in a work accident at the lumber yard just before Dean started college. As an only child he had led a solitary existence growing up, but by the time he left for college he was officially an orphan, no parents to cheer him as the starting safety on the University of Illinois football team, and no siblings to share the empty and confused feelings of losing the only responsible adults he had ever known. His hometown of Summersville, West Virginia, was near the banks of the Gauley River, one of the most famous whitewater-rafting rivers in the East, and the gray, small-minded, and cruel little town resembled what Mayberry may have looked like if Andy hadn't been born. Until he was seventeen, Dean had never met a college graduate outside of a classroom, and growing up with his nose stuck in a book most of the time, his peers, and even most of the adults he knew, looked down on his habit as a sign of either homosexuality, laziness, or both. Maybe it was resentment for not living the fantastic and interesting life of the characters in the books that he read, or maybe it was the bullying that he experienced from his literature-averse peers, or maybe it was his sense of insecurity and inferiority from his hillbilly background, or maybe it was just his nature—for whatever reason, there was a well of anger deep inside of Dean.

The bullying stopped the first time he stepped on a football field. He loved to play defense, and putting the hammer to the ball carrier or receiver was equally pleasurable to him, whether in practice or during an actual game. He loved the rush of power he felt when a body crushed beneath him as he delivered the blow. As he would take aim at his target coming across the field, he imagined his body as a sledge hammer and he would launch himself, helmet first, at his opponents, relishing the pain he received nearly as much as the pain he delivered. As his scrawny adolescent body matured into a six-foot, one-hundred-ninety-pound defensive back, his football hits became ever more fearsome, and attracted the attention of a recruiter for the University of Illinois. Football would end for him upon college graduation for, as a pro scout told him, "Son, you sure have the meanness for pro football, but not the speed." But that was all right; football had served its purpose.

The first time his dad had taken him along to run the rapids of the Gauley he was only nine years old, but after that he was addicted to the river. Working as a gofer for one of the rafting companies, imagining himself as one of the cocky swaggering guides, he would do anything to be near the river. The owner of the company took a liking to him, and broke the rules to put him on as a guide at sixteen. He worked on the Gauley through high school and college. But, with the death of his father, West Virginia held too many painful memories; he needed to get away. He heard from some fellow guides that the Snake River in Wyoming, south of Jackson, could be fun. Sure, its mostly Class 2 and 3 rapids were nothing compared to the Gauley, but he had always wanted to see the Rockies, and it was about as far away from West Virginia as he could imagine. That summer on the Snake, in the Tetons, revealed another side that he didn't know he had. He learned how to cap that well of anger, to regulate the flow, to use it instead of letting it use him, and for the next decade was able to let it out only when his job demanded it. He discovered that there was another well, an untapped well, within him. A well of love and sweetness, of kindness and generosity. And the auger that tapped that well was Sara.

He'd just sent some food back at the Pioneer Grill, the coffee shop in Jackson Lake Lodge in Teton National Park. His order of sautéed Rocky Mountain rainbow trout appeared on his plate as buffalo meatloaf. His anger rising at this inexcusable display of disrespect and incompetence, he called over the pretty blonde server and pointed at the food in front of him. "Miss, do you think you would recognize a Rocky Mountain rainbow trout if you saw one?" She'd looked first at the gravy-smothered brown glob, and then directly into his twisted angry face, and behind her best smile said, "Apparently not, but I can recognize an asshole when I see one."

Dean was overmatched by the spunky girl with eyes of a deeper blue than the summer skies over the Grand Tetons, and he fell in love on the spot. They laughed at the story forever, and she still called him "meatloaf asshole" on occasion, either when she was feeling especially fond or, more often, particularly annoyed with him. She loved to tease him and ridicule his quirks, calling him "schizo" for the many paradoxical elements in his personality: jock /intellectual, hot head/sentimentalist, loner/ showoff. But when she would call him "schizo" and flash him her irresistible smile, it would always soften his mood, and he was able to laugh at himself.

As a trust-fund baby of a power couple in Chicago's legal community, Sara's suburban childhood was exactly the opposite of Dean's. Her bookworm ways were admired by her parents, friends, and her community. The vivacious blond with the sharp wit and the ability to fit in with every social group was a psych major at the University of Chicago, less than a two-hour drive up the interstate from Champaign if you are a hormone-crazed college boy, more like three hours for everyone else. Her well of anger was only a fraction of Dean's and reserved exclusively for bullies and people who abused children, animals, and the less fortunate. But if you happened to occupy that territory, her fierceness could make even Dean flinch.

When he thought of their first summer, it played back in his head like some film made from a Nicolas Sparks novel. As he watched the movie, alone in the theater seat of his Jeep Cherokee, he smiled at the "meet cute" first scene in the coffee shop, marveled at the on-location, awe-inspiring backdrops of the Snake and the Tetons, was moved to tears by the scene where he makes love to Sara for the first time. And he couldn't criticize the filmmaker's decision to leave every love scene of the summer in the movie. There they are making love on the window seat in the tiny apartment shared by Dean and his four other river rat roommates. There they are making love after a picnic at Schwabacher's landing, the Tetons reflected like a painting in the beaver pond. And there they are on their last day of the summer, on a picnic in the alpine meadow they had discovered on their long hike into the mountains. The meadow they had named "Sara's Meadow." The meadow where Dean proposed. The meadow they pledged to return to each year on their anniversary. They talked of it often, and relived the moment every year on that special day. But they never came back. Life, and careers, and bullshit got in the way.

Careers included the single-minded ambition they shared. Dean's resulted in a meteoric rise to detective in the Chicago Police Department and, after being handpicked to join the Midwest Organized Crime Task Force as the only local police detective among FBI and ATF agents, his days and weeks became an unending blur of clues, criminals, and cases. Sara's graduate degree at Northwestern led to a tenure track appointment at Loyola University. But tenure track meant running never-ending, back-to-back-to-back marathons of teaching, research, and publishing. It seemed the little time they had together was spent discussing Dean's cases, as Sara served as his in-house consultant to analyze the psychological profiles of his suspects. Their career ambitions allowed no room for children, or travel, or a return to Sara's Meadow.

And then, over the last year, came the bullshit. Dean was working eighty-hour weeks on a high-profile case involving government and police corruption, and many of the Chicago cops whom he considered friends turned away from him. And then, just when they thought they were getting close to breaking the case, the investigation was shut down and he was reassigned. He was exhausted, disappointed, stressed, and his friends treated him like a traitor.

And then there was Sara. She had been diagnosed with cancer just as Dean began the investigation from hell. After her initial treatment, she received a clean report, and he was too preoccupied to notice when she continued to lose weight. A check-up a few months later showed that the cancer had returned. The rebound was aggressive, additional treatment failed to stop the spread, and she continued to get weaker and weaker in spite of what she would call "frequent invitations for happy hour cancer cocktails with my oncologist." She even made up names for the cocktails based on the side effects she would experience afterward. There was the Diarrhea Daiquiri, the Migraine Martini, and the Vomit-rita. No subject was out of bounds for her wicked and irreverent sense of humor. Once, when she was bedridden near the end, Dean asked her how she was feeling, and in her best Sally Field Mama Gump imitation, she said "Well, Forrest, I've got the cancer."

Dean wanted to take a leave to stay at Sara's bedside, but she made up her mind that that was not an option. And when Sara made up her mind about something, he had learned to let her have her way. So Dean was relegated to spending every hour that he wasn't working by her side, holding her close, imagining how they would live their lives differently when she was well.

The night she died, she asked him to describe that day in Sara's Meadow. And when he finished, she said, "Promise we can go there when I get well. Will you take me there next summer?" He nodded, unable to speak. She slept peacefully that night for the first time in quite a while, and in the morning she was gone.

Strangely, although she was the center of his universe, the only person that he could say he ever truly loved, he showed little emotion when she died. He didn't cry. He felt almost as if he were an outside observer of these terrible events. He experienced only numbness. An unrelenting, withering numbness. A numbness interrupted only by random bursts of anger that disturbed even the hardened cops he worked with. Dean was not unaware of his problem, and tried to channel the anger by hooking up with Manny Cohen, a mixed martial arts coach and self-proclaimed king of "Jew-Jitsu". He loved the physicality of the MMA bouts, and that the jiu-jitsu moves he learned permitted him to disable much bigger and stronger fighters, even if he was on the ground being pummeled. He justified the training as part of his law-enforcement skills, but he knew what it was really about—the ability to inflict some of the horrible hurt he was feeling on others.

The changes in Dean since Sara's death were most troubling to his boss, Carlos Alvarez. Carlos had been crushed when, on the verge of busting a Chicago mob guy who had both political and police connections, which evidently reached all the way to Washington, the whole operation had been shut down. In his heart, he knew it was those same connections he was investigating that had defeated him. He looked at Dean and watched one of the most competitive spirits he had ever known flicker out, starved for the oxygen that Sara could no longer supply. The case they had put their hearts and souls into for the last year was ripped out of their hands and Dean, who normally would be just as pissed off as he was, seemed to be only going through the motions.

But the most disturbing problem, as far as he was concerned, was Dean's refusal to mourn Sara. Carlos watched as Dean's isolation became extreme, and he refused all offers to talk or socialize. Dean's robotic demeanor and increasingly unpredictable violent outbursts were scaring him. When Carlos sent him to meet with the psychologist assigned to their department, he refused to cooperate. He insisted that he was fine. But Carlos knew he wasn't fine. He saw a man on the brink of a breakdown and finally decided that drastic action was needed to rescue the man from himself. One morning he walked into Dean's office and handed him a letter worded as an authorization, which was actually an order, to take a three-month leave of absence.

"But where will I go? What will I do?" Dean said, seemingly incapable of entertaining any change to his barely functional routine.

Carlos looked toward the picture on his desk, the one taken twelve years earlier. It showed Dean standing on a whitewater raft. Sara was sitting in the boat looking up at him with a combination of love and lust in her eyes. In the background, the grandeur of the Tetons loomed. "You have to get out of town. You have to get away from here, from all this. And I know where I would go if I had no obligations and three months off. I've been envying that picture since the day you moved in here."

What his boss didn't know, and what Dean couldn't tell him, or anyone else for that matter, was the real reason that he wouldn't see the psychologist—something that would make him seem crazy to outsiders. Hell, he often had that thought about himself. Not every evening, but maybe two or three nights a week, he would spend the night with Sara. He would wake up a couple of hours after he went to sleep, and she would be there, sitting in the chair next to his bed. He would get up, and they would talk just like they used to, about everything, what was happening in his life and in his job, or what was going on in the news. They would make love, and it was every bit as passionate and real as before she was sick. When he would wake up in the morning, she would be gone. At first, he tried to convince himself that it was all a dream, until one night he washed the sheets before he went to bed, and the next morning her perfume lingered on the bedding. She was really there, and she was as real as anything he had ever experienced.

He had nothing against psychologists. He had seen a therapist in college after a particularly hard break-up and had found it very helpful. In fact, he visited that same therapist when Carlos was pushing him to see the department shrink—he wasn't about to have his craziness officially certified to his employer. And his own therapist confirmed what he instinctively knew himself. "Your hallucinations of your dead wife will go away when you allow yourself to fully mourn her." But that was exactly the problem. Her very real apparition was the only tangible thing he had left of her. Her visits were the only thing that let him get through the day, that kept him from becoming totally out of control, and he wasn't going to let anyone take that away from him. He was determined to hold on to whatever was left of her, for as long as he could.

Sara was the one that convinced him to take the trip. She told him during one of their nocturnal visits that he could use the time off; that she knew he was stressed out. He agreed on one condition. That she would come with him. She gave him her mischievous smile, the one that had captured him that first day in the coffee shop, and said, "That's not a problem. I'm not going without sex for three months. And the ghosts here are too creepy to sleep with."

That first summer twelve years ago, he had come into town from the south, getting off I-80 west of Rock Springs, approaching Jackson via Alpine and driving up through the Snake River canyon so that he could view the white-water section he would be working. Wyoming is mostly high plains except for the northwestern part, which is an endless vista of scrub grass, prickly pear, sage brush, with occasional red-rock battleships and gargoyles. On that first trip he was able to view the Wind River Range in the distance outside his window, but he didn't really get a good view of the Teton Range until he reached the outskirts of the town of Jackson.

This time he had decided to take the Northern route via I-90, because he wanted to see the Black Hills, one of the few topographic areas of interest that is easily accessible from the interstate. So he was not really prepared for what happened when his Jeep rounded the bend on Route 26, east of Teton National Park, and he looked west. The fragrance hit him first. He had the windows in his Jeep rolled down and, as the road increased in elevation, the air turned cooler and became infused with snow runoff blended into mountain streams and the bouquet of lodgepole pine forests to form the unique perfume that his unconscious associated with his first summer there. He was looking down for a station on the radio when he felt the jolt, as if a switch was flipped in his brain, and when he turned his face back to the road, the windshield was suddenly and magically filled with the panorama of the majestic purple, snow-tipped peaks of the mountain range that symbolized all that had been true and pure in his life. All that was lost and would never ever return.

The image struck him like a bullet in his chest, sucking all the air from his body. The next thing he knew, he was out of his car, on the side of the road, on his knees, gasping for air, heaving, sobbing. "Oh, Sara. My sweet, sweet, Sara."

Chapter 3

THE Teton County Sheriff stood next to her Jeep, her hazel eyes following the gap in the guardrail, down the earthen scar to the bottom of the slope. A late-model sedan rested upside down in the Snake River, only its wheels uncovered by the churning waters. A Wyoming highway patrolman stood next to her, and together they watched the paramedics move a gurney along the river bank to reach the launch where their ambulance waited.

"At first light, we got a call from a passing car," the patrolman said. "Looks like some time during the night he hit a deer, lost control and went over the ledge. Took the deer with him— it's halfway down the bank and has part of his fender attached to his antlers. Both of them were long dead by the time the paramedics got here. Most likely he was knocked unconscious and drowned—he was still strapped into his seat belt when they pulled him out."

Danella Cody had been the Teton County Sheriff for the last ten years. She was a tall woman, and still possessed the athletic build that made her an all-conference power forward at the University of Wyoming. Her face, as wide and welcoming as the Wyoming sky, and her garrulous personality were definite advantages for an elected law enforcement official, but her gender often led her overwhelmingly male "clientele," as she referred to them, to severely underestimate her ferocity. Making the unfortunate decision to resist arrest, they'd find themselves face down on the ground, hogtied with a face full of dirt, wondering what the hell had happened. That toughness had allowed her to be accepted in the all-male Sheriff's office, but she was not under any illusions, she needed to prove her toughness every day, and her strategy was nearly the opposite of walk softly and carry a big stick; it was more like "talk tough, but act fairly." Sheriff Cody was only the second female chief law enforcement officer in Teton County, and the first since 1920, when the women of Jackson Hole, just after the ratification of the 19th amendment, took to the polls and elected a female mayor and all female town council, which at the time was thought to perhaps foreshadow a national electoral revolution. The route Sheriff Dani had followed to become the chief law enforcement officer of Teton County had been a quite traditional one. Her family had been ranchers in the valley for over a hundred years, their homestead founded by her great-great-great grandfather, who'd been one of the thousands of cowboys roaming the West after the Civil War. Land was free, or nearly so, in this remote valley in the late 1800's, but today Teton County is one of the richest in the country, and the family ranch was worth millions. Her perfect-sounding Western surname was owed to her grandfather Vincentas Codikov, a Lithuanian immigrant who'd wooed her grandma and been forced to shorten his name to sound more American as a condition of their nuptials.

Sheriff Dani, as everyone called her, had risen quickly through the ranks at the Sheriff's office after she graduated from the University of Wyoming, a rise attributable not only to her skills, but also to the high turnover in the force due to the astronomical cost of housing in the county. She knew that not everyone was a fan of a female sheriff, and some referred to her as the Queen of Teton County after she'd run unopposed in the last election. Most of Wyoming is as red as Alabama clay, but Teton County is almost like a foreign country within the state, occupied by wealthy progressive, tree hugging, NGO founders, conservationists, and young people looking to experience the outdoors, and they were perfectly open to electing a personable, smart, tough talking, homegrown female. They aren't all liberals in Teton County, but even the Republicans are socially aware. Teton County is a colony of the last surviving Rockefeller republicans, of which Dani was a member.

Sheriff Dani's eyes didn't move from the wreck in the river. "Any ID?"

The patrolman was busy scraping the mud off his hiking boots, the official footwear of the Wyoming highway patrol who cruise the thirty-mile stretch through the Snake River from Jackson south to Alpine. "Ma'am, the car's a rental out of Avis at Salt Lake City airport. The deceased has an Illinois driver's license. That's why I called you in. No warrants on him, but it seems he has quite a criminal record in Chicago. Called my supervisor and he said to hand it over to you, that you would probably be interested in what the hell this guy was doing out here. I'll file the accident report. We'll send his records over to your office."

"Shit." Dani knew damned well why the highway patrol was pushing the case back on her. She'd raised holy hell when one of the investigations last year had been compromised by an overlapping state investigation and had taken the issue all the way up the chain of command in Cheyenne. She'd told them, "They'll be no state investigations in Teton County without my knowledge." She'd been a grizzly protecting her cub. Under normal circumstances she'd have been happy to take over the investigation, but there were only four detectives in the department, and one was recuperating from bypass surgery, and another was in the hospital in Idaho Falls with a fractured pelvis from a nasty fall while rock climbing. Neither was going to be back any time soon. And this was the middle of the busy tourist season. "OK, I'll call the

ME and tell him to send the autopsy report to me. You documenting the accident scene?"

"Yes, ma'am. I'll write it up and email you the report and the pictures. I'm having the car towed in a little bit."

Dani trudged back to her car. *It's going to be a long summer season*, she thought.

Joanie Marks's smile bothered some people, as it made her seem unnaturally and perpetually happy, which to some seemed an indication of insincerity or dullness, but she was far from either, and she flashed that smile as she always did when Dani marched into the office in Jackson.

"The file just came in on the deceased guy from Chicago. Also, you have a call from a man by the name of Carlos Alvarez from a Federal agency"—she looked down at her notes to get it right—"from the Midwest Organized Crime Task Force. He wants to talk to you. Want me to get him on the phone?"

"Having a bad day, Joanie?" Dani liked to tease her assistant about her relentless cheeriness, but down deep she really appreciated the antidote to her own realism that often teetered on pessimism. "Give me ten minutes to look at the file, then get him on the phone," Dani said.

The Sheriff wasn't fond of Chicago. To Dani, Chicago and Illinois represented dirty cops, dirty politicians, dirty streets, and dirty air. Never mind that Dani had never visited Chicago and had never even met a Chicago law enforcement officer. She'd read a magazine article once that had chronicled so many sordid stories of crooked cops, politicians, and judges in the Land of Lincoln that she half-way believed Al Capone was probably one of the good guys there when he was alive, that maybe his real crime had been not paying off the right people. Dani picked up the file on her desk that described the dead man in the river.

Edward Torino was forty-two years old and lived at an address Dani deduced might be on Chicago's Northwest side, judging only from the fact that the address was on Northwest Highway. In the twenty-four years since Edward's eighteenth birthday, he had spent fourteen of them in prison, though he had been out of prison nearly three years at the time of the accident; maybe he was turning his life around— he did have a completely clean driving record. The file Dani was looking at fit perfectly the Wyoming sheriff's notion of a Chicago hood: youthful arrests for assault, auto theft, and petty thievery; adult convictions for assault, attempted murder, and armed robbery. The desk phone buzzed. "Carlos Alvarez on line one."

"Am I speaking with Danella Cody, Sheriff of Teton County?" The formal voice on the other end had a slight Hispanic accent. The Hispanic population of Teton County was about fifteen percent and, like the rest of the country, it was growing rapidly. Dani was well aware

that this group was the single largest demo-
graphic voting bloc in the county and she discreetly courted the Hispanic vote. Securing the
support of Hispanics without alienating the
Republican and anti-immigration electorate of
the county was one of her biggest balancing
acts. But the truth was that she truly enjoyed
the hospitality, old-world manners, and family
values of the Hispanic community.

"Yes, sir, how can I help you?"

"This is Carlos Alvarez of the Midwest Organized Crime Task Force. I doubt that you
have heard of us. We're a small group based
in Chicago, comprised of federal and local law
enforcement officials that work on a number of
select cases that require focused interagency
resources. The Chicago police department
called me this morning and said that a person by the name of Edward Torino was killed
in a car crash in your county last night?"

"That's right. Looks like he hit a deer and
flipped his car down a canyon into the Snake
River. Probably drowned, but we won't know for
sure until we get the autopsy back." The Feds.
There must be more going on here than a car
wreck.

"Mr. Torino has been involved in several cases
that we've worked over the years. I have no idea
why he might be in your county. But we would
definitely be interested in seeing whatever was
on his person, taking a look at his cell phone if
he had one with him, and being kept abreast of
what you find in his car."

Maybe this Alvarez could help after all. "I'd be happy to turn the case over to you, Mr. Alvarez. How soon can you get someone out here?"

Alvarez was wary. Was Cody being sarcastic? He wasn't sure, but he was used to local officers getting in a snit when his federal agency got involved. He didn't want the Sheriff to think he was taking over the case. And he, frankly, didn't have resources to spare for what might turn out to be just an auto accident. "Oh, no. We have no interest in taking over the investigation. Right now, this looks just like a car accident. And Mr. Torino isn't a subject of any active investigation. I just wanted to give you some background. And I wanted to ask you for a favor."

"What's that?" The biggest favor Dani could think of was that Alvarez would take the whole thing off her hands.

"We have an agent, happens to be vacationing in your area. His name is Dean Wister. He's very familiar with Torino. Maybe I could send him over? He could look at the car, Mr. Torino's possessions, and his cell phone. We just want to make sure he wasn't carrying anything incriminating that could help us with anything we're working on in Chicago."

Dani paused for a minute. This whole conversation was strange, and she was becoming skeptical of everything about Alvarez. Clearly there was something Alvarez wasn't saying. But she could use another set of hands and eyes. "Sure, have him contact me today and I'll get him set up."

"Thank you very much, Sheriff Cody. If you need anything else from me, don't hesitate to call. Miss Marks has my number."

Dani hung up the phone and sat and thought. *We have a Chicago low life, probably a Mafia-connected guy, dead in the river. Unless he was out here with his family on vacation, chances are he was up to no good. The Feds suspect that, too, or they wouldn't be calling me.* The more she thought, the more it looked like maybe she could have it both ways. Dani smiled and called out, "Joanie. If a guy named Dean Wister calls, he works for Alvarez. Put him through to me right way."

Chapter 4

DEAN Wister sat in Sheriff Cody's office in an uncomfortable metal chair in front a large and cluttered metal desk. He thought the decor was odd. Every other building—the retail shops, the grocery stores, even the Kmart—was decorated in tourist Western, logs, rough-hewn beams, and the Wyoming bronco rider logo on everything. The furnishings of this office shouted army surplus 1955—gray metal desks, tables, filing cabinets. The only nod to their current location was a huge elk head mounted on the wall. With a full rack and a bonus antler sticking straight out from the middle of the animal's head, the elk looked as if he had a rhino in the family tree somewhere. Joanie brought in a giant mug of coffee. "I understand you're on vacation, Mr. Wister. Is this your first time here?"

"Actually, I was here about a dozen years ago. Worked as a river guide one summer when I was in college."

"You here with your family?" Joanie asked, giving him a big smile.

Dean wondered if she was sizing him up for herself or for one of her friends. She was a little old for him, and it was just a fleeting thought, the kind of not really serious fantasy that devoted married men indulge in almost every day. "No family, just me. Thought I would see how things have changed. Seems they haven't changed much at all."

"It's true. They haven't torn the mountains down. But there sure are a lot more houses and condos and development here in the last ten years."

Sheriff Cody appeared at the door, gave Joanie a glance and she discreetly disappeared, closing the door. "Mr. Wister. Pleased to meet you."

"Please, call me Dean. Nice elk head. You take him yourself?"

"And you can call me Dani, or Sheriff Dani if you prefer, we're pretty informal here. No, that's not my trophy. I'm not much of a hunter. Bought Elmer at an estate sale. Thought I should have something Western in here. Dean, I thought you were from Chicago, you sound like you're from Tennessee."

"I grew up in West Virginia. Went to school in Illinois and ended up in Chicago. I'm afraid I never completely lost my accent. But when I go back home, they all say I sound totally Chicago."

"West Virginia." Dani thought of what she associated with West Virginia. "You like Bluegrass?"

"Let's see. Do I like Bluegrass?" Dean considered the question. "Do you mean West Virginny Bluegrass, like the Samples Brothers, Hazel Dickens and the Lilly Brothers? Or are you talking about the Jackson Hole Newgrass I've been listening to in the bars here all summer, like Steam Powered Airplane, One Ton Pig and Poot McFarlin? To tell you the truth I kind of like them all. But don't tell that to my relatives back in Honeysuckle Hollow."

Dani laughed. "I guess you're a little more hillbilly than Chicago then and that's more than OK with me." Then she paused and began what seemed to be a rehearsed monologue. "Mr. Wister, I mean Dean, I'm not sure how familiar you are with the demographics of Teton County. Our county covers over four thousand square miles and some of the richest and most powerful folks in the country are full-time or part-time residents. Because of Teton National Park, and Yellowstone just to the North, and because of the most extraordinary mountain range anywhere in this country, our county attracts—and when I say attracts, I mean attracts like one of them super magnets that they use in *nucular* research—an amazing cast of characters. We got movie stars, billionaire businessmen, cabinet members, and we also have ranchers, shopkeepers, transients, ski bums, tree huggers, mountain climbers and, in the summer time we have the added burden of a couple million people passing through here on their way to Teton or Yellowstone Park. Now I am entrusted with the sworn duty of protecting all these folks from any harm which may come from each other, themselves, the animals they try to kill or may get killed by, the mountains or rivers they might fall off of or run into or get lost in, and any and all the other dumb ass things people do when they are in close proximity with people who have much more, or much less than they do. Now, Dean, I'm a very straightforward woman and I generally just come out and say what I mean. That may not be what you're used to back in Chicago, but that's the way I run my office and people out here seem to appreciate it. Now, I want to apologize in advance if I seem rude. But it's not rudeness, just directness. I am going to ask you a direct question, and I expect you to give me a direct answer."

Dani paused, as if asking Dean's permission, and Dean nodded, wondering where the hell this was going.

"Are you chasin' him or is he chasin' you?"

"What?"

Dani thought she'd had been perfectly clear and repeated the question, this time a little louder, a little slower, and a little more force-fully, as if this would import clearer meaning to Dean. "Are you chasin' him or is he chasin' you?"

Running the risk that his response might put him in an endless loop, Dean took the risk any-way. "I'm afraid I'm not sure what you mean."

"Here's the way I see it. I have me a dead Chicago gangster at the bottom of the Snake

River. If he was on vacation with his family then they probably would have reported him missing by now and no one has called reporting their husband or daddy missin'. So I'm assumin' he was not here on vacation. And by some incredible coincidence, you're here at the exact same time, on vacation. Now I am going to repeat my very direct question, and I would appreciate the professional courtesy of an equally direct answer. Are you chasin' him, or is he chasin' you?"

Dean could feel his face reddening, that familiar burn of rage he was seemingly born with working its way from his gut to his brain and out his mouth. "Sheriff, you don't know me, and I don't know you. Until I got here, I hadn't had a day off in over a year. And I've been out here the last month or so to get some peace and quiet. I got a call about an hour ago from my boss in Chicago, and he said that this guy, a guy that I know from some previous cases, was dead in a car wreck and he wondered if I would come over here and take a look at a few things and see if there's anything that I could help you out with. I am definitely not out here chasing anybody, and I can't think of any reason anyone would be chasing me. So if you don't want my help, just say so and I will walk out that door, get in my Jeep, and drive up to Yellowstone today like I was planning."

Dani softened. "So you're not out here working a case?"

"Nope."

"And you can't think of any reason that this Torino guy would be following you?"

"Nope."

"In your gut, what do you think he was doing out here?"

"Well, he doesn't have any family. And he's not an outdoorsman. But from time to time we have tracked his travels, and there were three occasions when he left Chicago."

"And where was he headed to those times?"

"Never to the Rocky Mountains. Florida once, Detroit once, and Cleveland once." Dean paused and smiled at the sheriff. "And although we can't prove it, we're pretty sure we knew what he was doing on those occasions."

"And what was that?"

"Murder."

The contents of the items on Edward Torino's body and his car were spread out on a table in front of Dean in a room in the basement of the Teton County Sheriff's office. It had amused Dean to drop the "hit man" bomb on the sheriff. Especially after Dani's "Are you chasin' him or is he chasin' you" speech. Sheriff Dani had looked stunned. And all of a sudden everyone couldn't be more helpful to Dean. It wasn't hard to understand why. A hit man had come to town, and Dean had the resources and knowledge of the hit man's network to potentially find out his target. And if Dean was in charge of the investigation instead of the Sheriff of Teton County, the Feds could always be blamed if things went wrong. Even better, it wouldn't be hard for Dani to claim the credit in the local press if things went right. Dean had experienced this before and it was fine with him as long as he got what he needed. The last five weeks of exploring had been fun. He had acclimated to the altitude and long daily hikes in the mountains had gotten him in the best physical shape of his life. But the truth was, he had cleared his head, at least a little, and now he was bored. The circumstances of Torino's death had intrigued him and gotten his juices running. And convincing Carlos that he was rested and willing to go back to work wasn't as hard as he'd expected.

He had prepared an inventory of the items found in the rental car and on the body: a wallet containing an Illinois driver's license; ATM card; VISA card; five hundred and fifty-seven dollars in cash, mostly twenties; frequent player's card from Rivers Casino, DesPlaines, IL; maps of Utah and Wyoming; car rental documents from Avis, Salt Lake City Airport; and a key chain containing ten assorted keys on a "StarButts Vegas" key chain.

Had Torino completed his mission or was his target still alive, unaware that the man sent to kill him was taken out by a curvy road, a steep hill, a fast moving river, and a reckless mule deer? Was the secret to Torino's mission contained on this table? Probably not, Dean thought, but it was a place to start. Dean considered the contents. What was missing? No possible murder weapons, no cell phone. Seldom would you find a person of Torino's age traveling without a cell phone. Lack of a cell phone by itself was incriminating. He would have thrown away the burner after he committed the crime, maybe even called who hired him to confirm the hit. There didn't appear to be any blood in the car, but the evidence technician had gotten some fingerprint samples and was matching those, along with a few hair strands on the seats, either to Torino, or possibly Torino's unknown victim.

Dean thought about the first time he'd met Eddie Torino. It was his first real case after he made detective nearly eight years ago, right after Thanksgiving. There had been a rash of UPS packages disappearing from suburban home porches. Turned out that Torino and a couple of his buddies were following UPS delivery trucks in a van of their own all day, every day. Packages left on the porch for absentee homeowners were scooped up by Eddie and his crew and stashed in the van, and they would move on to the next delivery. Given the pattern of the theft, it was pretty clear what was happening, so Dean held a short training session for the UPS drivers to show them how to detect a tail. Sure enough, on the twelfth day of the investigation, a UPS driver called in a suspicious white van following him. Dean caught up to the UPS truck and the white van and followed them through the streets of suburban Chicago for the rest of the day, observing the UPS deliveries, and watching the plain white panel van as it pulled in front of the houses and made the package pickups. That evening, Dean was waiting when Torino returned home. His house and attached two-car garage were filled floor to ceiling with Christmas presents: televisions, computers, blenders, mixers, toaster ovens, microwaves, fruitcakes, mobile phones, hams, jewelry, gift cards, lingerie, video games and consoles—a complete cross-section of American holiday consumerism all in one place. The Chicago *Tribune* dubbed the story "The Twelve Darkest Days of Christmas." Eddie had spent the holidays in Cook County jail and the next three years in a federal prison, received the Chicago mob-worthy nickname, Eddie "The Grinch" Torino, and Dean began building his rep as a pretty savvy detective, in spite of a speech pattern that seemed like a foreign language to the rest of the Chicago police force.

The next step was to get his data analyst back in Chicago to start working his magic with the organized-crime database. There was clearly a Chicago-Teton County link and the Task Force had access to the FBI's sophisticated database that contained detailed information on all individuals and their associates that had been involved in recent investigations. Dean's thoughts were interrupted by Sheriff Dani calling out to him: "Dean, let's go. I think we might have found Torino's victim."

Chapter 5

HAYDEN Smith's office was in a gray-clapboard office building just off Jackson Town Square that housed a Reiki practitioner and a taxidermist as well as Hayden Smith, LLC: Attorney, Real Estate Brokerage, and Property Management. When Dean and the sheriff rolled up they found a deputy standing guard outside the front door. Several people, who Dean assumed worked in the building or nearby, were milling around outside as their patrol car pulled in.

Deputy John Rogers looked relieved when he saw them, nodding toward the woman dabbing her eyes in a chair just inside the door, obviously upset and in distress. "One of the real estate agents, Kate Wheeler, found Jordy Smith, Hayden Smith's assistant, when she came in this morning. The front door was unlocked, the lights were off, and his body was in the back room. Looks like a single gunshot to the chest. The evidence tech is on his way. We tried Hayden's home and cell phone, but his cell phone goes straight to voicemail, and no one picks up at his residence. We've got someone there now, but no one answers the door."

Sheriff Dani and Dean walked into a large open-area office that was divided into about a dozen small cubicles. Nothing looked disturbed. With the exception of the large framed photographs of mountain homes hanging on the walls, the space resembled a real estate office that could be found anywhere else in the country. They walked quickly to the private office in the back. That office had been ransacked and, amongst the emptied drawers and scattered mounds of paper, a rust-haired man lay on his back in a pool of blood, his pale blue eyes in a fixed stare. The Sheriff and Dean kneeled and looked quietly at the body for a moment. "This isn't Hayden?" Dean asked. "Looks a lot like the picture of the real estate guy in the front window."

"Jordy is Hayden's cousin. He's about ten years younger than Hayden. Most agents never change their picture after they get into the business. We've got some seventy-year-old female real estate agents in town who look like they're still using their high school prom pictures. But, yes, there is a strong family resemblance."

They spent a few minutes looking around the office, but there were no obvious clues, no bloody fingerprints or footprints. No signs of forced entry. "Let's talk to Kate," Dean said.

Kate Wheeler was an attractive, perfectly coiffed woman and, like many real estate brokers in the upscale Jackson Hole resort market, had had enough cosmetic surgery so as to be of indeterminate age. She looked as though she was about to cry but was holding back to save her eye makeup. "Kate," the sheriff began softly. Dean recognized the tone. This was the caring, compassionate cop-voice. Dean had one himself that he took out in situations just like this. "Kate, this is Dean Wister, and he's going to be working with me on this. I know this is difficult, but we need to ask you a few questions."

Kate coughed and seemed to regain her composure. "I can't believe it. Who would do such a thing?"

"That's what we're going to find out, Kate. I promise you that. What time did you get here and how did you find him?"

"Well, I'm showing properties later today and I came in to print out listings and make some appointments. I got here about an hour ago. Our office isn't officially open until ten, but the door was unlocked. I thought nothing of it because Jordy is often here early and opens the office."

"Did you notice anything at all amiss or unusual? Did you see anyone at all in the area, coming or going, when you got here?"

"No, nothing at all. I said, 'Good morning, Jordy.' I could see the light on in his office. He didn't answer, so I walked back there, and there he was." Her voice quivered.

"Kate, do you keep any money or other valuables in the office?"

"Not really. I think Hayden keeps about two hundred in petty cash in the top desk drawer. But we don't keep any other money or anything here."

Dean spoke up. "Ma'am, do you know if Jordy had any enemies, or any friends or associates who might not be the most savory characters, if you understand my meaning?"

"No, not at all. Jordy is the sweetest young man in the world. I can't imagine why anyone would want to do this."

"How about Hayden... does he have any enemies?"

"Well, of course, everyone loves Hayden, too. Except, you know, Fletcher."

"Dean is new here, Kate. He doesn't know Fletcher, but I'll fill him in later. When was the last time you saw or talked to Hayden?"

"I haven't seen him for about a week. I've been out of town. But I talked to him the day before yesterday and he seemed fine."

"This sort of thing is a big shock. And you may remember things in an hour, a day or a week, that you don't recall just now. If you remember any little detail at all that seems unusual, you give me a call, OK?"

"OK. Can I go home now?"

"Sure, and it might be best if you didn't talk about what you saw here today. Not just to the press, but to your fellow agents and friends, too. This is an active investigation and we don't want information getting out until we catch the guy."

As she got up to leave, a short, plump man dressed head to toe in camouflage walked in the door. "Hi, Sheriff, I got here as fast as I could."

"Dean, this is Rusty Jackson, our evidence tech. Rusty, this is Dean Wister. Dean's a new deputy on loan from another department and he's going to be the lead on this. Fill him in when you get the scene processed, and keep him updated through Joanie. Help him out any way you can. I'll be at the station if you need me. This is the first murder in three years here, Rusty, so I don't need to remind you that this is the most important crime scene you have ever processed. Don't fuck it up."

Rusty looked around. "I appreciate your vote of confidence, Sheriff."

In the car, Dean turned to Sheriff Dani. "So, I'm in charge?"

"Completely. As soon as we get back to the office I'll inform the entire department. Joanie can get you anything you need. Rusty is very good at processing a crime scene. I just wanted to put a little pressure on him." She paused for a moment. "So what do you think?"

"Well, obviously someone wants us to think there was a robbery, but I seriously doubt it. No one thinks there's any cash kept in a real estate office. I'm not saying that it's out of the question for some tweeker to kill a guy for two hundred bucks. But it would be a gas station or convenience store. He wouldn't think of holding up a real estate office to do it."

"You think the Torino guy did it?"

"Possibly. For it to be a robbery, the dead hit man in the river would have to be a coincidence. Now I'm more of a believer in unrelated coincidences than most police. Too often I've seen cops substitute coincidence for evidence. But in this case it just seems like the coincidence is too strong."

"But why Jordy? I have to tell you everyone thinks he's a great kid."

"Well," Dean scratched his head. "I can't get past the fact that maybe Hayden was the target. Our boy Torino isn't generally hired to take out office managers in real estate offices, unless Jordy was involved in some pretty serious shit. Which we can't entirely discount. Even the best of us have secrets. I'm sure you've seen your share of fine upstanding citizens with things in their backgrounds they'd rather their neighbors didn't know about. But the fact that he and Hayden look so much alike...Torino probably didn't know either of them personally. And if he was hired to take Hayden out, he could easily have mistaken Jordy for Hayden. Is Hayden pretty high-profile in the community?"

"Hayden knows pretty much everybody in town."

They drove a few more minutes, each of them rolling it over in their heads. "I guess my theory right now would be that someone hired our boy Torino to come looking for Hayden, he mistook Jordy for Hayden, shot him dead and headed out of town. Of course, that's until I find out that Jordy is Wyoming's biggest drug lord."

The sheriff nodded but said nothing. Dean said, "So who is this Fletcher guy?"

"Fletcher Barns was involved in a real estate development project over in Wilson last year called Raptor Landing. Fletcher's been doing construction in the valley for decades. He's pretty rough around the edges, and his operation doesn't look like much, but you can't let that fool you. He's done all right for himself. Well, he got ahold of some land over in Wilson, and he wanted to build a mixed-use development, a few shops, a little office space, some condos, on this five-acre plot. So he put together this investor group, mostly rich guys who have vacation homes here and think that real estate development is their way of giving back to the community. Well, Fletcher got into it with Hayden over it. Hayden is a county commissioner in addition to his real estate business. The commission killed the plan mainly because Hayden opposed it. So Fletcher loses his own money and the money of his investors. And just as important, Fletcher is a proud, hot-headed SOB and he loses face in the community. The commission was split and Hayden was the deciding vote, though I think the bad blood between them goes back awhile even before that. Anyway, Fletcher and Hayden got into a shouting match at Mountain Man Days over at Teton Village over Memorial Day. Fletcher threatened to kill Hayden and had to be restrained by a few of his friends. It was the big story in the valley for about a month."

"Do you think Fletcher's capable of it?"

"My theory is that about ninety percent of the human race is capable of murder in the right circumstances. But the thing is, the bullet wound in Jordy looked like a nine millimeter to me. Hardly anyone around here carries that. The cowboys around here consider it a gun for girls," Dani smiled. "The thing is, women in Wyoming are pretty tough and most of them know how to shoot. Hell, I don't even know any women that carry a nine. It's all forty or forty-fives out here."

Dean thought about that and said, "Well, Fletcher knows Hayden and it's unlikely he could have mistook Jordy for him. So, it would have had to be someone that Fletcher hired who did the shooting, if Fletcher's the one behind it. And then there's Hayden. If he doesn't turn up, then he's probably skipped, or dead, too."

The Sheriff paused. "Going into Hayden's house is sticky. We have no evidence that it's a crime scene, and no one has reported him missing. I know a couple of people close to Hayden. I'll make a couple calls. If they don't have any info on his whereabouts, I'll authorize an entry into his house for a well-being check."

Dani pulled off to the side of the road. "One more thing." She pulled a badge from her pocket and tossed it to Dean. "I assume you have your own gun, but you'll need this. Now, raise your right hand. Do you swear to uphold the laws of Teton County, the State of Wyoming, and the United States of America?"

Dean picked up the badge. "I do."

"Welcome to the Teton County Sheriff's office, Deputy."

Back at the sheriff's office Dean picked up a portable police radio from Joanie and got on the phone with Alvarez in Chicago, updating him on the body they'd just found.

"Do you think this maybe leads back to one of Our Boys?" Alvarez asked. He had the habit of calling all the organized crime thugs they dealt with "Our Boys," as if they were delinquents in Alvarez's School for Wayward Youths. Dean thought it was pretty ridiculous, but he had learned to humor his boss on certain of his quirks.

"Probably," said Dean. "There must be a link between Teton County and the Boys. I was thinking we should put Mark to work crunching the data and see what he comes up with."

Mark Jeffrey's official title was "Analyst." But his real job was to maintain, develop, and care for the most important asset of the Midwest Organized Crime Task Force: Data. The Task Force had access to the FBI data warehouse and over the last few years had assembled a sophisticated subset containing information on thousands of individuals investigated for a specified list of crimes that were loosely described as "organized crime." The data was searchable by dozens of specific criteria and Mark's specialty was to access and manipulate the information to find patterns that could help them understand the informal and often unintentional networks that inevitably resulted from these criminal enterprises.

When Dean got hold of Mark, he got right to the point: "What I'm looking for is the link between Edward Torino and someone in Teton County, starting with a guy named Hayden Smith. I'm looking for not just a direct link to Torino, but also a link between any of Torino's associates and someone in Teton County. Can you come up with something?"

"Nice talking to you too, Dean," said Mark. "I thought you were supposed to be on vacation. I knew Alvarez would find something for you to do. Last year when I was in London, he called me every day for ten days straight. Yeah, let me put together a 'network analytics' on him. I should have something in your email by tomorrow."

Someone knocked on the door of Dean's makeshift office.

"Mark," Dean said, "got to run. Give me a call if you need any more info."

Sheriff Dani walked in. "No one has any idea where Hayden could be. A patrolman is waiting for you at Hayden's house. Why don't you go on in and see what you can find? From this point on, the case is all yours. Just keep me up to speed." She turned back and smiled, as if she'd thought of something that amused her. "Oh, if people ask where you're from, you might get a warmer reception around here if you say West Virginia instead of Chicago."

"I'll keep that in mind, Sheriff," Dean said, exaggerating his Southern drawl.

Over the last month in the valley, Dean had spent time obtaining a certain amount of local geographical knowledge, driving around and fantasizing about where he would build his mountain mansion when he won the Powerball. The ridge on which Hayden Smith's home sat was on his short list. As Dean drove up the winding road to get to the house, he wondered how difficult it would be to drive up and down when it was covered with snow during the winter.

A deputy approached Dean's car as he pulled into the driveway. "Looks quiet, no lights on, no one answers the door."

"Let's look around and see if we can find the best way in."

The house was a one-floor ranch style with only three ways in: the front door, the back patio door, and a service door to the garage. Dean and the deputy walked around the house and stopped at the garage door. "This looks like our best bet. Do you have a screwdriver in your car?"

When the deputy brought back the screwdriver, Dean took out his knife and wedged the blade between the door jamb and the latch. Taking the deputy's screwdriver he wedged that into the latch, jiggled it with a little force, and pop, the latch opened and they were in the garage.

The deputy laughed. "As you can see, our folks are not exactly into sophisticated security around here."

There were no vehicles in the garage. Like most people, Hayden didn't lock the door from the garage to the house and they entered the laundry room off the kitchen. The house was a three-thousand-square-foot, three-bedroom ranch, upscale, but not ostentatious by Jackson standards. It was tastefully decorated, but the real star of the furnishings was the full view of the summit of the 13,776-foot Grand Teton from the huge windows in the great room. The same five-star view was replicated in the master bedroom.

They walked through the house, room by room. Nothing appeared out of order. A typical Wyoming bachelor bedroom— king-sized bed, huge flat-screen TV you could watch while lounging, an unfired and unloaded Colt 45 revolver in the drawer of the nightstand. Dean looked through various papers on the desk and in the drawers in Hayden's office, looking for a calendar or day timer but didn't find anything of interest. There was a gun rack on the wall containing a 12-gauge shotgun and a 22-caliber rifle. A laptop sat on the desk and Dean made a note to get the sheriff's help to confiscate and review its contents. If Hayden did not show up soon, perhaps they could declare him missing and get a judge to authorize it.

Dean got on the phone to Sheriff Dani. "I'm at Hayden's house. No Hayden, no vehicle, nothing out of order. I think we should get the phone records for him and Jordy as soon as possible and look at who they've been talking to the last few days. Can you help out with that?"

"Sure, let me put Rusty on it. Rusty does most of our in-office investigative work as well as processing crime scenes. I'll tell him to get on it, and feel free to use him for whatever you need. He's working exclusively for you on this until you wrap it up."

When Dean left Hayden's house, he felt exhilarated. He was back in the game.

In his dream Dean was guiding a raft down the Snake, but he was the only one in the boat, standing in the rear with his long oar, steering the boat through the rapids. Suddenly, a huge wave crashed in, overturning the boat, wedging him between two rocks. Dean was trapped underneath the boat, completely under water. He pulled and squirmed, feeling smothered, trying to free himself, his lungs burning. Something else was pulling at him, pulling down his shorts, grabbing at him. He woke with a start, gasping.

Sara looked up from between his legs, his boxers bunched around his ankles. She took him out of her mouth with a pop. "Hi, honey. You always said you wanted me to wake you up this way."

Afterwards, he got up and made some tea for himself. When he brought the hot mug back to bed, she looked up at him and smirked. "Somebody got a job."

"The case looks pretty interesting. You remember that case with the hit man Torino a few years ago? They found him dead in the Snake River. The Sheriff called Alvarez and Alvarez called me in. The Sheriff, Dani Cody, is a woman. It's hard to believe they've elected a female Sheriff in Wyoming, but who knows, this place is a bit unique. I think she's more than happy to have me take it over. She can take credit if I solve it and blame me if I don't."

"You OK working for a female Sheriff?"

"What does that mean? Why wouldn't I be? You know I'm a feminist."

Sara laughed. "I'd hardly call you a feminist. I just know that you've never worked for a woman before, and those Neanderthals you work with in Chicago wouldn't be so OK with it."

Dean looked insulted. "I'm plenty OK with it, By the way, where have you been all week? I was afraid you'd abandoned me," Dean said.

"I've been around. I just thought you needed some alone time. But don't change the subject. So you're back to work. Just don't overdo it, mister. You were really burned out when you got here." She stroked the side of his face, and he was reminded of the hundreds of times he had felt that same caress. "So have you found anyone to hang out with yet?" Sara had been bugging him about making friends.

"Not yet. I've been enjoying the time alone. And I was hoping to spend the summer hanging out with you."

"Honey, I'm the only close friend you've ever had, and you need more than me now."

"You know that's not true; you aren't the *only* friend I ever had. I have lots of friends."

Sara looked at him. "You've always had plenty of friends, but no one that you were really close to until me."

"That's still not true. I had a best friend long before you. You know that."

"I apologize. I should say the only close human friend. I forgot about Buddy," she said softly.

"Since when does your best friend need to be human?"

"Look, I know that little mutt who followed you around from what, age nine to sixteen, was a great guy. And I know how hard it was to lose him. But it's not healthy that the two closest friends you ever had are a dead wife and a dead dog. So man up, baby, you need to start looking for a replacement for both of us."

Dean got quiet, and she knew to change the subject. "So what do you think Torino is doing here?"

"I have a theory, but you're the one with the super powers. I was hoping you'd be able to tell me something about it."

"That's silly, being dead doesn't give you super powers. Give me a little time, you only told me about the case just now."

Dean looked up at her and smiled. "Well, it seemed your powers were pretty super a few minutes ago."

She smiled back, grabbed him by his head and kissed him hard. "I bet you say that to all the ghosts."

Chapter 6

You might think that a man whose international business travels included side trips to his personal tailor on Saville Row to choose his suits, to Milan to acquire his handmade Italian shoes, and whose private pleasures included wandering through haberdasheries on cobblestone side streets in the City of Light to select his ties might find himself out of place at the Cheney auditorium in Cheyenne, Wyoming, where the best dressed businessmen find their sartorial selections in the men's department at JC Penney. After all, the great James Cash Penny himself, the unofficial men's clothier of middle-class America, opened his first store just down the road in Kemmerer. But, oddly, Charles felt quite at home in the room this morning. He felt at home in spite of being supremely self-aware of how obviously out of place he looked—actually, part of the reason he felt at home was because of how out of place he looked. He knew that he was being noticed, and even though part of him wanted to keep a low profile, why should he? The day in many ways did belong to him. The room was full of local and national media, Wyoming politicians, and local businessmen, none of them with his panache. His vanity extended beyond his fashion choices to his personal appearance—one of the reasons for his obsession with nutrition and fitness was so that his body could suitably exhibit his European finery—and, beyond that, to his business and political achievements. It was all part of his "Grand Plan", the carefully constructed life plan he had created shortly after taking over the Alton, Illinois bank that he'd inherited from his father twenty years ago. He was well aware that anyone reading his journals over those years would be amused or maybe even alarmed by his grandiose vision, but here he was, the epitome of the American archetype of the self-made man, taking a measly million-dollar inheritance and making something really big out of it.

Charles Kidwell, Chairman and CEO of Prairie Bankcorp, and founder of "America For All" Super Pac, was sitting in the front row of the Cheney Auditorium in Cheyenne, Wyoming awaiting the speech of his best friend, Senator Thomas McGraw. And in his mind, he owned the room. Certainly it was his work and vision as much as the senator's that was responsible for this day. This was the culmination of a decade of amazing accomplishments for the Chicago banker. He had engineered the transformation of his father's small-town bank to the twentieth largest bank in the United States with over one-hundred billion dollars in assets. When the housing meltdown precipitated the full-blown economic and banking crisis, he had parlayed his bank's complete lack of exposure in the residential mortgage sector, along with the leverage of the nearly free money offered during the Federal bailout, to build a dominant Midwestern bank conglomerate, cherry-picking the best of scores of failing banks, off-loading their bad loans to the Federal government, and installing his new banking blueprint of loaning money to solidly capitalized small and medium-size businesses. In other words, he had gone back to the simple formula that had worked for hundreds of years and made bankers some of the richest men in the world: making loans to customers who didn't need them.

Tom McGraw wasn't the first politician Charles had befriended. In fact, he had fostered political connections in both parties. But he had recognized in the senator something special, and he had become a close friend as well as an important business connection. They had met several years ago at a banking conference in Chicago and he immediately discerned that the senator had the charisma and agenda to transform a Republican Party devoid of big ideas and seemingly unable to win a national election. As they became closer, he took on the role of unofficial political advisor, and provided reinforcement that the senator's vision could be truly transformative for both the party and the country. Not coincidentally, the senator's contacts had enabled him to acquire an important banking group serving the Rocky Mountains and West Coast. With the help of his new best friend, Charles Kidwell was no longer a local banker, but the head of one of the few national banks not beholden to public shareholders. Eventually, the senator was convinced that he possessed three of the four key ingredients—ideas, charisma, and vision —to make a successful run for national office. But without the fourth key ingredient—money —ideas, charisma, and vision meant absolutely nothing. Charles had the money and the ambition to be a kingmaker. And it didn't hurt that his sister Charlotte was crazy about Tom, and vice-versa. Charles joked that the three of them were the unholy trinity.

Lydia McGraw sat next to her husband on the stage and finished flattering the man on her other side, who was to introduce the senator today. Her husband leaned over and whispered into her ear, "You look beautiful."

She didn't look at him but replied with a tight smile, "Thank you."

Tom still didn't know her even after being married to her for over twenty years. She knew she wasn't a beautiful woman, and his insincere compliment was both unnecessary and unappreciated. He didn't marry her because of her looks, or because of shared sexual chemistry, or any particular emotional connection. A tall thin woman with piercing blue eyes, she'd been something of a goody two-shoes at the University of Wyoming when the young cowboy from Casper caught her eye. Tom had worked as a roughneck in the gas fields after high school when he had no clue what to do with himself, but after two brutal years working through a couple of the coldest winters in Wyoming history, he knew what he didn't want to do with the rest of his life. After enrolling at the University of Wyoming as a history major, he met Lydia at a fraternity party. Her slender, somewhat fragile look, along with her family background, made her his type, and they immediately became inseparable. She saw Tom as something of a diamond in the rough and took to chiselling him into the proper cut with a deft, subtle touch that Tom appreciated. The irony was not lost on her that Tom had worked in the same gas fields that were owned by the company that her father was the founder and CEO of, but her father did not find the irony as amusing as she and Tom did. When her father saw that the apple of his eye was not going to give up on the young man, however, Tom started to grow on him. It was his father-in-law-to-be who got Tom a position in the office of Senator Carson, the man sitting on the other side of Lydia today, and with the support of his influential father-in-law and Senator Carson, Tom's political career was launched. Lydia frowned as she looked down and saw the thin, drawn face of Charles Kidwell in the front row. Lydia was suspicious of Charles. Tom had met him at some conference and, the next thing she knew, Charles had virtually taken over Tom's political career. She was ambivalent about the run for President; she loved the idea of being First Lady but wasn't so sure she wanted the obligations that would go with it, and she felt it was her ambivalence that had permitted Charles to push Tom over the edge with the decision to run. And now here he was, at the most important event of their lives, sitting in the front row with that smug smile on his face, as if he was the one running for President instead of her husband. It was OK that he was around for the time being, they certainly could use his money and fundraising skills, but after the election she intended to use all of her influence to freeze him out of the inner circle.

Former Vice President, and Wyoming's favorite son, Carl "Kit" Carson stepped to the podium. Kit was a legend in Wyoming, serving as senator and governor before his appointment to Vice President when the former Vice President was caught in a bribery scandal. With his rugged good looks and full head of gray hair, he could be Clint Eastwood's long lost brother. Tom McGraw had worked on Carson's staff when he was Vice President, and the older man had become not only a mentor to Tom but also something of a father figure. Carl paused before he spoke, looking over the crowd and enjoying the limelight that he had forsaken when he retired from public office. "Only once in a generation does a man come along who has the potential to change the course of a party. To change the course of a country. To change the course of the world. To even change the course of history. Some say the last time that happened is when I made my own announcement for President thirty-two years ago this week." The audience laughed and then erupted in raucous applause and cheers. "But today is not about me. Today is about the future of all of us. The future of our children, our grandchildren. And insuring the legacy of freedom for future generations. I have the honor and privilege of introducing to you a man I have watched grow from a smart young cowboy to a true statesman. A man who will bring back honor and family values and prosperity to our great country. A man who will energize and inspire conservatives all over this great country and will be a new force of unity not only for our party, but for America. I give you Senator Thomas McGraw."

The moment was so historical and overwhelming to Charles that he couldn't really focus on Tom's speech. When the senator's announcement was over and the audience erupted in deafening applause, he couldn't recall hearing a word of it. But he had read so many drafts, and listened to so many rehearsals, that it didn't really matter. What mattered was that on this day, he had arrived. His friend had arrived. How he wished his overbearing, disapproving father could see him now. His role on this day surpassed anything the small-thinking, penny-pinching son of a bitch could ever have imagined.

But the senator's platform was risky. When Charles had initially discussed a run, Tom was reluctant and skeptical. "I'm convinced that my party cannot win a national election without a change in our approach. And a change in our approach may not get me nominated." But eventually he concluded that he wasn't running for the nomination, he was running for President, and he didn't want the nomination if he didn't think he could win. Finally, he came to the conclusion that his run was really a no-lose proposition. His new approach would result in one of two outcomes. Either he would win the nomination and the election. Or he would lose the nomination and whoever beat him would lose the election. In that case he would be in the "I told you so position" and maybe the party would be ready for his ideas four years from now. He could live with either of those outcomes. Tom's political theory was that Americans bought into the conservative economic views, but conservatives had lost enough of three components of the electorate to make it impossible to win a national election. If his party could win back just enough of those groups, they could form a new majority. His speech today was the first step in bringing back those three groups to his party: women, gays, and immigrants. He didn't need a majority of any of those groups, he just needed to do well enough to add some of them to the existing base. His chief political consultant, who had been with him since his earliest political run, argued that he would lose more of his base than he would gain. But Tom was convinced that "the people are always ahead of politicians on social issues." And even more importantly, he was convinced he could reframe those issues as, if not conservative, at least libertarian. He intended to wield a sledge hammer and swing it at anyone in his own party who accused him of abandoning traditional conservative principles. "Let's keep the government *and* our politicians out of our personal business." He would frame himself as not a "new conservative" but a "true conservative."

Today's audience, of course, was handpicked from the senator's most enthusiastic supporters. And their enthusiasm did not disappoint, from their thundering welcome to their equally thundering endorsement of his candidacy at the end. The speech was carried live by CNN and Fox News, and would be reported on every TV and Internet network by the end of the day.

As the senator walked off the stage, his wife by his side, shaking hands, smiling and enjoying the adoration, Charles looked down at his phone. Charlotte and Tom had spent the previous weekend at Charlotte's new home in Jackson Hole, and there had been a "complication."

When Charles read the news alert from the *Jackson Hole News & Guide*, his face turned ashen. "Jordy Smith, Assistant to County

Commissioner Hayden Smith, murdered, Commissioner Smith missing and foul play feared."
Holy shit. Could this be the result of the call to Mario? Charles felt nauseous, and then made the same decision that had served him well since he was a teenager: he took the piece of disturbing information and locked it in the compartment in his brain that contained the rest of the disturbing issues in his life that he promised himself to deal with at some future date. Besides, this was something the senator did not need to deal with right now. It could derail the entire day. The politicos in Tom's entourage, including Charles, were headed to the airport. They would stop in Chicago for a speech and then fly to Washington so the senator could appear on the Sunday morning news shows. Charles figured Charlotte could fill him in on the unfolding events in Jackson Hole in the hotel room tonight. She had a way of handling the senator that always kept him in a good mood, no matter what was going on around him. And with the senator's wife back in Cheyenne, the unholy trinity could run wild.

Chapter 7

THIS was the happiest day in the life of Oleg Petrov, which was ironic in that just two weeks ago he was diagnosed with inoperable lung cancer. But today he had traveled two hours on the train from his small village to Moscow to hear the presentation of a successful Russian-American businessman. And now he had hope. Not hope for himself, that wasn't possible for people like himself in the chaotic, corrupt environs of post-Communist Russia, but hope for his daughter. Hope for your children was also the rarest of things in his world, and for a dying man, knowing that his child might have a future, well, that was all he could really want out of life. Oleg had struggled to make ends meet for almost all of his sixty years, but when his wife died sixteen years ago, shortly after Tatiana was born, he decided, partly out of necessity but mostly out of desperation, that something had to change. He still had to work at his low-paying job at the post office to just barely put food on the table of the two-bedroom apartment he and Tatiana shared with his dead wife's sister and her husband and four children. But at night, after Tatiana went to bed, he would go to work in his computer workshop in the cluttered corner of the bedroom he shared with his daughter.

He was an easy mark for the big, good-looking Russian with the deep voice and seemingly unlimited knowledge of how to navigate the red tape of Russian bureaucracy, American immigration, and the confusing and almost incomprehensible system of getting an education and a job in the free-wheeling economy of America. And the big man brought with him a pretty Russian girl whose parents had entrusted to his care just five years before, and she told her story of how she got a university degree in Chicago and was now a computer programmer at an Internet startup there, with stock options and a one-bedroom, high-rise apartment overlooking Lake Michigan that she shared with no one but her cat. Her story was accompanied by slides showing her at work and at play in her fabulous new life in Chicago. He pictured his Tatiana standing up there telling her story in five years, and the pride of that thought, along with the knowledge that he would not be around to see it, would have brought tears to his eyes. Would have if his innate sentimentality had not been replaced by cold hard survival skills many, many years before.

It had taken him months of trial and error to master the skill of refurbishing the aging personal computers trashed by citizens of other, more well-to-do countries in Europe, mainly Slovenia, Poland and the Czech Republic—computers he acquired from a variety of nearly legal sources. But working with the set of computer repair CDs he'd purchased on eBay, the stoic determination passed down in the DNA of his people through centuries of suffering and survival, and the readily available black market software prevalent in his part of the world, he churned out a steady stream of somewhat outdated, but perfectly functional personal computers. Over the last ten years he'd squirreled away every penny of his profits from his ersatz computer business, minus a few rubles here and there to give Tatiana a new, or at least only moderately worn set of clothes, and some English lessons from the strange British ex-patriot who lived in their village. Now he carried with him to this meeting his entire life savings, every penny he'd stashed from more than a decade of toil at his American-style venture.

The opportunity presented to Oleg was simple and easy to understand. In exchange for a cash payment upfront, and monthly payments for two years, the Russian businessman would make all the arrangements to provide his Tatiana with the chance of a lifetime. A select few young Russian women were taken every month to America on a tourist visa that he obtained through his contacts in the Russian bureaucracy. The man assured everyone that once the young women were in America, they were enrolled in one of over a dozen universities in Chicago, given a student visa, and, after two to four years of training in the fields of their choice, they would receive offers of employment from some of the thousands of amazing companies in the land where a smart, hard-working immigrant could still rise to the top of society. While in Chicago, the girls worked part-time to pay their college tuition, and shared an apartment with up to three other Russian girls so they could more easily adjust together to their new life in America. Their employers would enable them to obtain work visas, and then they were on their way to US citizenship—or maybe they returned to Russia after making their fortunes in America.

Oleg approached the man at the end of his presentation and told him his story—and his problem. The next group was leaving in a month, and Oleg wasn't sure he would still be alive when that happened. He had no intention of telling Tatiana of his condition; he didn't think Tatiana would leave him once his condition became apparent. He told this to the man, and said, "I have brought with me all the money for the initial payment. I would also like to pay the two years of monthly payments in advance. I want to make sure that my daughter is taken care of when I'm gone." He held up the tattered briefcase that contained the cash.

"How much is in that bag, comrade."

"I have the amount you said. The upfront payment of fifty thousand dollars, plus another one thousand per month for twenty-four months."

The big man smiled. "Brother Oleg, your story moves me so much. This will be difficult, but I want to help you any way I can. I am leaving for Chicago tomorrow. If you get your daughter to the Moscow airport tomorrow afternoon, I think I can arrange to take her with me."

"Don't worry, I will have her there. I can't tell you how much this means to us. Thank you so much, Mr. Birkov."

Chapter 8

BUBBA's Barbecue was Dean's favorite break-fast spot in Jackson. It reminded him of one of the restaurants his father took him to when he was growing up in West Virginia, and he would often stop there for a breakfast of biscuits, gravy, and homemade sausage, and assuage his guilty gluttony by hiking the rest of the day in the mountains. Today he left Bubba's heading for the sheriff's office—he would have to find some other way to work off his guilt —hurrying to his Jeep when he passed a tall skinny man wearing a dirty red ski vest and a Wind River Casino cap. His face had the weathered, old leather-moccasin look of ranch hands who have spent most of their lives work-ing on the range, and the disproportionately developed forearms that Dean had observed in men who had spent time working on the docks. He was standing over a Border Collie with tan-gled, matted fur, and the man was screaming at the dog and throwing fake punches at the dog's face. The collie would cower and the man would laugh and back away, and then come at the dog again, as if the Border Collie was his opponent in some strange universe of man-versus-dog boxing matches. Dean stopped and stared at the guy, and the dog looked directly up at Dean with the kind of look that ignited his protective instincts. It was only with some difficulty that he ignored the dog, deciding he didn't have time to counsel a crazy redneck cowboy on animal care, and hurried on. But for the rest of the day the image nagged at him. He could sense Sara's disapproval that he couldn't take a minute to help the dog—and something about how the Border Collie looked at him reminded him of Buddy.

When Dean arrived at the office that morning, he discovered a rumpled and droopy- eyed Rusty devouring the largest sweet roll he had ever seen and washing it down with one of those gigantic quart mugs of coffee they sell to truckers. "You look like you pulled an all-nighter," Dean said.

"Yep." Dean had to look away because Rusty did not stop chewing as he continued. "Made a lot of progress, such as it is. All the hair in the car belongs to Torino. There's a bunch of fingerprints that are not his, but probably belong to other rental customers. No hits on the fingerprint database. Otherwise the car looks clean. No bloody fingerprints or footprints at the real estate office. Jordy was killed with a single nine-millimeter shot to the chest, sometime between eleven PM and two AM. One of our guys surveyed the neighborhood and no one heard anything, not surprising since the direct neighbors are businesses that wouldn't be open at those hours. So not much to go on at the crime scene. But I put together a spreadsheet of the phone calls that Jordy and Hayden have made. Maybe you can piece together their activities from that."

"Anything jump out at you from the phone records?" Dean asked.

"Not at first look. Almost all local calls. Many calls back and forth to each other. Last call from Hayden was about six PM the evening of Jordy's death. I also downloaded their voicemails and text messages and I'll put together a transcript of them this morning for you. Oh, also, Sheriff Dani got a warrant to look at those computers we took from the real estate office and Hayden's place."

"Thanks. Let me know when you have the phone transcripts, then go get some sleep. You've given me plenty to work on."

Dean got Mark on the phone in Chicago and updated him on the case. "Morning, Mark. I need to get you to go through a couple computers, Jordy's desktop and Hayden's laptop. The Sheriff just got a local judge to issue a search warrant for them. Should I FedEx them to Chicago so you can analyze them?"

Dean heard what sounded like a cough, then hysterical laughter from the line. "Dean, how long have you been doing this job? Just hook both computers up to the Internet in the Sheriff's office and I should be able to access the desktops and hard drives from here. Should only take me a few minutes to get access."

"Thanks, Mark." Although only a half generation younger than Dean, that half generation meant, in computer skills, the difference between learning a language as a member of a bilingual household and learning a language in middle school. Like most of the techno snobs of his generation, Mark had the ability to make anyone without extraordinary computer skills feel like the dumbest person on the face of the planet. So Dean changed the subject to hide his chagrin. "How are you coming with that Six Degrees of Kevin Bacon chart you're working on?" Although Dean found the new computer technology useful, he couldn't help but be skeptical. He teased Mark that he spent his days downloading the profiles of the Facebook friends of every bad guy into his database.

Mark easily ignored Dean's jab. He had broken several big cases using the software they had nicknamed "Six Degrees of Kevin Bacon" and knew the comment was just part of the old school breaking-balls culture that cops can't get away from. "I'm wrapping up the network analytics right now. I'll email it to you as soon as we're off the phone."

Rusty's spreadsheet of Jordy and Hayden's phone calls was certainly complete. He had included the name and address for each of the phone numbers for the last few days, along with the length of the call, and a brief description of the person spoken to, if known. Jordy had had thirty-six calls over the last three days. About half of them were to or from Hayden. Most of the rest were to names in the office directory, so probably real estate agents or tradespeople. There were half a dozen calls to a number listed to an A. Gathers, in Alpine, the little town about thirty miles south of Jackson. He decided he would put Rusty on tracking down A. Gathers.

Hayden had about twice as many calls. And Dean could see it was going to be a bigger job tracking them down. Maybe the Sheriff could get someone to call these numbers for him, find out the nature of the relationship Hayden had shared with their owners, and the subject of the conversations they'd had with him just before he disappeared. Then Dean could circle back and follow-up if warranted.

The person who had made a threat on Hayden's life kept coming back to him. Maybe he should make an unannounced visit to Fletcher Barns and see if he could stir the pot a little bit.

Joanie provided Fletcher's contact information and Dean updated Sheriff Dani, who said she would put someone on telephone canvassing and have the computers brought into the office so Mark could connect. On his way out, Dean made a visit to Rusty's desk and found him dozing. "Rusty!" Rusty jumped up and Dean laughed. "Go home. I'll touch base with you later. I'm heading out to talk to Fletcher Barns. And can you put together a list of the investors in Raptor Landing and send it over to Mark in Chicago? After you get some sleep, of course. I have plenty to keep me busy right now."

Rusty responded slowly. "Maybe I should come along. Fletcher can be a cantankerous son of a bitch."

"That's OK. I think I can handle it. I can be a cantankerous SOB myself."

"Fletcher Barns Ranches." That was what the sign said underneath a steel branding iron with FBR in big, antique-style letters. But the term 'ranches' would have to be applied liberally to accurately depict the hodgepodge of machinery, the functional pieces sitting in a row next to another row of seemingly identical half-eaten cannibalized machinery, mounds of construction materials that looked as if they were left over from dozens of projects, assorted working and non-working vehicles, and ramshackle buildings, some of which may have even housed humans at some point. As Dean pulled his jeep slowly through the FBR gate, a skin-and-bones yellow retriever bounded toward him, tail wagging. Dean parked the car and was wading through the junkyard when he was jabbed in the back by a large metal object. A very deep voice accompanied the jab. "Now, you turn around real slow. You have thirty seconds to tell me what your business is and why you are trespassing on my property."

Dean did just as he was instructed, expecting to see a 12-gauge shotgun pointing at him. Instead, he saw a very large man whose physique and scowl gave the impression of a man who'd been an NFL defensive lineman say twenty years ago and who had given up working out but still retained much of the muscle mass of his younger days. The man was holding in his hand a six-foot-long piece of four-inch-diameter galvanized pipe, waving it at Dean as if it were a walking stick.

"Mr. Barns?"

"Who the fuck wants to know?"

"My name is Dean Wister. I'm a deputy with the Teton Sheriff's Department. I came out here to ask you a few questions about an acquaintance of yours, Hayden Smith."

The mention of Hayden's name seemed to put him in an even more disagreeable state. "What the fuck would you want to ask me about that piece of shit?"

"Well, I figured you heard. His office manager Jordy was murdered yesterday and Hayden is missing." Dean stared directly at Fletcher's eyes, but Fletcher didn't flinch.

"I heard. Now Jordy was a real nice young man. And I was sure sorry to hear about him. But his cousin Hayden was a no-account son of a bitch. I suppose you heard that me and Hayden have some bad shit between us and you come out here to find out if I killed him, is that about it?"

Dean noted that Fletcher was already using the past tense when referring to Hayden. "Mr. Barns, I'm not here to accuse you of anything. Yes, people are talking that you and Hayden are enemies, but what I'd really like to do is rule you out as a suspect, and then I can move on to other areas of the investigation. Can you tell me your whereabouts night before last, say between about nine PM and five AM?"

"I can. But I don't think it'll be enough to rule me out. Me and the wife spent the whole evening alone at home, watching TV. She'll back me up, but I know that won't mean nothing to you."

"Anyone else can verify that? You talk to anyone on your home phone for example?"

"Don't think we talked to anyone that night. Just a nice quiet evening at home."

"When is the last time you saw or talked to Hayden?"

"Well, you probably already know that 'cause I ain't never seen you around here before and someone must have sent you out here on me. Was at the Mountain Man Days at Teton Village, Memorial Day weekend. Had harsh words with him that day, and haven't seen or talked to him since."

"OK. Since you and your wife were having a nice quiet night at home when all of this went down, do you know of anyone else who would want to harm Jordy or Hayden?"

"Look, I knew Jordy. And I don't think you can find a person around here who would have a bad thing to say about him. But in my circle of friends, you couldn't find anyone who had anything nice to say about Hayden. And I'll admit to you right now, you won't find anyone around here who had a more profound disgust for that greasy realtor than me. At least that I know of."

Dean couldn't decide whether Fletcher's unflinching honesty about his hatred for Hayden was evidence of his guilt, or that he was innocent and had nothing to hide, or that he had such fundamental disdain and disrespect for the new deputy he had never heard of that he figured it didn't matter what he said. Dean figured it probably was the last. He wasn't going to get anything useful here and would do just as well moving on. "Well, Mr. Barns, I'll leave you to your business. It seems like you had some affection for Jordy, so if you can think of anything that might help us catch his killer, give me a call down at the sheriff's office."

"I'll do that." But as Dean got in his car, Fletcher said something to Dean that stopped him in his tracks. "Deputy, have you thought of the possibility that the fucking asshole killed his cousin Jordy, and then took off?"

"Of course, we're looking into that theory as well," Dean lied, and then he drove off.

Chapter 9

AFTER Senator McGraw's speech to the National Association of the Self-Employed at the Palmer House in Chicago, he had dinner with Charles Kidwell and the Governor of Illinois, whose effusive flattery revealed his desire to be considered as a vice-presidential prospect. As Charles and the senator walked back from the restaurant to the hotel, Charles gave him the news of what had happened in Jackson. "I didn't want to tell you until after the speech this afternoon. I didn't want anything clouding your mind."

"Holy crap. I assume you think Mario is involved in this?" Tom said.

"I called Mario earlier. He said he didn't have anything to do with it. But he also said it in a way that made me think he wanted us to think that he did. He said you should definitely not contact him, and that I need to limit my calls to him to legitimate bank business."

"Oh, my god, Charles. Do you realize that we could now be considered his accomplices?"

"Tom, calm down. We don't know if he did anything. I seriously doubt that he was involved. The phone call Charlotte made from Jackson was vague, and he said nothing about how he was going to take care of it. Plus, there's no record of that call, it was on a disposable phone. And you only met him that one time, in private, and there is no record of it anywhere. There's no link from him to you."

Tom looked down for a moment, and when he looked up Charles saw an expression on his face he had never seen before. "I should never have let Charlotte make that call. I was in a panic and should have thought it through. I don't know how I can live with myself if someone was killed because of this."

"I really don't think murder would have been Mario's first move to ensure Hayden's discretion. You need to stop thinking about it. I bet we'll find out it was just a routine burglary gone bad. Now I want you to put this out of your mind and spend the rest of the night relaxing. Charlotte will be waiting for you at the hotel."

"I know." Tom put his hand on Charles's shoulder. "I've been looking forward to that all day."

Charlotte sat next to Tom on the bed, lightly stroking his hair, listening to his relaxed breathing. He had fallen asleep almost immediately after his orgasm, and that was fine, Charlotte thought. He was exhausted from his amazing day, but the most amazing thing about the day to Charlotte was the way his face lit up when he saw her come into his room. And what he said. A few minutes earlier, for the first time in her entire life, a man had told her that he loved her. And not just any man, but a man who, in a little over a year, could be the leader of the free world. Each time they were together he made her feel like the most desirable woman in the world. As she sat there and looked at him, her heart began to ache. She tried not to think about it, but she knew that if he was elected, he would have to give her up. She tried not to think of the fact that each time they saw each other, it was one time closer to the last. But she was determined not to let that darken their time together, so she lay down next to him, melded her body into his, and slept.

Chapter 10

DEAN walked into the sheriff's office and was greeted by Joanie wearing one of her world-class smiles and a red, embroidered Western shirt. "Morning, Dean, we have the computers set up for Mark in Chicago and he's working on them now. He said to tell you he has no idea how long it will take him to go through everything, but he'll let you know when he finds something interesting. And that he knows you're in a hurry so you don't need to call him to tell him that."

"Thanks, Joanie," Dean said and stuck his head in Sheriff Dani's office.

"Well, did Fletcher do it?" the sheriff asked.

"I have no idea. But he sure hates Hayden. And he has no alibi. And he is one mean SOB. What's his criminal history?"

"Nothing too serious. Bar fights. Threatening people. Generally, just being an asshole. But as I said, I think most of us are capable of violence, and Hayden cost him a lot of money. And that's one of the Big Four criminal motivations in my mind."

"Big Four. I don't think I've heard that one. What are the other three?"

"Sex, power, and love," Dani said, "and as the Good Book tells us, the greatest of these is love."

"Well, then, I guess I better start looking for the other three," Dean said, and headed down to his basement office.

Rusty had gone home to get some sleep but had left Dean with some notes: Multiple phone calls from Jordy to A. Gathers. A. Gathers is Amber Gathers. Resides in Alpine and works five nights a week as a stripper at the "Grandest Tetons" strip club and bar in Alpine. Multiple calls from Hayden's phone to Kara Winston, CPA, and to an Elizabeth Nelson of Jackson. Transcript of all text messages from the phones of Jordy and Hayden. The only ones of apparent interest are explicit sexual text messages between Jordy and Amber and between Hayden and Elizabeth.

Dean thought he would make a visit to Hayden's CPA. Maybe she could shed some light on the money motivation.

Kara Winston's accounting office was just across from Pinky G's pizza in the Pink Garter Theater plaza downtown. The aroma of fresh pizza crust and garlic arrived at Dean's nose first, then headed directly to his stomach. He thought he would make a stop in there after he talked to Kara.

Entering Kara's office, he encountered an athletic blonde woman wearing running shorts and trail-running shoes. Dean wondered if all the women in Jackson were so fit and athletic; it could be intimidating for an out of shape single man. The only couch potatoes he had noticed since he arrived were tourists.

"Can I help you?" she asked.

"My name is Dean Wister, I'm a deputy with the Teton County Sheriff. Are you Kara Winston?"

"Yes, I am. I heard about what happened at Hayden's office. I still can't believe it."

"I was wondering if you'd have a few minutes to talk."

"I was just getting ready to run up Snow King." She looked Dean up and down, seemingly gauging his fitness level. "Would you like to come with me? We can talk while we run."

"That sounds like fun. I've been in town about a month and I've been meaning to run up Snow King, but I haven't gotten around to it. I've got some shorts and shoes in my car. Just give me a minute to change."

They took Kara's Jeep Wrangler and drove the mile or so to the base of Snow King Mountain. As they began running side by side at a moderate pace along the trail, Kara said, "Snow King is the old ski mountain. The big ski resort is over at Teton Village, but there's something about this one that I like. They have lights for night skiing. Have you ever skied at night?"

"No, I haven't, but it sounds like fun. How long is the run?"

"Oh, not very long. It's only about two and a half miles, but it's sixteen-hundred feet up to the top. The slope is what makes it a good workout. I try to do it every day, but realistically I can only make it out here three or four times a week. Once we get to the top, we can take the ski lift down."

"Wow, I've never run such a steep slope before. Take it easy on me."

"Oh, I will." And with that, she sprinted off ahead of him.

By the time Dean caught up with her, Kara was sitting on a rock about halfway up the hill, sipping from her water bottle. "I thought you were going to take it easy on me," he said.

Kara grinned at him. "Oh, I am. Normally I would be done by now. So where are you from?"

"I'm from Chicago. This is actually the first case I've worked on in the county."

"Chicago? I would never have guessed it from your accent."

"Well, the accent is fake. It's left over from my last undercover case."

Kara looked at him, unsure. "Really?"

"Just kidding. I grew up in West Virginia. Never really lost it. But I need to ask you a few questions about Hayden. How long have you been his CPA?"

"Quite a while. Let's see, I guess about five years. He was one of my first clients when I opened my office."

"Were you working with him on anything unusual?"

"Normally, I only work on his books at the end of the year. But Hayden came to me a couple of weeks ago and asked me to look at some things in his records. He isn't hands-on with his bookkeeping. He leaves everything to Jordy. He felt that maybe there was some money missing, and he wanted me to take a look, but discreetly, so that Jordy wouldn't think he didn't trust him. He and Jordy are very close."

"And what did you find."

"Well, that Jordy has stolen about fifty thousand dollars from Hayden over the last year. Some from Hayden's client trust funds, and some from Hayden personally. It wasn't a very sophisticated scheme, but it didn't have to be because Hayden never looked at anything. I have a report detailing all of the stolen funds. I can email it to you if you want."

"So what did Hayden do when you told him?"

"Of course he was really upset. He treated Jordy like a little brother and felt incredibly betrayed. He said he didn't want to go to the police. That he was going to confront Jordy and make him pay everything back over time."

"Do you know if he had confronted Jordy before he was killed?"

"No, I don't. We talked about it before he disappeared, and I know he intended to talk to Jordy in the next day or two, but I don't know if he did."

"How angry was Hayden? Do you think it's possible that he confronted Jordy, they got into an argument, it escalated, and Hayden shot Jordy?"

"Deputy, I think that is just about the most ridiculous thing I have ever heard. Now, Hayden was really, really mad. As he should be. He was kind of in a state of disbelief until I showed him all the evidence. I tried to get him to file a police report, but he wouldn't do it. He swore me to secrecy. He said this was something he had to handle himself. But Hayden is not a violent man. He is actually very gentle."

Her use of the word "gentle" gave Dean pause. Perhaps her relationship with Hayden was more than professional.

"Do you have any idea what Jordy was doing with the money?"

"It looks like most of it went into either his personal bank account, or he would write checks to 'cash.' But I have no idea what he was doing with the money. Hayden said he would find out. Have you heard anything from Hayden yet?"

"Not yet. Do you have any ideas about where he might have gone?"

"No, I don't. I just hope he's OK."

"Me, too. When we get back to the office, I'll give you my email address and you can email that report to me."

"Sure, no problem."

Dean looked up at the trail. "Well, are you going to sit there on your ass, or are you going to run?" And then he sprinted up the hill, as fast as his flatlander legs would take him.

On the way back to his car he walked over to the pizza place and had a slice of thin crust with sausage and extra garlic. He thought of the pretty, athletic CPA, and then tasted the strong garlic remains in his mouth. He figured his garlic indulgence was one of the few advantages of his celibacy.

Chapter 11

THE Grandest Tetons was a restaurant, bar, motel, liquor store, and gas station smack dab in downtown Alpine, thirty miles south of Jackson, through the Snake River Canyon where Torino's body was found and along the rapids that the guides run many times a day throughout the summer. Strangely, as Dean drove through the canyon, he didn't feel the draw of the river that he had all through high school and college. It was almost as if his love of the river had been replaced by something else, but he couldn't quite put his finger on what it was.

Alpine, Wyoming sits at the intersection of the Snake, Salt, and Greys rivers, which flow into the nearby sixteen-thousand-acre Palisades reservoir. Completely surrounded by national forest, its thousand or so residents reside there for the world-class snowmobiling, backcountry skiing, hunting, and fishing as much as for the housing costs which are about a fourth of the price of living in Jackson. Downtown consists of a dozen or so log buildings, including a gas station, hardware store, grocery, coffee shop, bank, and post office. It wasn't difficult to find The Grandest Tetons club and bar. The river rock and timber building and attached motel sat in the center of town and dwarfed the buildings around it. A neon sign out front flashed everything you needed to know: Food, Dancers, Cocktails, Dancers, Lodging, Dancers, Package Liquor, Dancers. It was eight in the evening when Dean pulled into the parking lot. Drinks, lodging, food, and package liquor were available any time, but the dancers didn't go on until nine. The owner of the establishment viewed himself as something of a clever wordsmith, and so he came up with the name as a play on the name given the mountain range by the nineteenth-century French fur traders, who went for months or even years without female companionship. They referred to the three largest peaks in the range as "les Trois Tétons" or "the Three Breasts."

Inside, the establishment featured a large, well-stocked bar, an eating area with a couple dozen tables surrounding a stage in the middle of the restaurant, and a dancer pole in the middle of the stage. A sign that read "I Heart Mormon Boobs" hung on a mirror over the bar, which had stools for a dozen or so students of the female anatomy, Mormon and otherwise. Dead animal heads hung on walls facing the stage, one with a collection of panties dangling from his antlers, and Dean thought there were worse views you could have for your eternal landscape. Dean took a seat at the bar and ordered a Snake River Ale. When the bartender brought his brew, Dean said, "Amber dancing tonight?"

The bartender looked confused, then suspiciously at Dean. "Amber? We don't have an Amber dancing."

"Amber Gathers is her legal name. I don't know her professional name," Dean said.

The bartender looked at him skeptically. "Who wants to know?"

Dean flashed his badge. "Teton County Sheriff. I'm not here to interfere with the show tonight. I just need to ask her a few questions."

The bartender stared at him. He started to say something but changed his mind, and walked into a room behind the bar. Dean sipped his beer and, a couple minutes later, a young blonde came out wearing the uniform of the Grandest Tetons dancers: hiking boots, tattered denim shorts so short they were more like a thong in back, and a micro halter top.

"Hey, officer, I already told the Alpine cops I don't know nothing about Daryl selling nothing but EV products. He gave up that other stuff a long time ago, or I wouldn't be with him."

"I assume you're Amber Gathers? Is there some place we can talk in private?"

"Yeah, I'm Amber, around here I go by Cheyenne, though. We can talk back in the VIP room. Come with me."

The VIP room was a ten-foot-by-ten-foot room furnished with four small cocktail tables, each with one chair, apparently so that four dancers could entertain four customers at a time in semi-privacy. The room was accessed by a red velvet curtain that Amber pulled aside as they entered. "What can I do for you? I swear Daryl's totally straight now."

Dean assumed that Daryl was Amber's boyfriend. "This isn't about Daryl, Amber. Do you know a man by the name of Jordy Smith?"

At the mention of Jordy's name, Amber didn't speak for a moment, and Dean could tell she was deciding if she should lie or not, and if she should, what the lie should be. Eventually she said, "Yeah, I know Jordy, he's one of my regular customers."

"When's the last time you heard from Jordy."

"I think he was in here a couple of days ago. He generally texts me to see if I'm going to be working, but I haven't heard from him in the last day or two."

"Amber, Jordy was found dead yesterday morning." Dean paused to see how Amber would take this news.

Dean had seen his share of fake shock, and he thought the look of shock on Amber's face was not fake. She looked stunned. "Wha... what? No, no, no, you can't be serious. He was just in here a couple of days ago. He was happy." She looked confused, shocked, then sad. And then the tears came—big raindrop tears washing streaks of mascara and purple eye shadow down her cheeks. "He was so nice to me."

"Amber, did you have a personal relationship with Jordy?"

"He was one of my regulars—"

"You already said that. Did you ever see him outside of the bar?"

"A few times, but I wouldn't call it a personal relationship."

"But did Jordy consider it a personal relationship?"

"I don't know." Her eyes began to fill with tears. "Maybe."

"Amber, did Jordy ever give you money?" At that question, Amber put her head down and started sobbing. Her tears before were tears of sadness, but these breath-catching sobs were the cries of love and regret. Dean knew them only too well. He grabbed a handful of the paper towels that were on a stand at each table, offered them to her, and said, "Amber, this is a murder investigation, and right now I need to know the truth about what happened, the truth about your relationship with Jordy. How often did he give you money?"

"He wanted to help me. So he would give me money for my car payment or for medical bills. Daryl takes most of my dancing money for his business so I never have much. Jordy wanted me to have nice things."

"How much did he give you each time?"

"Maybe one or two hundred, that's outside of what he pays for the private dances when he comes in, maybe more if I had a medical bill or something."

"And how long had this been going on?"

"I'm not sure. I think I met Jordy about a year ago when he came in the bar. He started coming back a couple of times a week. We got to talking, and he was real nice and he wanted to help me out, you know?"

"And how does Daryl feel about Jordy?"

"He doesn't know about him. Daryl is real jealous. He says he wants me to quit dancing as soon as his business makes enough money. So I thought it best that he don't know nothing about Jordy."

"What kind of business does Daryl have, Amber?"

"He's a distributor with EV, you know the MLM Company. It's just about the biggest thing to get into."

"MLM?"

"Multi-level marketing. EV has vitamins and skin care and stuff. It's really the best stuff out there. Here look at my skin." She put her face close to Dean. *She really does have beautiful skin*, he thought. "It's how me and Daryl are going to get out of here and buy a place in Jackson or maybe Idaho Falls. That's why I don't mind giving Daryl my dancing money, even some of what Jordy gives me. He has to build a downline, and in order to do that he has to take them to dinner, buy them drinks, show them that he's successful. Daryl says that your downline needs to think you're already rich, and that's what sells them. Daryl's doing real good. He says in maybe six months we can get out of here."

"Amber, do you know where Daryl was Friday night between nine PM and two AM?" Amber had a look on her face like she was trying to do a math calculation but just didn't have quite enough brain power to complete it.

"Oh, that night. He was home all night long."

"Amber, how would you know that? Weren't you dancing that night?"

Amber didn't say a word to that, but looked up at the clock. "I'm supposed to get ready to go on in a couple of minutes. What do you say about being my first private dance of the night?"

Dean looked at the trailer trash girl with the full lips, a body that condemned her to a life of being hit on by men, and a mind that guaranteed she wouldn't be able to take advantage of it. And he was tempted. "Thanks, Amber, but I'll have to take a rain check. Pretty busy with the investigation. Now can you give me Daryl's last name and phone number? And I'll need your home address, too."

"Please don't tell him about me and Jordy."

"I don't want to get you into trouble, Amber. I just want to ask Daryl about his business. It sounds real interesting."

Dean left The Grandest Tetons and thought he would make a stop at the custom knife store he'd passed coming into town, but first he made a call to Sheriff Dani. "Sheriff, looks like Jordy was stealing Hayden blind and spending the money on a stripper in Alpine. I think I need to take a look at her boyfriend—you know, the love-triangle thing. Since I'm in Lincoln County, could you check with the police down here to see if they're looking at him already for anything? I don't want to step on any toes."

"Sure, Dean. What's his name? I know the Lincoln County Sheriff pretty well. I'll call him right now."

"Daryl Fay. Thanks, Sheriff. I'm going to look at some knives at a store down here, so I'll be a while yet. If the Lincoln County Sheriff is OK with it, maybe I can talk to Daryl before I head north."

The owner of the originally named "Knife Store" was getting ready to close but insisted on letting Dean look around when he came in the door. Browsing the rows of knives of all shapes and sizes, most with intricately hand-carved handles, Dean finally understood how Sara felt when she claimed she could hear that Michigan Avenue shoe store calling her name five miles away from their Lincoln Park condo. Although he could appreciate the workmanship and artistry of the pieces, he decided that owning a knife as a piece of art was a bit too serial-killer kitsch for him. He made it worth the shopkeeper's while to stay open late by dropping a grand on a Stryder tactical knife that would fit nicely in his boot, and a Leech Lake fillet knife that would last his lifetime, if he didn't drop it into the river.

Dani called on his way out of the shop, "As a matter of fact, Daryl Fay is the subject of an investigation. They're looking at him for drug trafficking down there. I said that we wanted to talk to him about a murder that could involve a love triangle with his girlfriend and you have the OK. Just stay away from anything to do with drugs. I have an address for him."

"Is it three-two-six-six Greys River Drive?"

"That's right."

"OK, I think I'll head on over and see if he's home."

"Be careful."

3266 Greys River Drive was a tiny but neat ranch home that sat on a street with about a dozen other tiny, neatly kept ranch homes overlooking the river that joins the Snake in Alpine. When Dean drove up he noticed that a spotless white Escalade sat in the driveway. In Chicago the Escalade was the vehicle of choice of gang bangers and drug dealers, but this one had a magnetic sign on the door that said, Daryl Fay, EV Products, Regional Distributor. Dean smiled. He hadn't ever seen that particular car with commercial advertising on the door, and he hoped the diversionary tactic wouldn't make its way back to Chicago.

Dean pounded on the door, waited a minute, and pounded again. He was just about to accompany the heavy pounding with a shouted

"Police," when a clean-shaven, twenty-something with a short haircut, wearing a pink polo shirt and khakis, opened the door.

"I'm trying to locate Daryl Fay?"

The young man smiled a salesman's smile. "I'm Daryl, what can I help you with?"

The shock almost floored Dean. He had met his share of stripper boyfriends on the streets of Chicago and most of them looked like they belonged either in a motorcycle gang, or were wiseguys or wiseguy-wannabes. Dean flashed his badge. "Deputy Dean Wister, can I come in and ask you a few questions?"

"Uh, what's this about?"

"There was a man killed in Jackson that you may know. I need to ask you a few questions." Dean asked again, "May I come in?"

The smile disappeared, but Daryl said, "Sure, come on in."

The interior of the house mirrored the well-kept exterior but was decorated in the same monotonous Western decor that Dean was finding tiring. Daryl motioned for Dean to sit down. "Who was killed?"

"A man by the name of Jordy Smith." Daryl stared at Dean and didn't say anything.

"You know who he is." Dean said it as a statement, not a question, so that Daryl would know that he already knew the answer.

"Yeah, I know who he is. He's one of Amber's regulars."

"Does it bother you that Amber had a relationship with him?"

Daryl laughed. "Relationship? Hey, a kiss in the car, a hand job, even an occasional blow job, that ain't no relationship. She was playing him like a bluegrass fiddle. Amber ain't as sweet and dumb as she plays. What she would do for him, that ain't nothing. Look, Deputy, me and Amber, we got something special. We both come from nothin' and she's doing what she's doin' so we can get a real business started and she can get out of dancing and we can have a real nice life together. So, what she's doing with Jordy or any of those other suckers down at the bar, no, that don't bother me. She's just paying her dues and it won't be long before I can get us out of here."

"So, it wouldn't bother you if Jordy was fucking Amber—if he wanted her to leave you for him?"

Daryl looked serious now. "Deputy. That would never happen. Amber loves me and we're going to have a family together. The thing with Jordy, it's just to help with the money. She thinks I don't know about Jordy. And that's OK. I let her think that. But I knew Jordy was giving her money. And most of it came right back here and into our business. If she was serious about him she wouldn't be helping me with the money for the business."

"OK, where were you the night before last between say nine PM and two AM?"

Daryl paused for a long time as if he too were deciding whether he should lie, or how much. "Here's the thing. I met with Jordy that night in his office at about seven-thirty. We met for about an hour. I gave him my EV presentation and signed him up for my downline. I think he was going to be real good at it." He paused again, then looked at Dean straight in the eye. "I know this don't look good. But I swear I never hurt Jordy. I have the paper work I can show you that I signed him up for my downline. And why would I hurt him? Why would I kill the golden goose? His money was financing our business and now that's gone."

"What happened when you left?"

"I drove back to Alpine. I spent the rest of the night working on EV stuff. Amber was working and didn't get in until about three in the morning."

"Did you see or talk to anybody after you got home?"

"I'm not sure. I'd have to check my phone records. But I'm sure I sent a bunch of emails and made some Facebook posts from my computer. You probably could check that." Dean thought that even if that was true, it didn't matter much. He'd confessed that he'd met with Jordy, he had a jealous-lover motive, even if he denied it, and he would have had time to kill Jordy and still drive back to Alpine and make phone calls and send emails.

"Deputy"—Daryl knew that the circumstances looked bad and was pleading now—"I have nothing to hide. I want you to know everything about me, and I can tell from your voice that you're from a different part of the country. Tennessee?"

"West Virginia."

"My great grandparents were from West Virginia. And I know that people from that part of the country are real. Not like some of the folks around here. I know if you talk to the Lincoln County police, they're going to tell you some bad things about me. I was a hellraiser in high school; I did do some things on the other side of the law, and I got me a bad reputation with the local cops. And I know they see the Escalade, and see that I've been taking people out to the steak house and entertaining them, and they think I'm selling drugs. They've been following me all over and I figured eventually they'd see I'm not selling drugs and give up. I've tried very hard to turn my life around. I'm not involved in anything outside the law, and I had nothing to do with harming Jordy. And I'm willing to swear that on the Bible and on the lives of my future children. Heck, I'm willing to take a lie detector test if you want."

When Daryl finished his speech, Dean was impressed. The kid had charisma and sincerity —a natural-born salesman. Whether he was innocent, Dean had no idea, but he did think he should take him up on the lie detector. Dean felt only true sociopaths or trained spies could beat a lie detector. And in his gut, Dean was pretty sure that Daryl would not want to kill the golden goose, at least until the goose had finished laying all of its eggs.

"You know what, Daryl? I think I believe you. But I'm going to try to arrange for that lie detector test. We should rule you out as soon as possible as a suspect, and it also might help you with the Lincoln County cops if you pass. Now, can you show me the paperwork that Jordy filled out? I'm going to have to take that with me."

Daryl took Dean into the back of the house, which had three small bedrooms. The bedroom that Daryl shared with Amber was decorated fully in pink and looked like the bedroom of a ten-year-old girl. A second bedroom was an office, which contained a desk, computer, printer, and motivational posters all over the walls. Daryl noticed Dean looking at the posters. "You know who Tony Robbins is? He is amazing. He's the reason I turned my life around. I went to one of his seminars in Salt Lake City and it changed my life." Daryl took the paperwork signed by Jordy from a folder on his desk and handed it to Dean. "There's no way I would actually document my meeting with him if I killed him, right? Or if I did, I would have burned this."

Dean had to admit that Daryl had a point. Innocent people talk like Daryl was talking. The guilty understand that stupid incriminating mistakes are an occupational hazard. "Where do you keep your products?"

"In our other room." Daryl opened the door to the third bedroom and Dean could see that this bedroom was larger than the other two. It was stacked floor to ceiling with packaged boxes and jars of varying sizes, all with the EV label. "Wow, how much money do you have invested in inventory?"

"Well, there's about a hundred grand here, retail, but I get a sixty-percent discount on retail, so there's about forty thousand in inventory. So there's sixty thousand of profit right here." Daryl smiled his biggest MLM smile.

"How did you get involved in MLM, Daryl?"

"Well, partly it was Tony Robbins, and partly it was I read this article in Business Week that said that Mormons are crazy for MLM. And they are. They just eat this up. Most people associate Mormons with Utah, but we have a lot of Mormons here in Wyoming and also just across the border in Idaho, so I've been having a lot of success with the Mormons. Heck, I'm even thinking of becoming Mormon."

Dean thought about the "I Heart Mormon Boobs" sign in the bar and wondered if there were any Mormon strippers. "So you mostly recruit here, or do you also recruit in Jackson?"

"Well, besides Jordy, I found another group that loves MLM in Jackson. There's been a lot of Russians that moved into Jackson in the last few years and they're almost as crazy about MLM as the Mormons. And I met this Russian guy, Boris Birkov, who is my downline into the community, and he's doing great."

"Thanks, Daryl. I'm going to try to get you set up with that lie detector. I want you to be in the clear on this," Dean said, and he meant it.

"I really appreciate it, Deputy Wister. Here, let me get you a catalog sample bag." The catalog was divided into a men's side and women's side, so if you turned the catalog over you had half a catalog devoted to products targeting your gender. He handed the bag to Dean. "There are four samples in this bag. There's the YR Supplement—YR stands for youth rejuvenator, it's a special formulation of vitamins, minerals, and herbs that increase your energy level and help your body remove toxins that cause aging. There's the T Factor Booster—these are enzymes that enable your body to boost its testosterone level. Now you look like you have plenty of testosterone, but give it a try—we can all use a little more, especially in your line of work. The third product is NV, or Nature's Viagra. Works even better than those little blue pills. Even though I don't need it at my age, it's kind of fun to be able to go four or five times in a row. And finally, there is EV youth cream. It's anti-aging skin cream for men. Deputy, if you try these products for the next two weeks, you will be calling me asking how you can become a distributor. It's my gift to you. All I ask is that you give them a try for two weeks. Deal?"

Dean couldn't help but laugh at the earnest sales pitch. "Deal."

Dean had a strange feeling on his way back to Jackson. Daryl had motive, means, and opportunity, and had even confessed to meeting with Jordy in the time frame in which he was killed.

Still, he had been able to overcome Dean's natural cynicism with his earnestness. More importantly, Daryl needed Jordy's money for his business, and that had just gone away. He understood where Daryl had come from and he wanted him to be innocent. But he would have to see the lie detector results. He called and asked the Sheriff to set it up.

Driving back, he stopped for gas and a six-pack and noticed "The Modern West," a resort magazine, on a stand at the checkout. There was a picture of Sheriff Dani Cody on the cover. Back home he sat on the couch, finished off the six pack and read the puff piece, detailing Dani's western roots, basketball stardom, Phi Beta Kapp membership, and her electoral successes. His mouth dropped when he saw her family also owned the largest bison ranch in Wyoming. He smiled to himself. The small-town country sheriff act was just that.

Dean awoke gasping. In the dream, he'd been guiding a raft trip, something had happened, and everyone was in the water and panicking. He was trapped underneath the raft, floundering and couldn't help his clients. The dream troubled him, and he lay there a bit trying to figure out its meaning. Looking up, he noticed a light reflecting from the hall bath in the cabin he was renting in an isolated drainage off Moose Wilson Road, just outside Teton National Park. Must have left the light on, he thought as he stood with a bladder full of Snake River Ale and walked into the bathroom. Wisps of steam rose from the big cast-iron farmhouse tub, mixing with the mountain air and pine logs. In the midst of the steam-infused smell of Christmas lay a naked girl, a cowboy hat perched on her blonde locks, with her leg angled on the side of the tub.

"Hi, honey," Sara said. "Want to join me?"

Dean sat in the nurturing waters, Sara leaning against him, his arms wrapped around her warm and slick body, and he told her about the dream. Sara had a theory. "Maybe it's about the case. You're back in Wyoming, but you're no longer in the same role you were when in when you were here the first time as a guide. This is causing you anxiety, and subconsciously you're afraid you won't be able to help the people affected by the case you're trying to solve. You're floundering, and you're afraid if you can't solve the case people might be harmed."

"Wow," Dean said. "That makes a lot of sense. So now that you've probed my subconscious fears, help me with the case. So far, my suspects are two people who have a motive to kill Jordy—Hayden, and Amber's boyfriend—and one person who has a motive to kill Hayden, Fletcher Barns. But you wouldn't expect any of them to hire a Chicago hit man to do the job. Out here you 'take care of them things yourself.'"

"You shouldn't try to imitate that accent," Sara said. "With your West Virginia drawl you sound sort of like a brain damaged cowboy.

No, actually, you sound exactly like a brain damaged hillbilly."

"Brain damaged hillbilly? Isn't that an oxymoron? I can say that cuz I'm one of 'em."

"Well, did that cute Mark come up with any Chicago connection in his database?"

"Not yet. I hope to have something in the morning."

"I'm sure the two of you will come up with something. You work really well together, The Geek and The River Rat. That would make a good sitcom. What do you think?"

Dean ignored her wisecrack. "I keep coming back to Dani's Big Four: money, power, sex, and love. Which one is it?"

Sara took the bar of soap, rubbed it between her hands, and soaped Dean's chest. "I don't know. Maybe it's all four. It's a place to start, but the Big Four thing is an oversimplification. You'd need to add control, betrayal, revenge, greed, and of course varying degrees of mental illness and personality disorder. Normally, none of these by themselves are strong enough for murder. Which suspect has the strongest motive?"

"That's a good question, but it's really too early to tell." Dean looked at her. "It feels like it used to back in Chicago... before. When I was stuck, we'd take a bath together, and you'd help me work it out."

Sara pulled him close, and Dean closed his eyes and could feel a heartbeat, not sure whose it was.

Chapter 12

WHEN Oleg entered the tiny living room of their apartment later that evening, Tatiana was sitting cross-legged on the floor reading a children's story in English to her two youngest cousins. Her English was excellent; her tutor had said that she had reached a plateau and her fluency could only be increased by studying abroad in an English-speaking country. "Tatiana, darling. I have some great news. As soon as you finish the story, I need to speak with you alone."

Oleg had just finished installing Windows XP on one of his refurbished computers when Tatiana came into the bedroom. *She looks so much like her mother*, Oleg thought. She was a small girl, under five feet tall, with dark hair and clear blue eyes, and so thin that most people imagined she was fragile, but her small frame disguised an unusual strength; she had just missed being selected for a national gymnastics team when she was younger.

"What is it, Father?" She looked at him in her calm, quiet way and again Oleg thought of her mother.

"I have some wonderful news. You are leaving for college in the United States tomorrow!"

"What? What are you talking about?"

"I've arranged for a man to take you to Chicago and enroll you in college there. He will get you a part-time job to help pay for college and you will live in an apartment with three other Russian girls. It's already paid for."

Tatiana looked stunned. "How can you pay for this? We have no money."

"I've been saving for this for years. I've made a lot of money in my computer business over the last ten years. It was always for your future. I've just been waiting for the right opportunity for you and this is it."

"Papa, I can't believe you haven't discussed this with me. I can't go to America. Not right now." She burst into tears, pulled on her coat, and ran out the door.

Oleg sat and put his head in his hands, not knowing what to do. She had to get on that plane tomorrow, no matter what. There was no other plan.

Two hours later a red-eyed and subdued Tatiana walked into the bedroom where Oleg was again working on a computer, this time a ten-year old Dell laptop, trying to distract himself about their situation. "Papa, tell me how this will work."

The next day Tatiana and Oleg met Birkov at the front entrance of Domodedovo International

Airport in Moscow. He was standing there in his black cashmere overcoat with the attractive Russian woman who'd spoken at the presentation and three other young Russian girls who looked to be about Tatiana's age, or maybe a little older. "Comrade Oleg, you made it. I am so happy for you—this must be Tatiana." He looked her up and down as if he was evaluating a calf. "Aren't you a cute little thing? Are you sure she is really sixteen?"

Oleg, mistaking Birkov's comment for a query rather than a misguided compliment, responded, "I assure you she is sixteen; she has her birth papers in her bag."

Birkov just laughed. "Tatiana, you will be very popular in America, I assure you. Now, Oleg, say your farewell to your daughter, we don't have a lot of time to make our flight."

Oleg pulled her to the side and pressed some bills into her hand. "Here is some cash. Hide it in a safe place for an emergency. Please write when you get to America." Then he pulled out a small picture in a silver frame and handed it to her. "This is my favorite picture of your mother." He paused as if considering whether he could let it go, then he placed it in her hand. "You look so much like her in this picture. Since she has been gone, it has given me comfort that when I would look at you, I could see part of her. I have always felt she was watching over us. And you will need her to watch over you in America." Then he wrapped his fleshy arms around the little girl and hugged her so tight it took her breath away.

Birkov, now getting impatient, insisted, "Oleg and Tatiana, we need to go."

"Don't worry, Father, I will make you proud."

Birkov took her hand, and as they walked into the terminal with the three other women, Tatiana looked more like his child than a young woman who would be required to give up all vestiges of childhood in the next few weeks.

Oleg didn't move until the group disappeared into the terminal. As he turned and walked away, he did two things that surprised him very much. Things he hadn't done for many, many years. He prayed. And he cried.

The four young Russian women sat in the back of the plane, and Birkov and his companion, the successful protégé from Chicago, sat in the front, in business class. Tatiana learned from the other girls that they had known about their planned trip for over a year, and, like Tatiana, their parents had savings from black-market businesses that made the investment in their daughters possible. She was glad to see that her English was far superior to the other girls' and was competitive enough to think about the advantage it might give her over any other young Russians she might find herself pitted against at university and, later, in the super-competitive American job market. They had a two-hour layover in Madrid, where Birkov bought them sandwiches at the snack bar and then disappeared with his companion until just before they were ready to board their flight to Chicago.

By the time they reached O'Hare airport, Tatiana was exhausted and stiff from the long flight and the cramped seats. She couldn't imagine how the other passengers felt, all of whom were much larger than herself. After getting their baggage, Birkov led them to the transportation center outside the terminal, and two Russian men met them in a white panel van. Birkov said to them, "Girls, these men will take you to your temporary accommodations. I have other business and will see you in a few days."

The men opened the back door to the van, and the girls sat on the two wooden benches facing each other. There was a blacked-out plexi-glass panel separating the passenger compartment from two men sitting in the front. Without windows in the van, the girls could see nothing of their route, but twenty minutes later they heard the mechanical grinding of a door opening, and the van pulled into a warehouse. The men opened the door and led the girls into the center of the building, a large open area with four sofas arranged in front of a television, several tables, a couple dozen folding chairs, and a small kitchen. Tatiana counted twenty-two other young women staring at them, with sad, blank looks. A very good looking young man of about twenty-five walked toward them with a big smile. "Ladies, welcome to America. Let me help you with your bags."

Tatiana had been at the warehouse for a week and she was getting impatient. The men in the white van had come and taken away eight of the women, but there were still fifteen young women sleeping on cots lined up on the concrete floor of the aluminum building. Each day's routine consisted of the young women queuing up to use the single toilet and one of the two open shower stalls in the makeshift barracks. The rest of the day was spent writing letters home or perusing a stack of American gossip and fashion magazines that had been so thoughtfully provided by Boris. Tatiana would listen as the young women speculated about life in Chicago from stories they had heard or old television shows and Hollywood movies they had seen on some of the black-market videos available to them back home. Tatiana kept to herself, re-reading the copies of American classics—Hawthorne and Twain and Fitzgerald—that she had brought with her. The lack of privacy bothered her, and she was self-conscious of her petite, prepubescent-looking body as some of the other girls flaunted their voluptuousness during their morning grooming rituals. After a few days, Tatiana offered to give English lessons to break up the monotony, but most of the others took this as an insult to their knowledge of the language, and only a couple of them participated. The men would come around most nights with food and vodka, and they would play music on a boom box and dance. Some girls would get very drunk and the men would take them to another room in the warehouse and have sex with them. Tatiana would not join in these parties, instead going off by herself and wondering when she would be taken to the beautiful apartment in Chicago that her father had told her about. The girls talked among themselves about what might be going on, but no one knew anything definite.

Finally, after ten days, the good looking young man, who gave Tatiana the creeps, took her and four other girls into a room and told them to pack their things, they would be leaving in ten minutes. All of them were excited that their apartment was finally ready and that they would be able to begin their wonderful new American lives. They loaded their baggage in the van and before the door closed, the young man approached them. "I have a message that I have been directed to read to you from Mr. Birkov.

My dear young ladies,

There is a complication that has caused a change in our plans. A corrupt bureaucrat in American immigration has demanded a bribe in order to permit each of you to remain in the country. He has threatened to arrest each of you if this bribe is not paid, and it would result in each of you spending several years in American prisons, and subjecting yourselves to much torture and abuse. Fortunately,

I was able to pay this bribe from my own funds to secure your freedom. However, this means that I no longer have the funds for your apartment in Chicago and your university tuition. But there is good news. This will result in only a temporary delay in your plans. I have found jobs for you in a spa in Wyoming. After you work there for twenty-four months, you will be returned to Chicago and you can begin your education. I am very sorry for this delay, but I am enduring a severe financial hardship in order to help you young women.

I hope to see you all soon,
Boris Birkov

The young women sat stunned, staring at each other. Two of them began crying softly. Tatiana looked directly at the good looking young man. "What is this Wyoming?"

Chapter 13

SUNDAY morning was Thomas McGraw's coming-out party. He was featured on all five major national political talk shows—Meet the Press, Face the Nation, CNN, the Sunday morning political panel on ABC, and Fox News Sunday. Tom felt a little like Miss America as he gave the same abbreviated version of his announcement speech on each program, a speech that was viewed by the liberal news media as a break from traditional conservatism—which was exactly Tom's intention. But when the liberal reporters on the panel couldn't hide their glee that a candidate was stepping forward to challenge the right wing of the Republican Party, Tom got a sick feeling in the pit of his stomach. Maybe he had been too aggressive with his message, and he knew there would be a price to pay with the conservative pundits for his challenge to the conservative orthodoxy that had taken over his party for the last several election cycles. When he got to his last stop, Fox News Sunday, his fears were realized. The Fox News panel interrogated him ferociously, all but accusing him of conservative treason. Actually, it was even worse than treason. One of the panel accused him of a metaphorical assassination attempt on the political views of the great Ronald Reagan, even going so far as saying that the liberal media was Tom McGraw's Jodie Foster. The conclusion they came to was that the conservative base would resoundingly reject this new "liberal libertarian."

Afterwards Tom's political war party gathered in a panicked meeting in a suite at Tom's Washington Hotel. Everyone looked glum. "That Fox thing. It wasn't a political talk show; it was more like a roast. I think we're going to be the laughingstock of the entire right-wing machine. I'm afraid we've lost the nomination on the first day," Tom's campaign manager lamented. "It's all going down just as I said it would. We're going to be hammered all week by every conservative media member, columnist, and all the conservative publications." He stared at Tom as if he were looking at a delinquent child.

Tom paused, cleared his throat, and stood. His normally calm, agreeable demeanor had morphed into a stormy, resolute anger that no one in the campaign had ever seen before. "I cannot fucking believe what I am fucking hearing in here. The same assholes that are attacking me are the ones that have not been able to win a national election in the last four terms. These are the ideologues threatening to make our party a permanent minority. Assassinating Ronald Reagan? They killed Ronald

Reagan's ideas years ago. I told each one of you that this campaign is not about the same old same old. I may not be successful, but I *do* have a vision for our party. And my vision *will* be put to a referendum to the American people over the next year or so. And if you didn't understand that these attacks were coming, then I misjudged your intelligence. Now we're going to reconvene this evening and before that meeting you all need to decide whether you believe in this campaign or not, and, just as important, whether you have the balls to withstand the fierce attacks we're going to have to weather from the establishment, and whether you believe that what we're doing is good for our country. And fuck FOX News!"

Tom went back to his room and returned some calls, most of them polite but clearly anxious about his performance on the shows. When he returned Charles Kidwell's call, Charles immediately picked up. "Hey, buddy, feeling a little ganged up on?"

"Are you kidding me? That was a political gangbang of epic proportions."

"Well, you shouldn't be surprised. You're throwing a wrench into an engine that's already sputtering badly. We talked about this many times."

"I know, I know. But it's one thing to talk about it theoretically, and it's another to actually experience it. Right now, I can't seem to find anyone in my party on my side."

"Well, that may not be a bad thing. At least for the time being. Since you're the only announced candidate, you're getting all the attention. That also means you have a chance to get your message out without having it confused by a bunch of other candidates' messages. And if your message starts resonating, there will be plenty of hacks jumping on the bandwagon. We just need to take this time to get you as much exposure as possible."

"I hope you're right."

"Aren't I always?"

At nine o'clock that evening, Senator McGraw walked into the computer-and pizza-infused mobile war room in the hotel, as much to see if there were any defections as to go over the schedule for the week. He was relieved to see that everyone was accounted for. He approached his campaign manager with kind of a sheepish look. "Did we lose anyone?"

"Not a one, sir." A young staff aide approached with his iPhone. The campaign manager seemed irritated with the interruption. "What?"

"Sorry, but I thought you'd want to see this right away. There's a video of the senator posted to YouTube a little while ago. It looks like someone recorded him when he talked to the team this morning. It's already all over the Internet."

Chapter 14

Mario Rosati sipped his morning espresso at the Starbucks on North Michigan Avenue and read the *Chicago Tribune* on his iPad. Mario wasn't exactly your father's Chicago mobster, but he was a Chicago mobster nonetheless. His empire was more befitting a mobster of the 21st century, and he saw himself not as a mobster but as a financial wizard, more of an out-of-the-box thinker than his counterpart CEOs of the major financial institutions. He liked to pose a rhetorical question to his inner circle—"Who are the real mobsters in our economy? No one gets hurt with what we do, or at least those who do get hurt are coming in with their eyes wide open." His argument was that his financial shenanigans, however questionable, didn't have the potential of crashing the entire world economy.

Mario financed those at the edges of society. He provided money laundering through his national chain of currency exchanges for a vast network of drug dealers, petty and not so petty thieves, and others on the edge of the law. Millions of illegal immigrants used his currency exchanges as their banks—to send money to support their families in Mexico, to pay their bills, and do all the mundane daily financial transactions that documented Americans take for granted. Some liked to criticize his transaction charges as excessive, but when compared to the gross margin on the ATM fees of the major banks, it would be hard for anyone to sustain that charge.

What got his attention this morning was that the front page of not only the *Chicago Tribune* but, in fact, every major news outlet was dominated by the candidacy of Senator Thomas McGraw from Wyoming. He had announced his candidacy for the presidency a couple of days ago and appeared on the Sunday news shows —now everyone seemed to be going apoplectic about the platform of the new Republican contender. The vicious attacks, interestingly more from the right than the left, were chronicled in the media with gleeful excess. The *Tribune* had a story entitled, "What the Top Ten Conservative Leaders Say About Thomas McGraw," followed by ten denouncements of him as a heretic to the cause. You could almost see the talking heads rubbing their hands together saying, "It's going to be fun feeding this guy to the dogs." And then there was the YouTube video that now had several million hits. Mario laughed out loud as he played it on his iPad. There was a foul-mouthed Senator McGraw cutting his staff a few new assholes. *I sure hope this guy knows what he's doing*, Mario thought.

His cell phone rang and it was his old nemesis, Carlos Alvarez. "Mario, it's Carlos. You remember me, right?"

"Carlos, how could I forget? How're you doing? I assume this is a social call, given the fact that your investigation of my organization was shut down. I wouldn't want you to put your job in jeopardy because of hard feelings you can't let go of."

Carlos ignored the jab. "Not exactly a social call, but I do need to talk with you about a fellow I think you know pretty well. Eddie Torino? He was found dead last week."

"Well, I haven't seen Edward for a long, long time, but I'm sorry to hear about him. What happened?"

"He was killed in a car accident in Jackson Hole."

"Jackson Hole, Wyoming? That's a hell of a long way from Chicago. What the hell was he doing out there?"

"That's why I'm calling you. I thought you might be able to tell me."

"I'm afraid I have no idea, Carlos." Mario had actually been expecting Carlos's call, and earlier than this. Even though he fully intended to stonewall Carlos, in cases such as this he felt an interview not only gave the impression of cooperation, but he often was able to glean information about what the authorities might or might not know about his involvement. "I don't know that I can help you. But it would be great to see you again. I'm available for the next hour or so. Would you like to join me for coffee?"

Twenty minutes later Mario opened the door of his penthouse condo in Trump Tower to the always impeccably dressed Carlos Alvarez and greeted him warmly. "Carlos, you look great. The last time I saw you, you didn't look so good. That misguided investigation had really affected your health. I am so glad you seem to have recovered."

"Thanks, Mario. I would say the same thing about you. The last time I saw you, you looked like a guy who knew his life was about to come crashing down around him. I do have to hand it to you, though. I don't know who you got to in the Bureau, but I have faith that your good fortune will eventually run out."

Mario smiled. "Let me give you some advice about faith—I know both our heritages are based in faith—but I've found that faith enhanced by powerful friends and money works much better than faith by itself."

Fed up with Mario's verbal games, Carlos got to the point. "When was the last time you saw Edward Torino?"

"I'm surprised you don't already know the answer to that question. I haven't seen him since before he went to prison the last time. Wasn't that at least two years ago? You would know better than me."

"So you've had no contact with him since then?"

"No. None. But I'm curious. Why are you investigating a car accident in Wyoming?"

"Well, the Wyoming police did a background check on Eddie and figured out he was a Chicago wiseguy. And then they did some more checking and saw that he was a hired gun. So naturally the cowboys out there got a little upset about a hit man coming to town. Sort of like the Shane thing, you know that old Western?" Mario had no inkling of the Shane reference, but nodded anyway. "So they called me to see if I had any ideas. I asked myself, of all the guys I know, who might know what Eddie Torino would be doing in Wyoming?"

"Well, I'm afraid I can't help you. Like I said, I haven't seen or talked to him in years."

"Assuming that's true, you do know people who know Torino. If you could check around I would be indebted for any information you could come up with."

"I'll check with my sources, Carlos. I'm a little curious about what he was doing out there myself. I never knew Eddie to be a lover of the Old West. If I hear anything, I'll let you know."

When Carlos left, Mario got on the phone with one of his boys. "Fucking Carlos Alvarez is trying to link Torino to us. We need to talk."

Chapter 15

Dean was a morning person. This was unfortunate in his line of work because almost universally criminals were evening people. Very few violent crimes occur before noon, and it is often difficult to interview witnesses in the morning. Still, Dean liked the solitude of the morning and he liked to use that time to catch up on paperwork, go through his emails, plan the day, and think. Sara never understood that the most important part of his work involved thinking. She would see his inactivity when they were both home as an invitation for conversation. And if she wasn't up for discussing a case, he would have to leave the house and go for a walk or a run when he wanted to do his serious thinking. Since she'd been gone there was no one to interrupt, but now he had trouble concentrating. He would start thinking about work, his mind would begin to drift to Sara, and the darkness would start to envelop him. This morning, when he felt the creeping darkness, he grabbed a cup of non-organic, non-fair-trade cowboy coffee, black, and picked up the morning edition of the *Jackson Hole News and Guide.* The front page was dominated by the murder of Jordy and the disappearance of Hayden. The dead Chicagoan had not yet been connected to the murder. Sheriff Dani was quoted making a few generic comments about pursuing several leads but did not say that an arrest was imminent. Today Dean wanted to follow up on the remaining telephone contacts of Jordy and Hayden, and see if Mark had anything for him yet. He closed the paper and checked his email. Apparently Rusty was an early-morning person as well. He had already gone through the remaining emails and text messages and set up an interview with Hayden's girlfriend, Eliza Nelson.

On the way to Eliza's house Dean stopped at McDonald's for a caffeine top-off and once again saw the man in the red ski vest with the dirty Border Collie sitting on a bench in front of McDonald's eating Chicken McNuggets. He stopped and got out of his car. "How you doing? Nice dog you got there." As he reached down to pet the dog, he saw that the dog's paw was swollen. The swelling was enough to shock him, and the dog was holding it up, not willing to put any weight on it. "Looks like your dog has a problem with his foot. Tell ya what... I'd be happy to give you money to have him looked at by a vet if you want. It looks pretty serious."

The man stared at Dean for a moment and then said, "If I was you, I would go on about my business. Just 'cause I don't dress like you don't mean I can't take care of my own animal. I saw that piece of shit you just crawled out of. See that truck next to yorn? That's mine, and it's paid for, so I can afford a vet if I want one."

Dean glanced over and saw a new silver F-250 with a crew cab and custom lights next to his 10-year-old Jeep. "I see it. You mean to tell me you can afford a fifty-thousand-dollar truck but you can't afford to take care of your dog? You should be ashamed of yourself."

The man grinned at Dean, showing a mouthful of tobacco-stained teeth. "That's right. You must be one of them city boys. The animal will either get better, or he will die. That's how I see it. Now get the fuck away from me and let me finish my lunch."

The blood was running to Dean's head now, and he clenched his fists involuntarily. Should he take this guy on? Take him in? He thought about the paperwork, and how he would justify it to the sheriff—after all he hadn't seen the guy do anything to the dog—and so he pulled out his badge. "Look, I don't want to make trouble for you, but I'm a deputy sheriff. I've seen you around town before, and I could take you in right now for animal cruelty, but I don't have time. So, here's how it's going to work. I'm going to keep my eye out for you, and the next time I see you I'm going to look at your dog's foot, and if it still looks like that, I'm going to arrest you. And the county will take the dog. Do you understand?"

The man's lips moved but no sound came out, as if he wanted to say something but knew better.

"I need you to acknowledge what I said to you. Do you understand?"

The man spit a wad of tobacco on the ground next to Dean's foot. "I understand."

Eliza Nelson's home was on a ridge north of town, not far from where Hayden lived. It resembled Hayden's home in its design—that is, if Hayden's home had been taking architectural enhancement drugs. Everything in the house was super-sized—the rooms, doors, windows, and even the furniture. Dean thought that it looked like a house built for a race of people where everyone was NBA-sized. Eliza greeted him warmly, and then led him to a corner of the great room which felt surprisingly intimate to Dean, considering it was a thousand-square-foot room with an open-beamed ceiling. Eliza sat next to Dean and put her hand on his arm. "Do you have any news about Hayden?"

"No, we haven't. He hasn't used his cell phone or credit cards and we haven't located his car. When was the last time you spoke to him?"

Eliza's face dropped a bit, and she paused before she spoke, allowing Dean to study her. Eliza looked like almost all the women he had met in Jackson—amazingly fit, as if she hiked, ran, or climbed every day. She had a striking, dark sultry look, Dean thought Italian or maybe Armenian, and the blackest eyes he had ever seen. "Hayden and I spent the evening together before he left. I'm afraid we had an argument. We went to bed, and when I woke up, he was gone. I tried to call his cell phone many times that day, and texted him, but there was no answer."

"What was the argument about?"

"Well, we have sort of a volatile relationship. I thought it was really no big deal, until I couldn't reach him. It was stupid, really. Like most of our arguments are. I had planned a private evening with him, had gone to a lot of trouble and cooked a big meal. Hayden was over an hour late, didn't call, and the meal was ruined."

"Why was he so late?"

"Hayden is always late, but his last stop of that day was at this new client's house, some big banker who built a new house across from the Elk Refuge. Something happened there, but Hayden wouldn't tell me what it was. And that made me even more pissed off and he just stormed out of here."

"When you say volatile, were any of your arguments physical?"

"Oh, no, never. We could yell and scream at each other, but neither of us have ever been violent."

"Do you have any idea where he might have gone?"

"I don't know—his only family was Jordy. Hayden likes to get out in the mountains by himself. He would go for long hikes sometimes when he was upset, but he's never been gone for more than a day or so before."

"How long have you and Hayden been together?"

"Well, we've known each other for about a year, but we've been involved only a couple of months. I should tell you that I'm still married, though my separation from my husband is very amicable, and I wasn't involved with Hayden before we separated. My husband and I had been living virtually separate lives. He travels a lot, and I just decided I wasn't happy."

"Is your separation mutual?"

"Not really. My husband, Matt, he's the nicest guy in the world. The nicest guy I have ever met, really. In retrospect, probably too nice for me. I like a guy with a little edge, you know? Matt put me on a pedestal. This house was a wedding present. But he treated me, I don't know, like his mother. When I told him I wanted a divorce, I could see the hurt in his face. But he said, 'I just want you to be happy.' Can you fucking believe that? Here I am walking out on him and he says, 'I just want you to be happy.' He insisted that I keep the house. Like I need a house this big."

"What does Matt do for a living?"

"He owns a chain of auto parts stores. He travels most of the week and is here only on weekends. He's renting a place over at Teton Village right now."

"And what does he think of you and Hayden? Does he think maybe you were seeing him while you were still together?"

"Well, when Matt and I separated, I told him that there was no one else, and that I would never, ever cheat on him, that I have too much respect for him, and I'm sure he believes me. Even though it's true, I think Matt would believe anything I would tell him. When I started to date Hayden—this was pretty fast, only a couple of weeks after he moved out—I had lunch with Matt and told him I was dating Hayden. I wanted him to know that I hadn't so much as kissed Hayden while we were married, but I wanted him to know everything that was going on so that he wouldn't think badly of me. Matt was totally OK with it."

"Is Matt paying spousal support? Is this divorce going to cost him money?"

"Oh, no, I have my own money. I won't take a penny from Matt. I even offered to list this house, not with Hayden, by the way, and split all the sales proceeds with him. But Matt is insisting I keep it."

"Did Hayden ever mention he was having trouble with anyone, or anyone who was his enemy?"

"Well, just that awful Fletcher Barns. Everyone else I know loves Hayden." Eliza stood and took Dean's hand in hers. "I really appreciate all your help, Deputy. Please find him."

On the way back to the office, Dean left a message for Mark in Chicago. "Hey, how are you

coming on my analytics? I haven't seen anything yet. I also need to know what can you find
out about a Matt Nelson, rich guy who lives in
Teton County? And some banker, I don't have
his name, who just built a new house, probably
a multi-million dollar one, on a property north
of town, across from the Elk Refuge. Can you
give me anything on him?"

Chapter 16

DEAN's cell phone rang and he could see it was Mark on the other end. "What do you have for me?"

"I just emailed you the analytics report. But I wanted to give you a heads-up. It seems that one of the investors in the Fletcher Barns venture is a guy named Boris Birkov. He was the subject of a federal investigation last year, but it was closed for lack of evidence. I pulled the file and found some very interesting shit. Boris runs what you could call an employment agency for Russian immigrants, some of it legal, some not so much. But here's the thing— most of these immigrants don't have bank accounts and Boris has a deal with Mario Rosati to buy thousands of prepaid phone cards, pay-as-you go phones, Visa cards, and such. He distributes them to his immigrant clients, and we assume takes a cut off the top from what he pays Rosati. He sort of acts as a middleman because most of Rosati's currency exchange employees speak Spanish, not Russian. Carlos came by when I was putting this together and he was nearly jumping up and down, saying this is the fucking smoking gun. You know what a hard-on he has for Rosati. So he said to call you and get you on this right away. Boris also has a home in Jackson, actually Wilson, and get this, his house is right next to fucking Dick Cheney. Kind of funny, huh? Cheney living next to a Russian gangster?"

"Hilarious."

"I'll text you his address and phone number."

Dean wondered if Cheney still had Secret Service protection and if he could even get near the house. He would have to check with the sheriff. "Thanks, Mark. But I don't know about the smoking-gun thing. Looks like I have more suspects already than I thought I would. But tell Carlos I'll get on Boris right away."

Sheriff Dani informed Dean that Cheney still did, in fact, have a small, unofficial security detail, but not Secret Service. She laughed when he said, "Obama was always scared shitless that someone would kill Cheney and the conspirators would blame him for pulling his security and allowing his Muslim friends to come after Cheney." Dean thought she was joking but wasn't entirely sure. "Anyway, I'll tell them that if they see a beat-up Jeep Cherokee in the neighborhood with Illinois license plates not to shoot you."

"Thanks. I'm heading out there now to meet one of the Russian investors in Raptor Landing, a guy named Boris Birkov. I'm really surprised to find Russians in Jackson Hole." "I was, too, when they first started coming in about ten years ago, but we have a thriving Russian community here, believe it or not. We even have a Russian Club. They arrange social events, that kind of thing. I attended one of their parties during my last campaign. I'm not a big drinker, and I have to tell you, I was in pretty bad shape the next day. So watch out if Boris brings out the Stoli."

"Will do, Sheriff."

Dean didn't see anyone who looked like part of a security detail as he drove through Teton Pines, the exclusive golf course development a few miles south of the ski village in Wilson, the town that sits in between downtown Jackson and the ski resort at Teton Village. He expected the homes to be situated on bigger pieces of property, but since the development was built around a private golf course, the lots were generally on the smallish side. There were even some cluster homes with very little land at all. He pulled into the driveway of a huge estate. The home looked dark, and Dean thought that maybe no one was at home. He parked his Jeep on the circular drive and walked up to the huge wooden double door, accented with heavy iron hardware. He sort of expected something that looked, well, a little more Russian. He rang the doorbell and could hear the loud chimes inside. For a long time, nothing happened, then he heard some fumbling and the door opened. For one of the first times in his life, Dean was speechless, and totally confused. For in front of him was the familiar face of the former Vice President of the United States. "May I help you?" the Vice President asked.

Dean's mind at first went blank. Then his next thought was, "What is Dick Cheney doing at the Russian's house, and why is he answering the door?" And then he looked up and saw the number 435, not 438. The older man was not unfamiliar with the speechless reaction when someone encountered him, either expectedly or unexpectedly, and repeated, "What can I do for you?"

Finally, Dean attempted a recovery. "Mr. Vice President, I am very sorry to disturb you. My name is Dean Wister, and I'm a Deputy with the Teton County Sheriff's office." Dean's normal modus operandi would be to then show is badge, but it occurred to him that if he reached into his pocket, the hidden security detail just might put a bullet in his head. He was glad he had decided to not carry a gun in Teton County. "Let me show you my ID, Mr. Vice President." And he very slowly and deliberately pulled his badge, and shakily displayed it to the Vice President.

"I know who you are. The sheriff called and said you might be stopping by. Won't you come in?"

This wasn't exactly the turn of events that Dean had been expecting, but he decided to take advantage of this unexpected audience with an undeniably historical figure, probably the only historical figure he would ever have an audience with. Cheney led him to his office off the foyer. Later, Dean could not describe anything about the foyer or Cheney's office. His attention was focused entirely on the Vice President, his height, shorter than he thought, his weight, skinnier than he thought, but understandable after his heart transplant, and his gait, surprisingly more steady and youthful than he thought it would be. The Vice President offered Dean a seat, and for a third time, patiently and calmly said, "How can I help you?"

Dean explained that he was investigating the murder of Jordy Smith, the disappearance of Hayden, and then told Cheney about the hit man in the Snake River. The Vice President was the first person outside of the law enforcement community he had talked to about the hit man, but he felt he needed to tell him to explain the possible connection to Fletcher and Boris, and he figured that the one secret tidbit from the investigation was nothing compared to the national security secrets that Cheney was still harboring. "So what can you tell me about your neighbor, Boris Birkov?"

Cheney at first seemed not to hear the question, or at least he ignored it. "Deputy Wister, where are you from?" He stroked his chin and said, "Let me guess, West Virginia, and I think I hear a little Chicago in there, too?"

Dean was somewhat astounded at Cheney's ear for American regional dialects. "I cannot believe that. How did you hear that? I can understand how you got the Southern part, though most people say Tennessee, but how did you get Chicago? And, please, call me Dean."

"Well, Dean, as I was listening to you, I could hear a perfect mixture of Brad Paisley," Cheney paused, "and Barack Obama."

Dean just stared, speechless. Then Cheney grinned. "I'm fucking with you, Dean. Sheriff Cody said you were on loan from Chicago, but that you sounded like a West Virginia hillbilly."

Dean laughed more loudly than the joke deserved. "OK, you got me. So what can you tell me about your neighbor?"

"Not much, I'm afraid. He moved in after I left office. If it had been prior, there would have been a formal vetting. As it is, I know he's involved in some kind of import-export business, and I know he helps Russian immigrants get through the red tape, finds them jobs, that kind of thing."

"Have you heard any rumors about him?"

"Well, honestly, you hear rumors about any first generation, rich businessman. I try to ignore the noise. I'm afraid I can't offer you any useful information. The one thing I do know about him, though, is a big point in his favor."

"What's that?"

"He hates that fucking Putin."

When Dean left the Vice President and headed next door, he was armed with no more information than if he had not pulled into the wrong driveway, but he had come away with a couple of great stories.

His purpose in visiting Birkov was not to get information, and he was not naïve enough to think that one of Rosati's associates would give him any. Rather, his purpose was to let Birkov know, and therefore at the same time let Rosati know, that they had made the link from Rosati to Torino to Birkov to Fletcher. Hopefully, this would put into motion damage control by any of the three living members of this group. And damage-control actions often left trails of evidence that could unravel a conspiracy.

This time when Dean rang the doorbell, it was answered by a young, tall, model-thin woman with short black hair and heavy makeup.. She looked at him coldly and said in a heavy Russian accent, "Yes."

Dean flashed his badge. "Deputy Dean Wister, Teton County Sheriff. Is Mr. Birkov home?"

"What do you want?"

"I'm afraid I would need to speak with Mr. Birkov about that. It's a very serious law enforcement matter."

The woman eyed him suspiciously. "Wait here."

Dean looked around the house while he waited. Now this was what he expected when he was next door—everything made from glass, steel, and glossy laminate, modern sculpture and artwork. Not a piece of barn wood in the entire place. In a few minutes, a heavy-set man waddled through the door, his frame encased in a blue silk warm-up suit.

"What can I do for you, Deputy?" Another heavy Russian accent.

"I need to talk with you about Mario Rosati."

Boris looked a bit startled. "Well, I have a business relationship with Mr. Rosati's company, but I don't really know Mr. Rosati."

"Mr. Birkov, we have reason to believe that Mr. Rosati may be involved with the death of Jordy Smith, and the disappearance of his cousin, Hayden Smith. I'm sure you've read about them in the papers. You're a known acquaintance of Mario Rosati, the only known acquaintance who resides in Teton County. I'm authorized by the Midwest Organized Crime Task Force to provide you with complete immunity in exchange for any information implicating Mario Rosati in these crimes." This was a complete lie, but Dean knew that Carlos would do just about anything to put Rosati in prison, and he had no doubt that immunity or other favors could be arranged.

"Deputy, I'm afraid you are being very insulting to me. So I am going to explain the situation to you and perhaps you will reconsider this very aggressive attitude you are taking. I have only a business relationship with Mr. Rosati's company. I have no knowledge of any criminal activity on the part of Mr. Rosati. As far as I know he is an honest man. If I had any knowledge of any crimes of Mr. Rosati, I would be more than happy to provide it without any favors or immunity or anything else. I also am an honest businessman."

"Do you know an Edward Torino?"

"I do not recall ever hearing that name. Perhaps you can refresh my memory on how I might have met him?"

"When was the last time you spoke with Mr. Rosati?"

"Well, as I am sure you already know, I speak with Mr. Rosati every week or so about my business account with his company. I am sure you can look up the phone records, I don't remember exactly the last time I spoke with him."

"Mr. Birkov, Mario Rosati is being investigated for murder. Any assistance that you may have given, even innocently, to Rosati in locating Jordy or Hayden Smith, or any assistance you may have given him or any of his associates in arranging travel or accommodations while these crimes were taking place, will be viewed as aiding and abetting crime. You could spend the rest of your life in prison. Please think about that."

"There is nothing to think about. I'm afraid that you are making me, how do you say this, guilty by association. Doesn't that violate your Constitution?"

Dean felt himself begin to simmer at being lectured to by a Russian criminal about his country's Constitution, but he kept his cool. "Well, if that's the line that you're going to take, please let Mario know about this conversation and he'll tell you what your next steps should be."

The pleasant meeting with the former Vice President was overshadowed by the contentiousness with Birkov, and Dean found himself in a sour mood on his way back to Jackson. His mood became even more sour when he pulled into the Sinclair station and observed from his side window the scrawny man in the red ski vest and baseball cap standing outside his truck in front of a gas pump. The man was sweating profusely and beating the shit out of the Border Collie with a thin metal piece of fence post. Dean got out of his Jeep and reacted immediately. "Hey, stop that!"

The man didn't look up. "Mind your own fucking business." He didn't even pause, just kept swatting the Border Collie, which was howling and cowering, covering its head with its paws.

Dean moved close to the man and yelled, "I've warned you before. Now stop or I'll put you under arrest. I'm a Deputy with the Teton County Sheriff."

This time the man looked up, stopped swinging at the collie, and pulled the fence post back in a threatening pose to Dean, "You want some, too, asshole?"

That was precisely the reaction that Dean had been hoping for. He was on the man in one second, his fists a blur on the man's face. When the man stopped moving, his face a mask of blood, sweat, and skin, Dean picked up the fence post and started striking the man on his torso, mocking him. "You going to be a good dog now, huh? Answer me. Answer me. Are you going to be a good dog?"

The man wailed and squirmed under the barrage but was unable to move out of the way, and angry red welts raised on his arms and face as Dean struck him again and again with the metal post. A few bystanders had gathered, and although none of them had interfered when the man was beating the dog, they now cheered as Dean gave the same treatment to the man. Someone said, "Cops are on their way." This broke Dean's tirade and he stopped, his fury spent. He picked up the bloody dog, put him in the back of his Jeep, and pulled away.

Five hundred dollars of x-rays, stitches, and medications later, Dean helped the dog into a corner of his bedroom and made him a bed of old blankets. "Everything is going to be OK." Dean stroked the collie's head. "The vet said you're lucky, nothing's broken, but you need to take it easy for a few days. You just stay here and I'll take care of you." He brought the dog a bowl of water. "But you're going to need a new name." Dean thought for a moment. "How about Cheney?"

Chapter 17

SENATOR Thomas McGraw stared down at his steel-cut oatmeal topped with a handful of blueberries and sipped his black coffee. He hated oatmeal. He was craving a cheese omelette with bacon and hash browns, but after spending thirty minutes in the hotel gym this morning, he was determined to exercise some dietary discipline. His campaign manager, who Charlotte had nicknamed "Tough Love" and Tom had shortened that to TL, had told him he needed to drop twenty-five pounds before debate season came around, and he reluctantly agreed. It wasn't entirely vanity and politics. Losing weight and getting in shape would make him a better lover. Although doggie style was his favorite position, especially with Charlotte, it was threatening to become a logistical necessity if he didn't get his belly under control. It wasn't just the oatmeal that was depressing him this morning, his blow-up with his campaign staff had gone viral on the Internet, and the media—in particular the most conservative members of the media—were labelling him an out of control cowboy who was self-destructing before he could even get started.

Tough Love marched into his room with a piece of paper in his hand, a Cheshire grin replacing his normal dour appearance.

"Why are you so happy this morning? Did you get laid? You know you need to stay away from those college girl volunteers," Tom said.

"Nope, even better than that. Got some overnight polling. How does it feel to be the latest YouTube sensation?"

"Well, up until thirty seconds ago it was feeling like crap. What do you have?"

"The American public loves you. The words they're using to describe you are tough, independent, straight shooter. This comes from all across the political spectrum, from left to right." He laughed. "The electorate is so strange and unpredictable. It's almost as if your swearing makes you more statesmanlike." Tough Love looked up to see Tom staring at him. "What?"

"This is the first time I've seen you smile since we decided to do this thing. You need to lighten up. It's going to be a long campaign." Tom took a sip of his coffee. "Say, could you do me a favor?"

"Sure, what?"

"Could you make an adjustment to my stump speech? I think you should add a half dozen 'fucks' and a 'cocksucker' or two."

"Ha, ha."

Chapter 18

In his dream, Sara is licking his leg, actually starting at his toes and licking her way up. He likes and dislikes the sensation, and finds that he is ticklish and starts squirming and laughing. "Hey, honey, that kind of tickles. Come on up here." But she doesn't say anything, just keeps licking, and eventually works her way up his thigh, to his hip, up his rib cage, and then she really starts going at it, lapping at his face. "What the fuck, honey!" He sat up quickly, and saw not Sara looking at him, but the furry black and white face of Cheney. "OK, OK, you need to pee, boy. Me, too, let's go."

After they both had peed, Dean walked back into the bedroom. This time it was Sara sitting in a chair next to his bed, wearing her usual smirk.

"What?" Dean said.

"I don't know where to start. Is it the fact that you have a dog? You never wanted a dog in Chicago. Or is it the fact that you named him Cheney? Dean, you used to call Cheney 'Darth Vader.' "

"First, I always wanted a dog, we just were never home. It wouldn't have been fair to the dog. Out here he can ride around with me every day in the back of my truck. Secondly, I never called Dick Cheney 'Darth Vader,' I called him 'Dr. Evil.'"

"I get the difference." And then Sara started laughing, and Dean jumped on top of her and licked her neck, imitating the manner of Cheney, and she laughed and laughed until she cried. Cheney studied the two of them, finally deciding that herding the pair would not be worth the effort and laid down by the side of the bed.

"So, Sara, let me bounce something off you," said Dean. "Right now, I have way too many suspects, more and more keep coming out of the woodwork, and there look to be at least four lines to this investigation. Jordy was stealing money from Hayden, so maybe Hayden killed him out of anger. That fits the money motive. But Jordy was having an affair with the stripper wife of a dicey guy down in Alpine, so maybe he killed Jordy, and that fits the sex-slash-betrayal motive. Fletcher Barns told me how much he hates Hayden, and Hayden cost him and his rich investor friends a substantial amount of money. Then we discovered that Mario Rosati, Torino's Chicago connection, is a business associate of Boris Birkov in Jackson who was also an investor who lost money in the Fletcher Barns project. So, which is it?"

Sara thought for a moment. "I think you're obviously in a hurry to wrap this up, but with this many possible suspects, it's just too early to draw any conclusions. For some people money is a strong enough motive for murder, for others it's not. The same for love, power, etc. It generally depends on the psychological profile of the criminal, and to some extent their propensity for violence. Sounds like you have some more investigatin' to do on this," she said, mocking his southern accent.

"Yes, I was afraid you'd say that. I was just hoping you'd see something I've missed."

Dean looked down at Cheney, and he jumped up between them on the bed, and all three of them went back to sleep until the phone rang at six. Dean answered, and when he looked up, Cheney was lying next to him and Sara was nowhere to be seen.

"Morning, Dean." It was Mark. "I have some of the info you were looking for. Matt Nelson owns Nationwide Auto Parts. Nothing out of the ordinary. Looks like it's a legitimate company. Stores in twenty-eight states. He's also a world-class poker player. He's won a bunch of tournaments. I also have some info on Charles Kidwell—"

"Who's Charles Kidwell?"

"You asked me to look him up, but you didn't know his name. Charles is the proud owner of that new house north of town you asked me to look up. I'll text you the address. He's the CEO of Prairie Bankcorp. It's like the six-teenth-largest bank in the country, something like that."

"I know, I have an account with them in Chicago."

"Well, I didn't find any dirt on him, either. But I added those two guys to your Network Analytics chart, with a soft link to Hayden. If you find anything about them that I don't know, fill me in so I can update the graphic. How did your interview with Birkov turn out?" Dean heard some background noise, then Mark came back on. "Wait a sec, Carlos wants to talk to you."

"Hey, Dean. Sorry you had to interrupt your vacation for this. Did you get anything from Birkov?"

"Not a thing. He's stonewalling, but I told him we were looking at Rosati for the murder, and that if we link him to it, then he's an accessory—trying to squeeze something from him, you know. Of course that isn't going to happen because, if he is involved, he probably brought Rosati into it himself. And he does have a pretty good alibi for his calls to Rosati: being a customer. But I figured it would get back to Rosati and stir things up for you."

"Well, based on the Birkov link, I'm resetting surveillance on Rosati. I'm going to have to give this some thought. There has to be a way we can leverage these two against each other."

"I have some ideas, but some of them may not be entirely legal."

Chapter 19

SHERIFF Dani had asked Dean for a case up-date this morning, so Dean walked into the sheriff's office with a cup of coffee and a notepad filled with notes. Dani looked up and with a completely straight face said, "Morning, Dean. Steal any more dogs today?"

Dean sat down and thought for a moment. Was he in trouble? Obviously the sheriff had heard about Cheney. "Actually, I rescued a dog that was about to be killed by some vicious lowlife. The scumbag tried to attack me when I suggested that he use positive reinforcement instead of a metal post to discipline his dog, and when he physically threatened me with the metal post, I subdued him with necessary force and then took the dog to the hospital. He was bleeding pretty badly and the vet said he wouldn't have survived without immediate medical attention. Sorry, I didn't stick around, but my first priority was to save the animal. Am I in trouble?"

"Do me a favor? From now on give me a heads-up when you're involved in any kind of altercation. The lowlife has a broken nose, and he looks like you took a mule whip to him. He's also missing some teeth, but they probably needed to come out anyway, so maybe you saved him a trip to the dentist. You messed him up pretty good, but we have witnesses as to what happened, and he decided to leave town. I think he was afraid he might run into you again."

"No problem. I'll keep you informed if I run into any more little spats."

"Thanks," she said, but Dean could tell by the way she was looking at him that maybe she wasn't quite sure what this incident said about him. "How's the dog?"

"I think he's going to be OK. Named him Cheney."

"Is that so you can tell everyone around here you rescued Cheney? Or so you can tell everyone that Cheney is your bitch?" At that, she started laughing so hard at her own joke that she had a coughing fit so intense she couldn't speak. Finally, she gathered herself, still red faced and still grinning at her own witticism, and said, "Well, that could be good or bad depending on who you talk to." Now, quickly getting down to business, she added, "OK, so where are you with the investigation, and when are you going to make an arrest?"

Dean updated her on Fletcher, Boris, Daryl, Amber, Eliza, Matt, and Charles. And on all of their potential links, using network analytics, to Mario. "The problem is, every time I talk to someone, they have some kind of relationship to someone else around here. It's like everyone in town is inter-married. I had no idea that Wyoming was so much like West Virginia."

"Well, the problem you're having is that Teton County isn't Chicago. This is a small community. Most folks here do have some relation in some fashion, through blood or business, to most other folks. If you keep using that network analytics bullshit you're just going to get more of the same. Seems to me you're nowhere with this. Just do it old school. Who wanted Jordy or Hayden dead and why?"

"You mean go back to the Big Four?"

"Damn right, it's always one or more of those."

"OK, I'm going to check out Eliza's ex. Does jealous husband meet one of your Big Four?"

"Sure does. Oh, and Dean, the polygraph tech is coming up from Cheyenne to talk to Daryl tomorrow. You might want to be here."

Dean walked up the driveway to the rented ski mountain chalet of Matt Nelson. After a while, all these rich people's vacation homes started to look the same. The house was considered "ski-in, ski-out"—which meant that that you could put on your skis right outside the front door, and ski down your private trail to a ski lift. There were two types of skiers who came to Jackson Hole—the hardcore types who came to challenge the mountain with one of the largest vertical drops of any resort in North America, and the rich wannabes who just want to say they skied the mountain with one of the largest vertical drops of any resort in North America. If you were the real deal then you'd love the personal ski path from the front door of Matt Nelson's home to a ski lift that would take you to the very top of the resort. But if you were the latter, you could just cruise down the path to lounge at the Four Seasons lodge for an afternoon of music and martinis with the real housewives of Jackson Hole. Dean wondered which category Matt Nelson fit into. On one of Hayden Smith's real estate brochures Dean had noticed that these homes were even more expensive than the places Dean had seen previously because, though they were a lot less grand and on much smaller lots, the price per square foot for the convenience was many times more than the homes a few miles away from the ski resort.

Matt answered the door himself, wearing tattered denim jeans with a designer label, and what appeared to be a very expensive western shirt and alligator cowboy boots. "Mr. Nelson, I'm investigating the murder of Jordy Smith and the disappearance of Hayden Smith and I need to ask you a few questions."

Matt seemed relaxed, personable, and friendly and he invited Dean in right away when he identified himself. "Please call me Matt. I've been reading about this in the papers, and I'm happy to help, Deputy, but I'm not sure I have any useful information. I don't think I ever met

Jordy Smith, and I met Hayden only a couple of times."

"I understand. I'm just talking to everyone in Hayden's circle. You never know where a valuable piece of information might come from. As I understand it, Hayden is dating your wife?"

"Technically, she's my wife. We're separated. Have you talked to her?"

"I have."

"Then I'm sure she told you we have a very amicable relationship. I know she's seeing Hayden and I have no problem with that. I just want her to be happy."

Dean's initial take on Matt was slightly effeminate and submissive. Soft-spoken, average-sized; everything about him seemed beige. Dean had seen this personality before, it was the Xanax-infused personality of an upper-middle-class woman of leisure. Dean wondered how an auto parts magnate could function with this personality. Maybe he should see if he could get his blood moving a bit. "Would it be amicable if you knew Eliza was seeing Hayden while you were married?"

Matt stared at Dean for a moment, as if he was mentally counting to five so as not to raise his voice. And he didn't. Actually, his voice went even softer. "I don't think that's true. Eliza says no. And I believe her. She has always been very truthful with me."

"Are you aware of any trouble in their relationship?"

"I really don't know anything about their relationship. As I said, I met Hayden only a couple times and he seemed a nice enough fellow."

"Can you tell me where you were the evening that Jordy was killed?"

"I was playing in a poker tournament in Atlantic City. I can prove it if that's what you're getting at."

Dean could see he wasn't going to get much here. "OK. Thanks for your time, Matt. If you hear anything you think could be helpful, even if it's a rumor, please give me a call." "I'll do that. I really hope you catch the guy soon, Deputy."

Chapter 20

DARYL Fay looked out the window of his Alpine home and saw that Boris Birkov's BMW X-5 was in the driveway. As he hopped in the passenger seat of the car, he glanced at the four young women in the back and, from their provocative European-style clothing, deduced they were Russian. "Hi, Boris, you bringing some more recruits to our meeting?"

Boris looked at Daryl as if that was the stupidest question he had ever heard. "No, I need to drop them off on the way. Just giving them a ride."

"OK." Daryl had learned not to ask too many questions of the Russian. He read somewhere that the Russian tendency to secrecy was due to the KGB culture, where almost any information that was volunteered could be held against you. So his way of handling Boris was to give Boris the information that he needed, and allow Boris to do his own thing.

His first EV recruits were from Alpine and the rural Mormon communities surrounding Alpine, but he knew the big money would be from breaking open the Jackson market that held most of the wealth of Teton County. He had recruited Boris as his first downline in Jackson, and in turn Boris had recruited about twenty or so Jackson-area Russians for his downline. Now Boris had arranged this evening's presentation to a group in Cheyenne. When Boris had told Daryl how many citizens of his mother country there were in Wyoming, Colorado, and Nebraska, Daryl had suggested they arrange a presentation in Cheyenne, an easy drive and overnight stay for anyone in most of those locations. Boris had put out the word and they were expecting dozens of entrepreneurial Russians to show up. Next month they were doing the same thing in Salt Lake City, and Boris said he could deliver twice as many at that venue.

Daryl's attempt at small talk, about the new EV product lines, was mainly a one-way conversation. After a few futile attempts, he stopped trying. He wondered how the presentation would go. The plan was that they would stand side by side; Daryl would work the power point presentation and give the pitch in English, and Boris would repeat what Daryl said in Russian. Boris had rejected all of Daryl's requests for rehearsal, and Daryl couldn't imagine Boris would be a good public speaker.

After about an hour and a half, they passed through Pinedale, and Boris turned onto a gravel road. They traveled about a mile before pulling up to a run-down but fairly large white farmhouse. Two of the girls got out of the car and went into the house with Boris. About ten minutes later, Boris came out of the house by himself with a canvas duffel and threw it in the back. The process was repeated an hour and half later just outside of Rock Springs, where they dropped off another girl and Boris picked up another bag. Around lunchtime, they stopped at a Wendy's, and Daryl, Boris, and the remaining girl ate in silence. After lunch they got on the interstate, and a couple of hours later exited to another country road, making their way to another farm house that looked abandoned. This time when Boris and the girl got out, Boris said, "Daryl, you come in with us."

The dilapidated exterior of bare gray wood decorated with chips of once-white paint camouflaged a clean and freshly painted interior furnished with a hodgepodge of cheap contemporary furniture. The focal point of the living room was a sixty-inch flat-screen TV displayed at the end of the room; the video playing on the screen was porn from the 70s or 80s. Daryl was able to deduce the vintage because the girls had pubic hair. One of Amber's duties at The Grandest Tetons was to indoctrinate the new girls into the finer points of stripper grooming. Many of the girls were trying to escape their Mormon upbringing and Amber would complain that she had to teach the "Mollies"—her nickname for the girls, combining their Mormonism with the hirsuteness of a Border Collie

—how to shave. Five girls dressed in Frederick's-style lingerie and stilettos sat on a large leather sectional, one eating a sandwich. Boris walked up to the girl eating the sandwich and slapped it out of her hands, shouting at her in Russian. She picked the sandwich up from the floor and ran into the kitchen. He then said something in Russian to the girl who'd been sitting next to her. Daryl had the impression that she was in charge. Boris looked over at him, said some more unintelligible words to the in-charge girl, then said something to a thin blonde on the couch, and she got up and strolled over to Daryl.

"Come." She led him by the hand into the back, past three small bedrooms, and up the stairs. There were four more bedrooms upstairs and they went into the last one at the end of the hall. Without saying a word, she started taking off her clothes. Once she was naked, she began removing Daryl's clothes. Daryl did not resist but tried to start a conversation. But she either did not understand English or, like Boris, just didn't want to talk. She pushed him down on the bed, got him hard with her hand, put a condom on him with her mouth, and mounted him. She pushed her breasts into his face, and brought him off in a steady, practiced rhythm, never so much as making a sound. After they were finished, she got dressed and left the room. When she didn't return, Daryl put on his clothes and opened the door. She was standing just outside the door and pointed out the bathroom to him, again without speaking.

As Daryl made his way back to the living room, he noticed that now all the rooms appeared to be full, the sounds of men and women creating a cacophony of ecstasy, real and fake, in the hallway. *Apparently all the girls are not mute*, Daryl thought.

When Daryl entered the living room, Boris wasn't there, but he could hear him yelling at someone in the next room—Daryl thought it was the kitchen. Although he didn't understand any Russian, he did recognize one word that was being shouted over and over again: "DYEHN-gee."

The MLM presentation in Cheyenne was completely surreal to Daryl. The meeting was held in the conference room at the "Old West Best Western" and the hundred or so folding chairs were filled shoulder to shoulder with first-generation Russian immigrants. The young men were dressed in tight dress pants and equally form-fitting shirts, the young women in dresses, stockings and heels—the group reminded Daryl of the young people in *Saturday Night Fever*. Few in the crowd spoke English. The buzz of conversation was indecipherable to him, except for the repetition of the same Russian word he had overheard Boris shouting in the house in Rawlins, a word he knew well: *den'gi...* money. Daryl set up the computer and powerpoint presentation and a table full of EV products, while Boris made the rounds. It seemed as if he actually knew most of the people in the room.

Boris made very brief introductory remarks in Russian, nodded to Daryl, and he began the power-point. Daryl would spend a couple of minutes on each slide, and then Boris would translate. The strange thing to Daryl was that his two-minute explanation of each slide was condensed to about fifteen seconds in Russian. Daryl was amazed that Boris could boil down everything he said to just a few Russian words. Maybe that explained why he had so many one word conversations with him.

After the presentation, Daryl passed out membership applications and order forms, and Boris collected money. Although he had brought a credit card reader with him, all of the fees were paid by the new downlines in cash, which Boris put in a large briefcase. When they got back in the car, Boris turned to him and actually acknowledged him for the first time since they'd left Alpine, "Very good, Daryl. Very good."

Chapter 21

THE polygraph tech from Cheyenne was already setting up in the conference room when Dean got to the station. The tech was wearing a grey suit, which kind of startled Dean. This was the first person Dean had seen wearing a suit and tie since he got to Wyoming.

Dean's perception was that polygraphs were part science and part magic. The magic part was that if the person taking the test believed the tech could tell he was lying, then he was more likely to tell the truth, or if lying, was more likely to show a non-truthful reaction. In Dean's opinion, the only people who could fool the machine were those who were trained, like spies, or pathological liars. Since pathological liars represented a sizable portion of the criminal population, the polygraph was not perfect. But based on his admittedly totally subjective observations of Daryl, he was convinced that he was not a pathological liar, and definitely not a spy, and therefore the results could be relied upon. As Dean reviewed the questions he wanted covered in the test, Joanie rang the room and told him Daryl had arrived.

When Dean went out to bring Daryl in, Daryl looked up and smiled, but he was a sweaty and fidgety mess. Dean had seen this before, which was his problem with the test's reliability. The anxiety felt by the innocent can often lead to a false interpretation of the results. Knowing he needed to calm Daryl down, he said to Joanie, "Tell the tech we'll be about ten minutes." Then turned and said, "Come on, Daryl, let's take a walk."

As they left the station, Dean said, "You know, I'm really pissed at you about those samples you gave me."

"Oh no, Deputy Wister, which one didn't you like?"

"Well, I took the Nature's Viagra before I went to bed one night. When I got up the next morning, I had a hard-on and it didn't go down the entire day. I couldn't even go to work."

"I've never heard of someone with that reaction before."

"I called the toll-free number on the bottle, but it must be misprinted. I described my problem to the woman who answered, but she said, 'Sir, this is AT&T, not the sex hotline.' Then she hung up on me."

"Oh, man..." Daryl looked truly concerned.

"Daryl, look at me. I'm pulling your leg."

"Oh. Oh. That's really funny. I thought you were being serious because that stuff really does work."

As they walked, Dean took Daryl through the polygraph process, to try to help him further chill about the process. "Daryl, just tell the truth and you'll be fine. I really want to rule you out as a suspect and this is the only way I can do it. Also, we're going to ask you some questions about dealing drugs and that will help get the cops down in Lincoln County off your back."

Daryl gave Dean a grateful smile as they started their walk back to the station.

The tech cleared his throat. "I have the results. Let me summarize." He picked up the graph paper on which he had made notes with a red felt-tipped pen. "On the questions regarding drug dealing, Mr. Fay stated that he has not bought or sold any illegal drugs in the last three years. The test indicates he was being truthful.

"On the questions regarding any knowledge about the death of Jordy Smith, Mr. Fay denies harming Mr. Smith or having any knowledge of anyone else who harmed him. The test indicates that he was being truthful.

"On the questions regarding any knowledge about the whereabouts or disappearance of Hayden Smith, Mr. Fay, denies any knowledge. The test indicates he was being truthful.

"On the question regarding any knowledge of any criminal activity of Boris Birkov...," Dean leaned forward, the other results weren't really a surprise to him, but he had no idea about how this one would go." Mr. Fay denies any knowledge. The test indicates that Mr. Fay was being untruthful."

The tech began packing up his equipment. "I think I'm done here, Deputy. I'll put my report in writing and email it to you."

Dean walked him out, avoiding eye contact with Daryl. He let Daryl sit and think about the polygraph results for about twenty minutes before he went back into the room.

"So, Daryl. Let's talk about Boris Birkov," Dean said.

Daryl put his head in his hands. Then he told Dean everything.

Sheriff Dani frowned for the first time since Dean met her when Dean sat down and said, "I just got some information that may implicate one of our suspects in an unrelated crime. What do you know about Boris Birkov?"

"Boris Birkov. Boris is very well respected in this community, by everyone except those people, and there are more than a few of them, who have a prejudice against immigrants. There are a ton of ignorant bigots around here who look down on the Russians and they have some pretty colorful names they can use, I assure you. Let me tell you something that not very many people around here know. My grandfather's name was Codikov, that's Lithuanian, but his mother was Russian. My granddad suffered his whole life in this county because of his name and his accent. You wouldn't believe the humiliation he had to put up with, so he changed his name to Cody. It didn't stop the bigotry because of his accent, but it did allow his children and grandchildren to be accepted as full blooded Americans. All because of a name. I have no doubt that I wouldn't be sitting in this chair if my name was still Codikov. Believe me it's much easier to get elected as a woman in this county than as a foreigner. I know Boris, not well, but I know him, and I know many of the Russians in Jackson. I have had nothing but positive interactions with him, and he is one of our biggest givers to charitable causes in the county."

This caused Dean to hesitate before moving ahead, but he really had no choice other than to tell the sheriff about Daryl's little trip to Cheyenne with Boris. This caused the sheriff's frown to deepen even further. She paused before responding.

"Damn. That's tough to hear. I'll call the sheriffs in those counties and let them know what's going on. But I suspect they already know. The areas that you're talking about are oil and gas fields, and we have hundreds of men working down there, rough men, away from their families for months at a time. The attitude of the law enforcement in those counties is that those men deserve a little diversion from the hard work. Hell, the people in those communities think those men are doing a patriotic duty for our country, reducing our dependence on Arab oil. So, I'll make the call. But don't be surprised if the reaction I get is just what I relayed to you. I think they'll probably tell me to mind my own business. The law enforcement types in the rest of the state view Teton County as elitist—some would say for good reason."

"So, it doesn't bother you, as a female law enforcement officer, that young Russian women, probably in this country illegally, may be being forced into prostitution."

"Whoa, whoa, whoa. Hold on there a second, Dean. You have no proof of anyone being here illegally or being forced into anything. As far as I know all the Russians in Teton County are here legally. At least we haven't found any that aren't. You have no reason to believe anyone is being forced into anything. Unfortunately, many immigrants who aren't fluent in the language take unsavory jobs. I said I'd make the call. If this were happening in Teton County, I guarantee you I'd shut it down. I have zero jurisdiction outside of this county. But you, Mr. big shot Federali, you can put all of the resources of the fucking FBI onto this if you're so concerned with sex trafficking. And don't you ever try to tell me how a woman should be doing her job as a law enforcement officer. Am I clear?"

"Very clear, Sheriff."

"Dean, I've given you pretty much free reign here. Now it seems to me you're straying pretty far from the original murder investigation. I would strongly advise you to focus your efforts there and find the son of a bitch that killed

Jordy Smith. Refer any sex trafficking evidence you stumble upon back to your Federal associates."

"Thanks, Sheriff, I'll do that."

"And another thing, keep this to yourself. Don't go around smearing the good name of Boris Birkov. There are enough people doing that crap already."

Chapter 22

Mario Rosati's foray into "Common Man Banking," the name he had proudly coined for his venture, came by accident. He had loaned money to an entrepreneur who owned a chain of "currency exchanges" in the Chicago area. Currency exchanges serve as banks for those who by choice or necessity live off the grid, who don't have or can't obtain bank accounts at conventional banks because of their immigration status or criminal history, or for those who have a profound mistrust of government and the mainstream banking system. This quasi-banking network had been forged into a true double-edged sword that ultimately the founding entrepreneur impaled himself upon. The business generated such large cash flow and leisure time for its owner that the man found himself drawn almost every weekend to the Vegas gaming tables, but the impressive cash-generating machine back in Chicago was no match for the cash-sucking machine that had been created in Nevada.

The man's banker at Wells Fargo didn't trust

the shady currency exchange business enough to loan him money against it—most of its profits were not reported on his tax return—and so the man turned to Mario to fund his habit. Mario made repeated loans to the man who would time and again spend a weekend trying to recoup his losses, only to see his debt to Mario steadily increase. Eventually, Mario became a minority owner in the man's business, with the provision that the debt must be repaid upon the man's death, and the loans were secured by a full one-hundred percent of the stock in the company and all of the personal assets of the owner.

After one too many losing weekends in Vegas, the man was found dead in his luxury suite, his wrists slit. With his "suicide," Mario became sole owner of the first legitimate business he had ever owned. And he was amazed at the profits that could be generated legally. His previous businesses involved mostly stealing in one form or another, with the attendant risks and costs of police bribes, attorneys, and sharing profits with the men who worked for him. But the new business, as he explained to Mario Jr. when he brought him in to help run the new, mostly legal enterprise, provided a true government-issued license to steal. With no product costs, minimal legal costs, no policemen or public officials to bribe, employee costs equivalent to minimum wage, and lax regulation of the fees he could charge, he was now making more money legitimately than he had through all the years of his life of crime.

There was only one problem. There was one cost of running a highly profitable legitimate business that was near zero in his criminal activities, and that cost was many times more than any of his other expenses: taxes. And so the gangster from Chicago found himself in the same position that all American tycoons have found themselves in since the creation of the United States income tax code. It was quickly apparent that, due to the sheer number of transactions and the critical requirement of keeping employee theft to a minimum in this cash-driven business, the tried-and-true method of tax planning for all red-blooded American small businesses—the double set of books—was impractical. So Mario reached out for professional assistance, and a large tax-planning law firm in Chicago came up with a complex arrangement of companies, some within the United States but also in tax havens outside of the United States, that would charge a myriad of consulting, management, and other fees that would result in a cascading flow of banking transactions, all of which would eventually end in most of the profits being deposited in an untaxed foreign bank account for the benefit of a company that Mario controlled. And, the lawyers explained to Mario, an effective tax rate of fifteen percent on the income that remained in the U.S. was the consensus fair tax rate arrived at by all the investors in the club of which he was now a member.

Mario had created this dizzying network of bank accounts and corporations at one of the largest international banks in Chicago. But little more than two months later, the bank had closed his accounts. He was told that the nature of his business transactions had been evaluated as "excess risk," and he should take his business elsewhere. He was in a panic. Until Senator Thomas McGraw, and with him Charles Kidwell, fell into his lap. One of Mario's men had a girlfriend who was a maid at the Four Seasons in Chicago. She recognized the senator as a frequent visitor to the hotel with a person who was clearly not Mrs. McGraw. When Mario showed the senator the video he was able to download from the camera that had been placed in his motel room, the senator came up with an easy solution to the problem. His good friend Charles Kidwell made a business call on Mario and convinced him that his bank could provide him with premium banking services.

It didn't take long for Mario to realize he was in over his head in the financial industry of Common Man Banking. He had thought that the man from whom he had acquired the company was just a bullshitter when he told everyone that he owned a chain of small banks, but to both Mario's delight and chagrin, it turned out to be pretty much the truth. The business was much more complex than Mario's skill set of stealing random shipments of merchandise and reselling the inventory to unscrupulous merchants could cope with, and he soon found that he needed someone with a more conventional background in finance to manage the business. His son, Mario Rosati Jr., became the answer to his problem.

Mario Jr. had been a good student, though something of a pretty boy, throughout high school and college and his father had shielded him from the details of his business, more from his evaluation of his son's lack of toughness than any misgivings about bringing him into the family business. After graduating from college with a degree in finance, young Mario had worked in the executive training program at Bank of America. An unfortunate misunderstanding between him and one of his female co-workers had been resolved by a payment from his father, and an "opportunity" for the young man to attend business school. The business with the young female banker had also exposed his father to a ruthless side of his son that he didn't know existed—and made him realize he had underestimated his son's predilection for the kind of life that his father had chosen. And so after receiving his MBA, Mario Jr. had joined his father in the business, and had done a magnificent job of learning the fundamentals. Unfortunately, like his father, Mario Jr. tired of new projects very quickly. As soon as he had mastered them to a sufficient degree they became uninteresting to him, and he was ready to move on to a new challenge.

When he noticed the challenge of managing the currency exchange business was beginning to wear off, Mario tried to interest his son in expanding the product line to include "payday loans." Payday loans are short-term loans that are advances secured by an individual's paycheck, and have interest rates and fees, mostly hidden, that result in an effective rate of 300-500% to the borrower. The old man had wanted him to start in on the payday project right away, but Mario Jr. had already started in on his next project—a young Mexican girl who worked at one of the currency exchange branches in Chicago. By the time Mario Sr. had discovered the problem, the girl had already had an abortion, which infuriated her gangbanger father, and so Mario Sr. decided it would be prudent to move his son entirely out of the family business.

An unsuspecting Charles Kidwell was about to come to the rescue once again.

The Italian Village lays claim to being the oldest Italian restaurant in Chicago, and it looks it. There has been little change in the decor or the menu that fed Capone, Sinatra, and a lineage of several generations of Mafioso, theatergoers, and tourists with traditional, old-world family recipes. The restaurant is a living museum of early-twentieth-century American-Italian cuisine that now sits alone amidst an archipelago of restaurants created by celebrity chefs and food chemists that have come and gone faster than women's fashions. It wasn't surprising that this was the first visit of the banker and new-age foodie, Charles Kidwell, to the Village.

Charles entered the dim foyer and approached the maître d'. "I'm here to meet an associate, Mario Rosati?"

"Of course, Mr. Rosati is already here. Come with me."

Charles followed the formally dressed maître d' up two flights of stairs into a small private dining room decorated with photographs dating from the restaurant's early days during the Al Capone era of Chicago. Mario was seated next to a very good looking young man who looked to Charles to be in his mid-to-late-twenties.

"Charles, so great to see you. I'm so glad you could make time in your busy schedule. I thought we needed to catch up. This is my son, Mario Jr. He has been managing most of the operations in the currency exchange business and is very interested in banking, so I thought you two should meet."

Mario Jr. stood, smiled broadly, and offered his hand to Charles. "Mr. Kidwell, I'm a huge fan of yours. I did my thesis in business school on your company. I really admire so much what you've accomplished."

"Why, thank you. I'm glad to meet you as well."

"Sit, Charles, and have some wine. I took the liberty of ordering for us. This is my favorite restaurant in the city and I wanted to share some of my favorite dishes with my favorite banker." As if on cue, several servers entered with plates of salad, pasta, seafood, bread and cheese.

They dug into the food and Mario Sr. and Charles talked Chicago and Illinois politics. After a waiter had opened their second bottle of wine, Mario Jr. asked Charles about his acquisition strategy that had resulted in the phenomenal growth of Prairie Bankcorp. This led to a complex discussion of how to gain efficiencies when integrating acquired accounts and the advantages of wholesale versus retail banking, which Mario, Sr. was not equipped or inclined to participate in. Finally, he interrupted. "As you can see, Charles, Mario Jr. has a passion for banking. But you and I have some other business matters to discuss." He turned to his son. "I'll see you back at the office in a little while."

The truth was that this meeting was very inconvenient for Charles. He'd had to reschedule a business trip to make the meeting, but Mario had said it was urgent. And given the incident in Wyoming, and Charles's uneasiness about Mario's role in it, he could hardly refuse. "So, Mario, what's the urgent matter?"

"Let me ask you, what do you think of Mario Jr.?"

"He seems like a very nice young man. It's great you can have family in your organization. In the money business, it's important to have someone you can trust."

"I agree, Charles. And I've been thinking. Mario Jr. has a very strong passion for banking. Do you think you could find a place for him in your organization?"

Charles suddenly felt sick to his stomach, but the internal wrenching never showed through his professional polish. "How could you spare someone who is as close to you as your own son? Your business is really growing, too... how could you get by without him? Especially since so much of your business involves cash transactions."

"The truth is, Charles, I can spare him because I actually welcome a little theft once in a while. It gives me an opportunity to provide an example of what happens to people who steal from me." He paused to make sure that Charles understood the meaning of this, and then continued. "And I really want to give Mario Jr. the kind of resumé that will help him move up in the financial industry. I think he has the smarts and the drive to be someone like you one day."

Charles could see that he was not going to be able to refuse this proposal. He thought he probably could put young Mario in a junior position, maybe a low-level staff position in operations, or maybe an internship of some type with a department-by-department rotation so it would be several years before he would have any authority or critical knowledge of the Kidwell organization. "Mario, I would be happy to mentor your son. In fact, I will put him into the same junior management-training program that we require our highest qualified business school hires to complete. He will be able to go through a training rotation that will give him experience in all phases of banking."

Charles was surprised to see Mario frown. His voice changed from the charming Mario to the gruff Mario of their first meeting, when he told Charles why he needed to accept his business, and why he needed to look the other way at some of Mario's more creative business practices. "It's my fault, Charles, for not making the situation clearer. Mario Jr. is not some fresh-faced kid out of business school. He has been running a bank, maybe not a chartered bank but a de facto bank, for the last three years. And now he is ready for a senior position in a traditional bank. As you know, our business is facing greater and greater scrutiny from the Feds, most of it totally unfair, because we deal in cash and, quite frankly, because the clients we serve are not part of the one-percenters that you serve. If Mario was in a senior position in your bank he would be able to monitor our account more closely, and he would be able to locate business opportunities within your bank that would be lucrative for both of us."

Charles could feel the pasta and calamari and bruschetta and the Chianti crawling up his throat. He concentrated hard on swallowing the sour, acidic bile, forcing it back down. It would be bad to vomit in Mario's lap. Very, very bad.

"I hear what you're saying, Mario, but right now there really isn't a position on our executive team, and I wouldn't know how to explain adding a senior position to our Board."

Mario rapped his fist on the table, causing the glassware to jump, tipping over a goblet of red wine and causing it to flow in a creek toward Charles's side of the table. "Charles, are you fucking stupid? Maybe you are, and that's why you're in this position. This is not a suggestion. I'm covering your ass. I'm covering the ass of the senator. I took care of that little problem in Wyoming. Your business is at stake here. My business is at stake, and the senator's presidential ambitions are definitely at stake. So here is what you are going to do. You are going to put together a job description and compensation program for a new member of your executive team, and you are going to send it over to me. After I have approved it, you are going to announce to your management team that you have the perfect candidate already for the job, and you are going to hire Mario Jr. Now is that clear enough for you?"

"Yes, it's very clear."

Charles was blinded by the bright Chicago sunshine as he exited the Italian Village, his head throbbing. He walked down the street, trying to process the events of the last hour. Everything had been going so well for him. Six months ago he had it all: respect in the banking community, important contacts in Washington—how had it all gone so wrong? *I took care of that little problem in Wyoming.* Could that be true? Surely Mario wouldn't have sent someone to kill Hayden. Wouldn't Mario use intimidation and blackmail, just as he was using right now on him? He couldn't tell Tom about this. His conscience was already going crazy. He stepped into an alley, unable to suppress the rising gorge in his throat any longer and, grunting in agony, he gave back the favorite dishes of Mario Rosati to the streets of Chicago.

The Jane Byrne Rehabilitation Center sat on Lake Shore Drive on Chicago's Gold Coast, right next to some of the priciest real estate in the country. Its residents received the finest care of any such institute anywhere in the world. With its individualized, gourmet food menu, personal maids, room service, and social director, it functioned more as a luxury resort than a nursing home. If you ignored the age and physical condition of the residents, and if the medical staff were not so obvious in their starched white jackets, a visitor might mistake it as such. Many of the residents on the higher floors enjoyed views of the lake and the city, and their rooms were furnished like one of the boutique hotels that had cropped up all over that part of town. Charles Kidwell visited the

Center often, and the staff was well aware of his stature in the community, as well as the level of fundraising support he provided in addition to the substantial out-of-pocket expenses he paid for the care of his loved one. As a result, the medical director left specific instructions to be notified promptly upon his arrival.

The medical director was a short plump woman with large glasses that made her resemble an owl and look a decade older than her chronological age. She caught up with him before he reached the elevator. "Mr. Kidwell, may I have a word with you?"

He stopped and backtracked to her office, which was right next to the front entrance.

"I just wanted to give you an update. Physically she's doing fine. But she's been agitated a lot lately and asking about you."

"I know it's been a couple of weeks since I've been here, but I've been traveling a lot for work."

"Oh, I know. You've been very devoted. But I just wanted to update you before you saw her. If there's anything she needs, let me know."

"I will, thanks," he said. He took the elevator to the top floor and walked down the carpeted hallway to her room. She wasn't there, so he walked farther down the hall and found her sitting in the solarium. The solarium was a huge community room with floor-to-ceiling windows facing east that afforded stunning views of Lake Michigan, Lincoln Park, and the entire Chicago lake shore. On a beautiful clear day such as today, the view included not only sunbathers on the Chicago beaches and sailors of every kind on the lake, but vistas as far north as Waukegan and, to the Southeast, the Indiana shoreline. A silver-haired woman with stooped shoulders sat in a chair looking at the stunning view. She shifted her gaze and smiled when Charles took the chair across from her. "I never get tired of looking at this view. Isn't it beautiful?"

Charles agreed. But he had exactly the same view from his office at the bank and the truth was that he hardly noticed it anymore. It had become the equivalent of background noise to him, and he used it primarily as a status symbol to impress his most important clients, politicians, or others who needed to understand how important he was. "Yes, it's stunning on a day like today. How have you been? I'm sorry I haven't been by in a while—I've been awfully busy. Do you remember that I'm working for Senator McGraw's presidential campaign?"

She ignored this comment, as she generally did when Charles tried to tell her about his present life, as she seemed incapable of conversation in the present tense. Instead, she took a large, worn leather-bound book from her lap and put it on the table between them. "Have I shown you these pictures before?"

Charles laughed. "Only about a thousand times. But why don't you show me again. Show me your favorites."

She opened the book and he noticed she was having trouble turning the pages with her arthritic fingers. He must remember to ask the medical director if a doctor had seen her lately. He wondered if his hands were destined for the same fate. A vain man, he dreaded the thought of the ruin of his manicured fingers as much any limitations on his physical activities. The book contained pages of photographs, representing the decades of her life. Charles had put the book together under the theory that it would trigger or stimulate memories in her damaged brain, and at times it seemed to work. She would point out a photograph and be able to relate a very detailed account of not only who the person was, but about the day it was taken, and how she felt, and other things that happened on that particular day. Other times she would have no clue as to who the person was—nor able to identify the person even it if was herself.

Today she picked out a picture of Charles to talk about. He was about four or five in the photo, and he was wearing one of his father's old suit coats, a tie that hung down to his feet, and a 1940s style fedora. "Look, Charles, it's you. You were such a cute little fellow. How you loved to play dress up! You would put on Dad's clothes and say you were going to the bank. You always wanted to be just like him," she said, and started giggling.

He looked at the picture, at his innocent face, and he remembered a time when he had admired his father. He'd done that right up to the time that he'd started to work for him and he saw what a bigoted, arrogant SOB he was. After he saw how he treated his employees, how he treated the women who worked for him, how he wouldn't listen to any of his son's ideas about how to grow the bank—after that Charles had no use for him. He'd just bided his time until the old man died of a heart attack and he could replace him.

She was laughing harder now and still pointing at the same picture. "Look, Charles, look at the shoes. You always wanted to put on his suit. But you would wear my shoes."

He looked more closely now and he saw that he was wearing a pair of black patent leather high heels. "What do you mean? I think they go very well with that suit." And he laughed with her. On the facing page there was picture of a young woman on a boat on a river near their home in Southern Illinois. She was wearing shorts and a halter top and the wind was blowing through her hair and she was laughing. "Look at this. Do you remember that day?" he asked.

She studied the picture for a moment. "Yes, I do remember that day. I was out on the boat of my girlfriend's family."

Charles looked at the woman sitting in her chair, and then down at the picture. He couldn't recognize the woman in the picture as the one sitting next to him. "You were so beautiful."

She looked up at him and smiled. "Yes, I was, wasn't I? I was very beautiful."

Chapter 23

TOUGH Love stood in back of the auditorium at Washington University in St. Louis. Senator McGraw finished his canned stump speech and was now holding a free-for-all Q&A session with the audience, and TL was worried. The viral video of Tom's rant at his campaign staff had bolstered Tom's poll ratings and increased his recognition throughout the country, but TL believed that Tom's shoot-from-the-hip style was bound to blow up at some point. TL had worked for George W. Bush and felt that a McGraw Presidency could be like what W's might have been if Iraq hadn't happened. But McGraw was all-in on bringing in new voters without losing the traditional conservative base, and TL knew this was a very delicate balancing act. He also knew not to underestimate the cowboy. People simply liked and trusted Tom, and TL knew that likeability in politics trumped everything else. TL was also skeptical of McGraw's insistence on a college lecture tour, but McGraw was adamant that young people were a totally untapped source of Republican primary votes that he could dominate. But the questions that were coming out of the audience appeared to TL to be plants from his opponents, the questions worded much too deftly for college students.

A pretty brunette stood up and read her question from a note card. "Senator, your party has been against gay marriage, can you clarify your stance on this?"

"First, I don't think you can say that my party is against gay marriage. There are many different positions on the subject within my party. My position, and I believe the position of all true conservatives, is that the government should not take away the freedom of Americans to marry who they wish, as long as the person is an unrelated competent adult. The government should keep its nose out of the private lives of its citizens."

This answer was met with resounding applause in the audience, and TL almost smiled. The phrase "true conservative" had been his idea. He hoped it would be an inoculation against charges of liberalism on the social issues, about which the senator held a more progressive view than most members of his party. The senator had embraced the phrase and was using it whenever he encountered a question where his position diverged from the conventional conservative line.

The answer to the question on gun control was not as popular with the young audience. "Where I come from, guns are a way of life. Most everyone, men and women, own guns. The gun problem in this country is complex and difficult. But I am not in favor of passing gun laws that will not reduce gun crime but will only serve to reduce our constitutional freedoms. I have outlined my three-point gun-crime plan that I think does that. One: comprehensive background checks that will make it very difficult for criminals and the mentally ill to lawfully purchase a weapon. Two: mandatory and severe prison sentences for crimes committed with a gun. And finally, and this may be the most important thing we can do, three: expanded treatment for the mentally ill. Most of the mass gun murders that have occurred over the last several years have been committed by the mentally ill. And a significant portion of the people currently incarcerated have untreated mental illness. This needs to change." When the answer was not met with boos from the young audience, TL smiled for the first time. This was more of his sleight of hand, modest gun control and redirection of the conversation to mental illness, which had broad support across the political spectrum.

A forty-something man stood, and TL thought, *This guy must be a plant from one of our opponents' campaigns.* "Senator, a lot of conservatives are calling you a fraud. Fox News referred to you as a 'liberal libertarian.' How do you respond to that?"

McGraw laughed, giving the impression that such a criticism was too absurd to be taken seriously. "Let's see, 'liberal libertarian', one of the Fox News talking heads actually said that? Are you sure it wasn't just a stutter? That phrase doesn't even make any sense." That got him a huge laugh and applause, and TL thought it was going to be a really good new sound bite. "But seriously, the word 'liberal' has been used way too often in our party to label anything that we don't like. I am officially banning it from my campaign vocabulary, though I think it does a disservice to our political discourse. Instead of debating the merits of a policy, it's much easier to label it liberal or conservative. When I evaluate a policy position, I don't ask myself if a position is liberal or conservative. I ask myself, which position increases the level of individual freedom for our citizens. The primary role of government is to maximize our citizens' economic freedom, while minimizing the intrusion on individual freedom. Let me give you an example. My friends on the other side of the aisle are making a big push to raise the minimum wage, and that makes me mad as hell. You want to know why?" When the audience didn't respond, Tom raised his voice. "No, seriously, I'm asking, do you want to know why?"

With that, the young audience, not sure where this was going, got caught up in his playful rhetoric and a few responded "Why?"

"Because it doesn't help poor people. Let me have a show of hands here. Does anyone in this room have parents who make eighteen thousand dollars a year or less? Please, if so, please raise your hands. We are all friends here." No one in the room raised a hand.

"Do you know what eighteen thousand a year is? That's the number the other party wants to raise the minimum wage to. Eighteen thousand a year. Now, can you raise a family on eighteen thousand a year? Hell, no. Can you send your child to college on eighteen thousand a year? Hell, no. Can you buy a house on eighteen thousand a year? Well, can you?"

Now he had gotten their attention. The audience responded in unison. "Hell no!"

And he said, "That's right. Hell, no, you can't."

TL was starting to get alarmed. They had had some preliminary discussions on this issue, but it was his understanding that Tom hadn't come to a final conclusion on it one way or the other.

"These minimum-wage jobs could never lift anyone out of poverty. They are intended as transition jobs, jobs for students, or part-time jobs to supplement a main job that pays a lot more than eighteen thousand a year. So what makes me mad—no, what pisses me off, and excuse my language, is that this minimum-wage increase is just a dirty trick that's going to be played on the working poor. It's just a tactic to take away from the real economic issue in our country. Do you want to know what the real economic issue in our country is? Well, do you?"

TL stood back, amazed. This was totally un-scripted. And Tom had the young people eating from the palm of his hand. They were engaged and interested, and responding to the senator's rhetorical questions.

"Well, do you?"

"Yes, yes," the crowd responded.

"The real issue in our country is economic freedom. The real issue is why we can't create enough jobs that pay a middle-class living. Why millions of people are so desperate they have no choice but to take a job that pays only enough to live on the margins of our society." And then the senator looked out on the crowd, and he raised his voice once more. "And this pisses me off and makes me embarrassed to be a lawmaker in the United States Congress."

The crowd screamed their agreement.

Tom waited for the crowd to quiet. And then he said very softly, "But the question is, what are we going to do about it? You know, my party likes to brag that we are the party of 'job cre-ators.' And so in this election, I am challenging my party, and I am challenging American busi-ness—big American business *and* small Amer-ican business. It's time to stop bragging and start doing. I pledge that I will do everything in my power to demand that the U.S. Congress create an environment that takes the handcuffs off the greatest economic engine in human his-tory. And when we take those handcuffs off, I expect American business to create millions of new jobs. Middle-class jobs. Jobs that will pay enough money that no one will talk about raising the minimum wage. Because companies that are paying minimum wage are going to have a hell of a time finding anyone desperate enough to take them.

"But let's get specific. Do you like specific? Do you want me to get specific?"

The crowd signaled by their raised voices and applause that they indeed wanted him to get specific.

"Two numbers for you. By the end of my first term, our country will generate ten million new jobs. Ten million new jobs that pay at least twenty-five dollars per hour. And for the rest of my campaign, whenever anyone asks me about raising the minimum wage, you know what I am going to say?" And he raised his voice again. "Do you know what I am going to say?"

And the crowd responded, "What?"

"Hell, no, I don't want no stinkin' minimum wage. I want ten million new jobs that pay twenty-five dollars per hour."

And with that, he walked off the stage to a standing ovation.

TL was stunned. His candidate had created pandemonium. He was sure there would be nothing else on the news today. But ten million new jobs at twenty-five dollars an hour? Where had that come from? The senator had shown rhetorical skills that TL didn't know he had, but this shooting from the hip, this improv political revival thing Tom was doing—it scared the shit out of him.

Charlotte joined the senator in his hotel that night. "I saw a clip of you on MSNBC at Wash U. You were terrific, and it seems even the leftwing democrats love you."

"Well, that's a big problem. As much as I enjoy pleasing the liberal pundits, the endorsement of any of them is the kiss of death. FOX News is killing me. I can't be seen as being the conservative lapdog of the liberal Democrats. I need to find a way around this."

"Hey, I thought you pledged today you weren't going to use the L word. But I have an idea—what you need is for one of the conservative political commentators to come out in your favor. Do you know of any of these guys who might do that?"

"Well, there are a few pretty crazy ones that might do it to make a name for themselves. Or maybe a bigger-name crazy who might want to be a king maker. I need a conservative mouth, a big mouth, in the media. One with an ego big enough that he actually thinks he could be a king maker."

They looked at each other and said the same name, at the same time, "O'Malley."

Charlotte laughed. "There's no bigger mouth than O'Malley."

"Don't you mean there's no bigger ego than O'Malley?"

"Why don't you ask TL about it? Maybe you could court O'Malley, use that irresistible cowboy charm. Kiss his ass as much as you have to. Go on his show. You haven't really done a one-on-one with any of the Fox guys yet. O'Malley's ego is so big he wouldn't feel he needed to prove his conservative credentials by raking you over the coals."

"That's a really good idea, but it will have to look like we're coming hat in hand, asking the great man to anoint me. TL is quite good at that kind of thing. I'll mention it to him in the morning. I guess you aren't just all delicious bootie and sex appeal after all."

She walked over to the couch and sat on his lap, facing him, put her hands on his face and kissed him hard. "Not all, but hopefully just enough."

The next morning, Charlotte was gone when Tom awoke and he had an early breakfast with his campaign staff before leaving for the airport. TL said he would reach out to O'Malley and see how receptive he would be. On the way to the airport, Tom got a call from Charles. "Good morning, Tom, I didn't want to spoil your evening last night with Charlotte, but I wanted to update you on my meeting with M in Chicago. I ran into a little problem and I wanted to run it by you."

"OK, shoot."

"He had a special guest at lunch he wanted me to meet. It seems there is an M Jr. who has been running his currency exchange operation and he wants to make him a banker. He wants me to give him a job."

"Well, that shouldn't be too hard. You should be able to put him somewhere he couldn't do too much damage."

"I'm afraid it's not that simple. He wants me to put him on my executive team. What he really wants is someone on the inside. Someone to look over my shoulder. And you know where that will eventually lead."

Tom didn't say anything for a few seconds. "Right. How long do you think you can put him off?"

"Not too long. Maybe I can stall him a couple of weeks."

"Let me think about it. This isn't good. For either of us. Did he say anything else to you about his role in the Jackson thing?

"No, nothing. I still don't think he had anything to do with it. But time will tell."

Chapter 24

DEAN was finishing a lunch of pulled pork topped with southern slaw at Bubba's when Sheriff Dani rang his cell phone. "Where are you? I need you to get over here right away. Hayden Smith just walked into my office with his attorney."

"Be there in five minutes," Dean mumbled through a mouthful of smoked pig, barbecue sauce, and cabbage.

When Dean walked into the interview room, the sheriff sat on one side of the table, across from a lanky, good looking, rusty-haired man whom Dean recognized as Hayden. Beside him was a much smaller man with dark, curly hair, in a sedate suit, who had to be the lawyer. Hayden was red-eyed and looked on the verge of breaking down at any moment.

Sheriff Dani introduced Dean as the lead investigator for the murder of Jordy Smith, and at the mention of Jordy's name, Hayden gulped and forced back a sob. "I didn't want to get started until you got here, Dean. Dean, this is Hayden Smith, and Judd Moran, Hayden's attorney. Judd just told me that Hayden has been on a camping trip. When he got back into town this morning, he heard about the murder and called him."

The attorney interrupted. "As you can see, my client is terribly upset about this, but he wants to help in any way he can with the investigation."

"OK, Hayden," Dean said. "I can see this has been a shock for you. Let me say that I'm relieved you're OK. We thought something might have happened to you since no one had any idea of your whereabouts. Let's start from the beginning. When was the last time you saw Jordy?"

"I saw him the night before I left for my backpacking trip. I met him at the office. I guess it was the night he was killed, from what I understand."

"About what time was that?"

"I think it was around nine."

"And how long were you there?"

"Around an hour, I think. We discussed certain business affairs that needed to be taken care of while I was gone."

"Did you argue about anything?"

At this question, the sobs could no longer be stifled, and they came with a force. His attorney patted his arm. The sheriff said nothing. In a few moments, Hayden answered. "No, we didn't argue, we just went over the things in the business that needed tending to while I was gone."

"And where were you going?"

"I've been on a backpacking trip in the Wind River range."

"Was anyone with you?"

"No, I went alone."

"Did you meet up with anyone while you were gone... who could confirm your whereabouts?"

"Actually, I didn't see a soul while I was gone. I just wanted to get away. Things have been pretty stressful lately in my business."

"Unusually stressful, or normal stressful?"

"Just normal business stuff."

"Isn't it unusual to start on a backpacking trip in the middle of the night?"

"No, there was a full moon, and I love hiking the backcountry in moonlight. I do it a lot, actually."

"Hayden, do you know any reason why anyone might want to harm Jordy?"

Dean looked at Hayden closely. Everyone handles the shock of the death of a loved one differently, and Dean liked to think he could tell if a reaction was genuine or forced. He knew his gut reactions were accurate only sometimes, but if Hayden had killed Jordy, it was the act of an amateur. And amateurs were generally terrible actors. He thought Hayden seemed genuine. He was now subdued, and his answers had a sad resignation. "No. That's the thing." And he used the same words Dean had heard time and again. "Everyone loved Jordy."

"Hayden, do you own a nine-millimeter hand gun?"

"No, I don't."

"And would you have any reason to want to harm Jordy yourself?"

At this question, Hayden looked up, his ruddy face getting redder. "I loved Jordy... he was family."

In support of his client, the attorney intervened. "Now, Deputy, my client has voluntarily come down here to try to answer your questions. And I have to say you're not treating him like a cooperative citizen. The tenor of your questions is accusatory and frankly uncalled for."

Sheriff Dani and Dean paused for a moment, letting the silence sink in. Then Dani spoke. "If our questions seem impolite, I definitely do not apologize. A young man has been murdered and your client is sitting here telling us lie after lie."

"What lies?" Hayden leaned forward and glared at the sheriff.

"Well, for one thing, you do own a nine-millimeter pistol. You bought it about a year ago at a gun shop in town. And for another, you said nothing unusual was going on in your business when you just found out that Jordy has been stealing a whole lot of money from you. You know what I think? I think you argued with Jordy about the money he stole, shot him with the nine-millimeter gun that you say you don't own, and then ran out of town in a panic. Is that about right?"

His attorney responded loudly, "Sheriff, that's total nonsense. This interview is over." Hayden, now pale with something more than grief, quietly said, "Sheriff, I did not kill Jordy. I would never do anything to harm him."

Dean decided that maybe it was time for him to play good cop. "Look, Hayden, I know how much you cared about Jordy—I've heard that from everyone. But we need to rule you out as a suspect. You were the last person to see Jordy alive, and we know he was stealing money from you. If we can rule you out, then I can move on to looking at other suspects. Would you be willing to take a polygraph test?"

Hayden didn't hesitate, "Of course, I'll take one right now."

His attorney spoke over top of him. "That is completely out of the question." He turned to his client. "Hayden, polygraphs are really unreliable, especially for someone in your emotional state. And it's a total lie that the deputy will rule you out if you pass. There are about another hundred reasons I can't let you take a polygraph that I will explain to you privately." Then he turned to the sheriff. "We're leaving now. My client has told you everything he knows. If you want any more information from him, put the questions in writing and send them over to my office."

As Hayden and his attorney walked out the door, Sheriff Dani sent the message that Hayden was now the primary suspect: "Make sure your client doesn't leave town again, Mr. Moran. If he does, I guarantee I'll issue a warrant for his arrest."

When they were gone, Dani turned to Dean. "He did it. The gun he bought is missing. He, by his own admission, met with Jordy at the time he was killed. Jordy stole a substantial sum from him. And he won't take a polygraph."

"What about the dead guy in the Snake? How does that fit in?"

"You haven't been able to link him to Hayden or to Jordy. Right now it's just a dead guy from out of town killed in a car wreck."

"You saw, he wanted to take the polygraph, his attorney wouldn't let him."

"He's a big boy. He can take the test if he wants. I think I might have enough for an arrest right now, but I'll hold off for a few days. If you think it was somebody else, you need to deliver him. My gut's telling me it's Hayden."

Chapter 25

DEAN was on his fifth beer at the Silver Dollar Bar, the honkytonk and former illegal casino inside the seventy-year-old Wort Hotel in downtown Jackson that was packed on Saturday nights all summer long. He thought the saloon-style bar probably looked pretty much as it had seventy years ago. The pine floor was worn down with the grooves of generations of cowboy boots and looked as if it could be that old, but the top of the bar held hundreds of silver dollars covered in plexiglass. That definitely was a touch that wasn't in the original. Dean imagined an after-hours robbery and wondered how difficult it would be to break up the bar top to steal the silver dollars, and whether it would be worth the trouble.

The case was giving him a headache. The sheriff was focused on Hayden, but Dean didn't buy it even if he didn't have anyone else to give up. And he was pretty sure the sheriff would arrest Hayden if he didn't come up with someone else soon.

Or maybe it was the Silver Dollar Bar that was giving him a headache. One Ton Pig was playing a foot-stomping version of some bluegrass tune and the standing-room-only-crowd was feeling it. Real cowboys from ranches all around Teton County were looking to get their drink on and maybe find a Saturday night girlfriend. The college girls working summer jobs in the park, and the middle-class women from out East looking for a sexy vacation experience to brag about back home, were only too happy to oblige. Dean was amazed as he watched the cowboys prance the two step and Western swing in dirt-and-sage encrusted boots with the outdoorsy park summer help in flip flops, and the middle-aged moms in their short skirts and rhinestone boots. He and Sara had loved Western dancing, though he'd always thought it was something invented by the Eastern elite, but these were real cowboys dancing steps that he knew weren't learned in some dance studio. Dean sipped his beer and watched the spectacle in front of him. It took him back to the time that he'd sat at the same bar with Sara, watching the couples dance. At that time Dean wasn't a dancer, but when they returned to Chicago, he and Sara had taken dance classes, and they'd grown to be pretty good as a couple.

His melancholy was broken when a pretty petite brunette stepped right up to him, held out her hand and said, "You dance, cowboy?" Dean was momentarily tongue-tied. Over her shoulder he could see a table of three of her girlfriends giggling and watching the two of them intently.

Ordinarily, his shyness might have gotten the better of him, but he was five beers into a mellow buzz and the woman was damned cute. "A little, ma'am. I'll try not to step on your feet." And for the next two hours, except for exchanging names, they hardly spoke. They danced. Holding a woman in his arms for the first time in a long time was a strange and exhilarating feeling. Amazingly, all the steps came back to him and, to Rose's credit, she was a great partner who could interpret his moves seemingly before he telegraphed them to her. As the band played the last song of the night, Dean held her close and whispered, "You're a great dancer. Thank you. It's been a long time since I did this."

She smiled up at him. "No, thank you. It's great not having to dance with these smelly cowboys." Then she grabbed his head and planted a huge kiss on his lips.

In the moment, Dean felt aroused, and then, instantly, confused and guilty. "I'm sorry, I have to go." He turned and pushed his way through the crowd to the door, stumbling out into the warm summer night.

"I'm here every Saturday night," Rose called after him.

Fletcher Barns had sat at the back of the bar all evening long, a bomb of testosterone, jealousy, and insecurity churning in the pit of his stomach. The bartender had tried to light the fuse by supplying him with one Jack Daniels after another. *So this is where she came with her girlfriends every Saturday night.* Well, she wasn't dancing with her girlfriends. She was out on the floor with that cop from Chicago, and she hadn't returned to her table for nearly two hours. He knew the look she was giving the asshole cop. It was the same look that she used to give him, back before she became such a bitch. But when she pulled the cop's head down and kissed him hard, Fletcher thought, *This will not stand*, and followed Dean out the door.

Still high and in a daze from the unexpected kiss, Dean was humming a bluegrass tune as he walked out of the bar and onto the wooden boardwalk. His reaction time dulled a bit by the alcohol, he couldn't get his head around in time to respond to the "Hey, asshole" from behind him. Suddenly a searing pain jolted his head forward, followed by his body, and his face landed with a crunch on the pine deck. If the deck had been concrete instead of wood, the blow would likely have given rise either to a great black void of unconsciousness, or maybe Dean would even have joined Sara in the hereafter, but instead, a giant paw grabbed him by the hair and bounced his face off the boards in a steady rhythm. It was the splatty, crunchy, bloody sound, as much as the pain, that cleared his alcohol fog and replaced it with adrenalin, survival instinct, and, equally important, the muscle memory ingrained by

Manny Cohen. Manny's mixed martial arts training actually had served two purposes—it allowed anger to replace the pain of his mourning, but it also taught him how to escape the situation he found himself in right now, flat on his face, his lungs and face being crushed by a much stronger man.

Dean turned his face just enough to the left to divert the blows landing on his forehead and his nose. His cheek promptly encountered a nail popping out from the sidewalk that penetrated his flesh and a fountain of blood began pulsating from the wound. Summoning every bit of strength in his body, he timed the rhythm of the pounding and, as his head was lifted for another downward blow, he rose to his knees and violently twisted his body so he was on his back facing his attacker. Due to the darkness, and the blood in his eyes, he couldn't identify the load on his chest as Fletcher Barns— it felt like a grizzly—but at least now he was facing him. As Fletcher lifted his right fist to smash Dean in the face once again, Dean twisted again, grabbing Fletcher's left arm and hooking it into an arm lock. Now if Fletcher had been more versed in mixed martial arts, and less versed in barroom brawling, the outcome probably would have been different. Such as it was, Dean had no trouble turning his body enough to convert his arm hold into a Kimura arm lock. He'd seen this maneuver in videos, and had even used it once or twice in amateur fights as a submission hold, but he had never taken the hold to its ultimate conclusion. Then again, he had never before found himself in such a desperate situation. His adrenalin now converted to a controlled rage. He leveraged himself against the wooden deck, pulled with all his strength on Fletcher's arm, and with a loud crack, the elbow dislocated and the arm splintered, a bloody white ragged bone ripping up through the skin. For a couple of seconds, Fletcher seemed not to realize that his arm was now a useless flipper, and he was able to land two more punches to Dean's head. But then the synapses delivered the voltage of pain to his brain and, as witnesses said later, his scream sounded like a teenage girl in a horror movie. He rolled off Dean and grabbed his maimed appendage, howling, moaning, and swearing as he squirmed like a gut-shot elk. He looked up at the crowd that had gathered and a rasp came from the bloody mask that had been his face. "Somebody call the paramedics."

Only one ambulance served Jackson, so Dean graciously allowed the paramedics to take Fletcher to the hospital. A physician staying at the hotel heard the commotion and came downstairs. He was able to borrow some supplies from the paramedics and put a dozen stitches into the back of Dean's head and another half dozen into his cheek. Then the sheriff showed up, and Dean told her what happened. "Dean, go home, get some rest. We'll talk about this in the morning."

Dean was awakened in the middle of the night by a cold cloth being applied to his swollen, sore face. Sara was looking down at him. "You had yourself quite a night, Cowboy. Dancin', drinkin', fightin'. Seems like you're fittin' right in." Dean couldn't tell if she was pissed or teasing. "Oh, and I forgot kissin'. I don't know if I should call you cowboy or playboy."

"I didn't kiss her, she kissed me."

"I know. I'm just teasing you. It's OK—about time you kissed a woman, anyway. At least I'm a better dancer than she is."

"Much better, and a better kisser, too."

Sara leaned over and kissed Dean a little too hard on his swollen mouth. "Ouch."

Dean awoke again late the next morning. He'd finished off a bottle of Wild Turkey before he went to bed to kill the pain and didn't recognize the swollen face that stared back at him in the mirror—he looked like a raccoon after a complete face lift. When he finally arrived at the station the next morning, Joanie's normal cheery greeting quickly turned to horror. "Oh, my God, Dean, are you OK? Should you be here?"

"I'll be fine, Joanie, there's a lot of swelling, but it's not as bad as it looks."

"It looks pretty bad." She shook her head. "Sheriff Dani wants to talk to you right away."

When Dean walked into Dani's office, he didn't get the same shocked reaction that Joanie had given him. The sheriff was all business. "Sit down. Dean, we need to talk."

Dean sat, and the sheriff paused before continuing. "First, the good news. We have witnesses and a webcam from across the street that shows the unprovoked attack on you. So there's no question about that. Now the bad news. Fletcher went into respiratory arrest on the way to the hospital. They couldn't revive him. He's dead. The doctor thinks that maybe a bone fragment from his arm got into his blood stream and went to his lungs. The autopsy will tell for sure."

Dean was stunned. Fletcher dead? It was just a bar fight. People weren't supposed to die from a bar fight.

"There's another problem. Someone located a YouTube video of you in a mixed martial arts match back in Chicago. Did you ever fight professionally?"

"No. I had a few amateur fights, but never got paid."

"Well, as you know, if you're considered a professional, then harming a non-professional in a fight is a whole different matter. I'm sorry, but I have to take you off duty until the county attorney finishes his investigation."

"You can't be serious. I've got a bunch of leads on this case. You can't pull me off in the middle of it."

"I'm sorry, Dean, but I don't really have any choice in the matter. Look, I really like you, but to be honest, you've been a bit of a loose cannon. I'm not really impressed with the leads or the results of the investigation so far, and then you get side-tracked with Boris? I talked to the sheriffs in each of those counties, and they're already aware of what's going on, and they told me to stay out of their shit. Sorry, Dean, I'm going to have Rusty take over. Go home and get some rest. You look like crap."

Dean froze, knowing what he wanted to say, but trying not to say it.

"I'll need your badge."

Dean didn't say a word. He stood up, took the badge from his pocket, dropped it on the desk, and marched out. He didn't look back. At home he took a couple pain killers and was awakened in the afternoon by a bell that wouldn't stop ringing. He rolled off the bed and fumbled his cell phone from his pocket.

"Dean, this is Carlos. I heard what happened. Are you OK?"

"Yes, I'm fine. Just a couple of shiners. But you should see the other guy." Realizing his joke wasn't right in the circumstances, he said, "I guess that's not too funny. Did you hear about him?"

"Yeah, I did. I actually saw the video. Looks like you didn't have any choice. I think he may have killed you. He was pounding on you pretty good."

"Yeah, I thought I was in deep shit."

"When you come back, I want you to teach that move to our guys. It was pretty awesome. Anyway, I know the sheriff took you off the case, but as far as I'm concerned you're still on it. Instead of working for her, you're working for me. Just try not to get in their way out there. I think this Boris thing is going to take us to Mario and, from talking to the sheriff, I know she's not going to follow up on it. Dean, this is ours now. Mario's slipped away before, and I want to make sure he doesn't this time. Are you up for that?"

"I'm plenty up for it, Carlos." Now his whole face was aching. "These assholes are pissing me off, getting away with murder and even more. Hell yeah, I'm up for it."

Chapter 26

TATIANA nervously opened the large envelope the man had given her. There were two smaller envelopes inside. She didn't see who'd dropped it off, but she assumed it was one of Boris's men. She was told that she was going to be working in a spa, but she knew there was no spa. The other girls filled her in on what was expected of her and she at first was stunned and depressed, but soon their resignation and acceptance began to rub off on her. None of the cowboys had picked her out yet—she had deliberately made herself look disheveled and undesirable. But the woman in charge had made her fix herself up and now she knew it was only a matter of time until one of the cowboys would choose her. She opened the first envelope; it was a letter from her Aunt Arina.

Dear Tatiana,

I am so sorry to have to tell you that your father has passed away. He was told that he had lung cancer last month, but he didn't want you

*to know before you left for America.
He was afraid you wouldn't go. His
passing was not painful. He got up
yesterday morning and was coughing badly. We put him in the car to
take him to the hospital, but he died
before we got there. I know he loved
you very much and was very proud
of you, as we all are.*

Love,
Aunt Arina

Tatiana was shocked and in disbelief. Surely,
this could not be true. She opened the other
envelope, and saw it was a letter from her father.

My Dear Tatiana,

*I wrote this letter and gave it to your
Aunt to send to you on my passing. I
am sorry that I did not tell you I was
ill, but I knew you would want to stay
and take care of me, and that would
not have done any good. There was
nothing that could be done. You can
honor me and your mother by making
a good life for yourself in America.
Finish your education, and maybe
you will meet a young man and have
a family. You are a very resourceful
young woman. Be strong. This is my
hope and my wish for you. Remember me, and remember your mother.
We both love you very much.*

Your Father,
Oleg

Tatiana sat for a long time, finding it difficult to process the news in the letters. Her disbelief blocked out the sadness. The last time she had seen her father, he had been so proud and so happy. It was impossible to imagine that this beautiful man who had raised her and loved her so much no longer existed on this earth. Gradually, grief began to edge out the disbelief, and as the enormity of the news overwhelmed her, she went to one of the bedrooms in the house and pushed a dresser in front of the door. She lay down on the bed and sobbed for hours, until the despair pulled her into a fitful and moaning sleep. Everyone left her alone through the next day and the next night. When she rejoined the women at the breakfast table thirty-six hours later, her face and eyes were swollen, but she wasn't sobbing any longer.

The woman in charge of the house took her aside after breakfast. "Tatiana, all of us are so sorry for your loss. Since you arrived here, I have not pushed you into being with any of the men. I know you are young, and this is a big adjustment for you. And now you have the death of your father to deal with. But I know what mourning is like. And I can't let you be alone with your dark thoughts any longer. It is not good. You need to be busy, and it is time that you started to work. Take the rest of the day off. Tomorrow, I will show you how to be with a man. Believe me, it is not so bad. And it is always better to work when you are sad."

The rest of the day, alone in her room, she cried again, until she could produce no more tears. When she was spent, a feeling arose inside of her that displaced the sadness. She knew there would be more time for mourning later. For now, she made herself concentrate on her anger, fueling it with resentment and despair for her situation, focusing it like the sun through a magnifying glass on the men who brought her here and cheated her father. Her wrath turned to rage as she brought every ounce of her being to bear on her hatred for those men. How she wished she could kill the lying fat Russian. Her father had not sent her to America to become a whore. She would rather be in an American prison than dishonor herself and her family this way. She looked out the window. It was starting to get dark.

It was early when Dean picked up Daryl in Alpine. Daryl hopped in the car, looking glum, and neither of them said a word for the first five minutes. Finally, Dean spoke. "Look, Daryl, I know you're not happy about this. But Boris may be involved in some serious shit, and this thing with the girls may be just part of it. You can't be in business with a character like this. I thought you were going straight."

"I just don't see that what he's doing is much different than what the girls down at the strip club in town do. And the Lincoln County cops leave the club alone."

"Well, for one thing, as I understand it, there isn't actual sexual intercourse going on at the strip club. For another, the girls working for Boris may be illegal and, in my experience, where illegal foreign girls are working in the sex business, it's generally against their will. That makes it human slavery, Daryl, which is punishable by life in prison. I'm sure you don't want to be involved in something like that."

Daryl didn't say anything for another minute. "Do you really think these girls may be doing this against their will?"

Dean looked straight at Daryl. "Yes, I do."

Daryl thought for a moment. "OK, then. I'll do my best to help you."

Tatiana waited in her room until all the upstairs rooms were full. She heard the boots of a cowboy walk past her door, and the voice of the woman in charge talking to him. When they entered the room next to hers, she slipped down the stairs. The living room was empty, and she quietly opened the front door. There were about a dozen trucks parked in front of the house. Creeping around them, she looked in the truck beds, trying to find the one most suitable. In the end, she chose one that seemed to provide the best place to curl up and hide, climbed over the tailgate, crawled between two tool boxes and pulled a tarp over her head.

Thirty minutes later, a drunken roughneck opened the door of the pickup, started the engine with a rumble, and accelerated sharply out of the driveway. Tatiana was jerked violently as the truck bumped across the gravel road. Ten minutes later, the truck slowed, the gravel crackling underneath her. The man got out of the truck, and she felt the jab of fear in her stomach. He walked around to the back of the truck and stopped for a moment, and she heard the splash of his urine on the gravel. She tried to make her body smaller as she listened for his zipper to close. When he finished, he reached into the truck, fumbling with the tool box next to her head. She was blinded as the tarp was ripped off her body and a flashlight pierced her pupils. Behind the stabbing brightness, she could see only a large hulking figure. "What do we have here? Are you running away, little girl?" She recognized the words as a drunken slur, even in a language that was not her first.

"Please, can you give me a ride to the truck stop at the highway?"

The man looked her over, and seemed to be considering her request. "Well, that might be possible. I sure could give you a ride to the truck stop. But what are you going to do for me?"

She took a look at the man. He was really old, even older than the big Russian man who had brought her to America. And he was very fat. He had on dirty blue jeans, and his belly hung in a huge slab over his belt. She looked up at him and smiled the biggest, sweetest smile she had ever faked. "Help me out of this truck, and I will do something for you that will make you very happy to give me a ride to the truck stop."

He pulled her over the side of the truck and Tatiana took charge. She put her body very close to his, ignoring his disgusting odor of sweat, tobacco, and whiskey, and pushed him back against the truck. "How about this?" She reached down to his belt, fumbling with the big metal buckle, struggling to find the catch underneath the mountain of flesh. The belt was so tight that she couldn't get it loose. Finally, the man pushed her away, and unbuckled it himself, and his pants fell to his ankles. Tatiana got close to him again and ran her fingers over his belly and his ham hock thighs. Reaching for the waistband of his briefs, she jerked them down. Now his pants were on his ankles, and his briefs were around his knees. "Now you just lean back against the truck, close your eyes, and I am going to make you feel much, much better."

The man grinned at her, and she could see a rivulet of tobacco drool exit the side of his mouth and begin to roll down his cheek. "Go for it, girl."

As if on cue, Tatiana turned and ran like hell into the field of sage and prickly pear that stretched for miles into the darkness. She didn't stop running until she could look back and no longer see the truck parked at the side of the road.

It took a moment for the whiskey-addled brain of the roughneck to understand what was happening. Finally, realizing he wasn't getting what he thought he was getting, he bent over, reaching for his underwear, and fell down. Leveraging himself against the side of the truck, he pulled on his pants, fastened his belt beneath his belly and got back into the cab. "That little bitch," he laughed, and drove off into the night.

Dean and Daryl took their time navigating the back roads from Alpine. Dean wanted to document every part of Daryl's original route with Boris. Daryl wasn't quite sure of the precise route, but after many wrong turns, he was able to locate each of the houses. Dean took pictures and marked their GPS coordinates. By the time they got to the last stop in Rawlins, it was dark.

Several miles past the brothel, on the road that joined the interstate, Dean noticed something moving through the bushes just off the highway. At first he thought it might be a coyote, but then he looked closer and saw the flash of purple, and a hand.

"Do you see that? Something's moving in that bush and I don't think it's an animal." Dean pointed to a clump of vegetation about fifty feet off the highway. They stopped the car, got out and approached the bush slowly. Dean pulled his gun as an arm covered in a purple sweater appeared from the vegetation. "I'm a police officer. I can help you. Please come out of there."

A slight, very young girl, covered in scratches and dust, emerged. "Please, don't give me back to Boris."

"Don't you worry, honey. It's going to be all right now," Dean said, holstering his gun. He put his arm around her and led her back to the Jeep.

At a fast food drive-thru they ordered some food and Tatiana was able to get cleaned up a bit in the washroom. Then they got on I-80, headed west back toward Jackson. On the way Dean got Tatiana's story, about how Boris brought her and the other girls from Russia through Chicago and then to Wyoming. She told him what she knew about the financial arrangements, too—which was plenty. She started crying again when she told about her father's death. Dean looked at Daryl's face and could see that her story affected him, and that he was feeling guilty he'd ever thought Boris's scheme was benign.

When Dean got on the phone and described the recent events to Carlos, his boss was as giddy as a schoolgirl. "This is it. We know Torino and Birkov are in business together, and we know the link is the girls out of Chicago."

"Do we want to bring in immigration?"

"If we do that, they'll just round up the girls. There's no assurance they'll nail Birkov. and almost certainly they won't get the Torino connection. Eventually we'll want to bring them in, but not until we can deliver the whole package."

"Right, but we have no idea where the warehouse is. There are hundreds, maybe thousands of places like that within twenty minutes of O'Hare."

"Well, if Birkov's people went there once for a pickup, I bet they do a pickup on a semi-regular basis. Maybe we can track him to the van they use to move the girls—but I don't think we have enough to get a warrant for a GPS tracker on his car."

"I'll see what I can do. But this still doesn't solve the murder of Jordy Smith."

"The murder of Jordy Smith is the problem of Sheriff Cody now. Your focus should be on Birkov and Torino and prostitution, kidnapping, and human trafficking. We're getting another chance to get to Rosati and I don't want us to blow it. Keep your eye on the prize, Dean."

Dean agreed. But there were two prizes that Dean had his eye on, and he wasn't going to let either one of them go. He sure as hell wasn't going to let the sheriff arrest an innocent man.

Chapter 27

Senator Tom McGraw sat in the dressing room of the Bill O'Malley show. He felt stupid and somewhat effeminate as the makeup girl worked on his face, but the stress of the campaign had caused his complexion to get blotchy and he was getting some dark circles from lack of sleep. He was also starting to lose some weight and his face was looking a little drawn. The makeup girl was good, and when he looked into the mirror he saw a man ten years younger than he was used to seeing.

Ben Greenberg, Bill's producer, walked into the room and held out his hand. "Welcome, Senator. I've been looking forward to meeting you. I just want to spend a few minutes with you going over what Bill wants to talk to you about. Bill doesn't like to meet his guests prior to the show. He feels it hurts the spontaneity factor."

"Not a problem. I understand perfectly." Actually he didn't understand. He had hoped to spend five minutes bonding with Bill before the show, one maverick conservative to another. TL had misgivings about the interview. He thought that O'Malley might use the show as an opportunity to take Tom down, instead of becoming the king maker, and thus become a hero to the right wing of the party. But Tom boiled it down to the hard truth: "If I can't win over O'Malley, or at least hold my own with him, I probably can't win anyway."

The producer was friendly and reassuring, but Tom was savvy enough to know it could be a trap and was wary. "Now, Bill is a big admirer of yours, but he knows what the conservatives are saying about you. Bill's going to give you a chance to answer all those charges. I don't think you'll be surprised by anything he asks. It's the same stuff that most of the guys on this network have been saying since you announced."

"Is there anything outside of those questions he may ask?"

"Bill prepares his own questions and often will go off the cuff during the broadcast, but from what he discussed with me I don't see any surprises. Bill's not here to ambush you. I'll come back and get you. About fifteen minutes."

Three minutes later, Bill O'Malley unexpectedly walked into the dressing room, a big smile on his ruddy Irish face. "Senator Tom McGraw …" He held out his freckled hand. "So you want to be president."

"It looks that way."

"But the right-wing establishment is kind of giving you a hard time and you're hoping Ol' Bill here will rescue you, is that about right?"

"Well, not exactly *rescue*."

Suddenly, O'Malley's smile disappeared. "Then, Senator, what the fuck are you doing here?"

So this was it. He was going to have to grovel and kiss this jerk's ring. Well, he had done worse in his life. "Bill, you're right. I think I have some great ideas for the country, but the conservative establishment is really threatened by me. I *am* a conservative, as I think you know, and I think it's important that conservatives take back the White House."

"So what do you want from me?"

"Well, I'd like your tacit support."

"And why would you want that?" He was going to make him say it.

Now was the time for the grovel. "Look, we both know that you have the ability to destroy my candidacy or make my candidacy. And that's why I'm here. If it goes well today, I guess I'm on my way. If not, then I go back to my ranch in Wyoming. It's all up to you."

Bill looked at him for a moment. Then he grinned. "It is up to me, isn't it?" He laughed. "Senator, that is the smartest thing you've said since you announced. Let's see how it goes. I'll try not to make you sound too stupid out there."

Then he left the room.

Tom had gotten used to stroking assholes. It was part of being a politician. Behind O'Malley's back, well, Tom's staff would have a good laugh when he told them the story. Right now, he was definitely nervous. This was his first interview since the conservative media had had a chance to regroup from his initial announcement. He spent his remaining time in the green room looking through his notes.

Right before the cameras were set to roll, Bill took his seat. Immediately he nodded to Tom and the interview began. "Tonight, presidential candidate and the senior senator from Wyoming, Tom McGraw, is with us. Senator, you've created more havoc within your party since Teddy Roosevelt at the turn of the century. How does it feel to be the favorite Republican of the left?"

Tom laughed. Laughing off criticism had become one of his strengths. It made him appear not to take himself too seriously, so he would often laugh first, which seemed to treat the question as frivolous, and then he would answer the question thoughtfully. "Well, Bill, first, it's great to be here. I've been a fan of your show for a long, long time. But to answer your question, I'm thrilled to be admired by Democrats. If our party is going to be the majority again, we need to win over more Democrats. If we can't win over more Democrats, our party may not get to occupy the White House again in our lifetimes."

Bill followed with questions that Tom had developed well-rehearsed answers for. His amusing one-liners, followed by thoughtful answers, showcased the McGraw charm.

"Are you a true conservative?"

"Actually I am the only true conservative from my party that has run for President since Ronald Reagan."

"Are you a liberal libertarian, as some conservatives are calling you?" O'Malley asked, giving him a chance to make the same joke that had worked for the college audience.

"That term doesn't even make any sense. It sounds like my candidacy has so unnerved my opponents that they're trying to find the right label for something that they really don't understand. Too many conservatives, and I am one of them whether they believe it or not, think attaching the label 'liberal' to anything is a substitute for debating the merits of policy, which I am looking forward to doing as this campaign progresses. So far, unlike you, most of the conservative media have been afraid to have me on their programs."

"Explain how your positions on gays and immigration are right for conservatives."

"In the last decade, people have taken over our party who seem to have forgotten what conservative values are all about. Where I come from, people want to be left alone, and don't want government telling them how to live their lives. Conservatives have traditionally believed that government should stay out of our personal lives, so I don't see how the government coming into our bedrooms limits government control. In terms of our immigration issue, no single group of people believes more in the conservative work ethic and family values than the people who bring their families to our country looking for a better life. I don't know of a single person in Congress who isn't the descendent of immigrants. Breaking up families is not a conservative value. Finding a way for the people in our country to become legal, by paying a fine and serving a probationary period, is good for our tax base, our work force, and America."

"OK, I just saw a video of you talking to the kids at Wash U. Great performance. But what's with the ten million jobs thing. How are you going to do this? More jobs on the government teat?"

"Not a single government job, Bill. These are going to be jobs all created by the private sector. Our private sector has been handcuffed by government. Businesses have taken millions of jobs overseas during the last twenty years while politicians have stood around with their hands in their pockets talking about who we should be able to marry or putting themselves in the middle of women's reproductive decisions. Government needs to be a true friend of business, with an understanding that the friendship can only continue if it provides good paying jobs for our citizens. The middle class in this country is slowly being destroyed and, eventually, that will destroy the fabric of our country. I am issuing a ten million job challenge. It won't be easy. But I believe in our ability to get this done."

It was a fantastic display of political skill, and Tom didn't have to be told that O'Malley had constructed all the questions for his benefit—and he knew that meant that O'Malley had made the decision to be kingmaker rather than pointing out the candidate had no clothes. At least, he thought he knew this, until O'Malley fired the last question at him. "I understand that your biggest supporter is the well-known banking magnate Charles Kidwell. Don't you think it's dangerous to take money from the industry that caused the greatest economic meltdown since the Great Depression?"

That was a question Tom wasn't ready for. If he had been ready, he could have pointed out that Charles's bank didn't take any money from the government bailout, and that Charles's bank had virtually no exposure in the residential mortgage market. But he wasn't ready for the question, and so he gave an unconvincing answer. "Well, Charles has not endorsed me yet. And he has been a supporter of many candidates in our party."

"Senator, that doesn't really answer my question. Will you accept money from his PAC and their endorsement if it's offered?"

"I am not prepared to make a decision on that at this time."

And then it was over. Tom leaned over and said to O'Malley. "Thanks for this. I owe you."

"Yes, you do, and if you're elected, I'll be reminding you and my audience of that for the next eight years."

They posed for pictures together and said their goodbyes.

In the car, he rang Charles. "What did you think?"

"You were great, but what's with O'Malley. He was fawning over you like a political groupie."

"Don't know. Guess he wants to hitch his wagon to a winner. Actually, I think he just wants the notoriety of being the first to endorse the next President."

Charles laughed. "You're getting pretty cocky, seeing how you're the only announced candidate."

"I'm just kidding. Maybe. Any more news on the Chicago problem?"

"Well, a new employee started today. Couldn't put if off any longer. He's a research assistant, helping me put together material for a book. I figured maybe I could get by with that with the rest of the executive team. His dad isn't happy, but I convinced him this was a way to get the younger one into the inner circle without suspicion, and I could work him into a different position once he gets familiar with the organization. I figure after the election you can take him off my hands and put him in your cabinet."

"Don't joke about that. I don't envy you. I'm sure that little turd didn't fall far from the asshole. Long term there needs to be a better solution to this, but I don't have time to think about it right now."

Chapter 28

DEAN pounded on Hayden's front door at seven the next morning holding two extra-large coffees. When Hayden finally came to the door he didn't look any better than he had the last time Dean had seen him at the sheriff's office. He opened the door halfway and growled, "What the fuck do you want?"

"I thought we should talk. I brought coffee."

"My lawyer said I shouldn't say anything to you guys."

"Look, I'm the only cop probably in the entire state of Wyoming that doesn't think you killed Jordy. I want you to help me find out who did. Let me come in and let's see if we can figure this out."

Hayden looked at him a moment, then apparently decided either he believed Dean or he had nothing to lose by talking to him. He opened the door and Dean handed him a coffee. "It's black, but there's cream and sugar in the bag."

"Black works."

They both took seats at the kitchen table. The news was on the flat screen in the kitchen and Hayden took the remote control and turned down the sound. Dean took a sip of his coffee and said, "I don't know how much time we have. The sheriff thinks she has enough to arrest you, but it depends on what the county attorney thinks. I think if nothing breaks in the next week or two, you'll probably be arrested."

"What about you? You killed that guy in the bar fight. You're not even a cop now, right? Are you going to face any charges on that?"

"Well, there's video of him attacking me, so I don't think I have any problem with that part of it. But you're partly right—I'm not working for the sheriff's office anymore. I am, however, a federal agent back in Chicago, and I'm still working the case independently of the sheriff in that capacity. Let me give you some background. The reason I was on the case in the first place is that a Chicago-based hit man ran his car off the road in the Snake River Canyon and drowned in his car the morning after Jordy was killed. His name was Eddie Torino and I have some familiarity with him and his criminal associates in Chicago. Since no one can give us any motive for anyone killing Jordy, except for you, of course, my theory is that maybe Torino was hired to kill you. And that he killed Jordy thinking he was you. The picture of you on your website and on the front of your building looks a lot like Jordy. And if Torino was only going by a picture, he could have made a mistake like that. Have you ever heard of Eddie Torino, or a man named Mario Rosati?"

"No, I don't believe so."

"Can you think of anyone who might want to hurt you?"

"The only guy I can think of who might want to hurt me is Fletcher Barns. He lost a bunch of money in a real estate development deal and blamed me for it. Are you aware of that?"

Dean nodded.

"But you took care of him. Thank you for that, by the way."

"Do you think Fletcher was capable of murder?"

"You should be able to answer that. I saw the video of him trying to kill you on YouTube. You're a pretty tough guy."

"What about Boris Birkov?"

"Well, Boris was part of the investment group that lost money on Raptor Landing. I don't know him well, but some people think that he's some kind of Russian mafia guy."

Suddenly Hayden looked up at the TV and froze. "I'll be damned. Of course. I can't believe I didn't recognize him before."

"What?" Dean looked at the TV.

"Do you know who that is?"

"Yeah, it's Senator McGraw, the Wyoming Senator who's running for President."

"Well, I should have recognized him, too. A couple of days before I went on the backpacking trip, I walked in on him fucking a woman at one of the properties I manage. I knew he was really familiar but couldn't place him at the time.

I guess I didn't recognize him with his clothes on."

"Are you sure it was him?"

"One hundred percent." Hayden laughed. "AC/DC was blasting from the stereo and they were going at it doggie style. He jumped up when I walked in and I have to tell you that he was laying some very serious pipe."

"He lives in the area?"

"No, the house belongs to Charles Kidwell, the CEO of Prairie Bankcorp. I assume he was letting the senator use it. I made my apologies and got out of there. We didn't talk."

"Did you recognize the woman?"

"I didn't. But she's a redhead, and I know his wife has dark hair. I only got a look at her from behind. I might be able to identify her ass though," Hayden said, then he laughed again. "Not sure if I could, but if you put together a line up for me I would love to give it a try."

"Somehow I don't think Sheriff Dani would appreciate that joke. What about Matt Nelson?"

"What about him?"

"Well, as I understand it, you've been screwing his wife. He wouldn't be the first man who wanted to kill his wife's lover."

"It's not like that. I didn't start seeing Eliza until she moved out."

"Does he know that? Or, more importantly, does he think that?"

"Well, you'd have to ask him. He's always been cordial to me, never an angry word, and Eliza says he's not giving her a hard time about it. She says he's the nicest guy in the world. Makes me wonder what she sees in me. From what she says, he's sure as hell a lot nicer than I am."

"Give me your number, Hayden. If you can think of anything else that could link Fletcher or Boris to this, or if anything else strange happens, please let me know. Also, if I were you I'd be careful. Whoever wants you dead may want to finish the job."

"Unless it was Fletcher and you took care of it already, Deputy. I guess I should call you Agent Wister now."

"Call me Dean."

"Anyway, Dean, thanks again for taking care of Fletcher."

"I'm skeptical that it was Fletcher who wanted you dead. By the way, do you have a gun?"

"Yeah, I'm going to be carrying my forty-five everywhere, and my shotgun's in the car. The reason I don't own a nine-millimeter is I swapped it at a gun show in Rock Springs for the forty-five."

"Do you have any paperwork on that?"

"Paperwork? This is Wyoming, Dean. Gun shows here are like garage sales in Chicago. Do you get paperwork when you buy a lamp at a garage sale?"

They swapped phone numbers and then Dean called Mark from the car. "Hey, Mark, how's it going?"

"Going well, Dean. How's your face? I understand you're going to have a nice scar. That's gonna make the bad guys here a little more scared of you."

"Right, I'm sure the mafia guys will be intimidated now that I'm known as Scarface Wister. Can you see if there's any link between a Charles Kidwell, CEO of Prairie Bankcorp, and Rosati or Boris Birkov."

Mark paused, and then said, "Done."

"OK, how long do you think before you might have something?"

"I said, done. Charles Kidwell met with Rosati for lunch two days ago at the Italian Village. Carlos has a tail on Rosati and we saw them together. Can't tell you what they talked about, but Prairie Bankcorp is Rosati's bank."

"No shit."

"No shit," Mark agreed. "I also emailed you some pictures for the Russian girl to look at. See if she can ID Rosati or any of his men."

On the way back to his house Dean stopped to pick up some shampoo and such for Tatiana. An idea took shape in the soap aisle and when he got back in his Jeep he made a quick phone call. "Hayden, don't you have to go into the properties you manage and inspect them periodically?"

"Yeah, most of our owners are here only occasionally. So we go in regularly to clean and to make sure everything's in order."

"Right. Well, I think it might be a good time for you to do an unofficial inspection of Mr. Kidwell's property."

Hayden paused for a moment. "Why would you think— Oh, I see. Yeah, I could do that."

"And I'm thinking I might want to familiarize myself with how one of these inspections work. Could I tag along?"

"I don't see why not."

Chapter 29

D EAN put Charles Kidwell's address into his GPS twice and nothing came up. He swore at the device and put it in a third time, still nothing. He took out his cell phone and looked at the text from Mark, "100 Granite Wayy." He had assumed the spelling was a typo, but sure enough, when he put the street name in as "Wayy", the address came right up. There was only one property on "Granite Wayy" and Dean was impressed as he drove up the long curving driveway. He also wondered what other affectations the owner might have in addition to his proclivity for creative spelling.

The entrance to the estate was proclaimed by a huge wrought iron gate dominated by a forged iron art deco CK. As he awaited Hayden's arrival, he got out of his Jeep and walked around the property. It was built on top of a butte and had 360-degree views—the Teton Range to the west, Sleeping Indian Mountain and the Elk Refuge to the east, the town of Jackson to the south, and the entirety of Teton National Park to the north. The dramatic landscape literally took his breath away, and he had to fight back the same feelings that had overwhelmed him when he'd seen the range from his Jeep as he drove into town two months before. Huge windows easily covered over half of the home, and the rest of the facade was supported with beautiful Wyoming sandstone. He wondered how much it would cost to buy a house like this, or how much the land alone cost. He couldn't imagine. The back of the property featured an open concrete and stone patio, with stone steps seemingly carved into the mountain.

Hayden arrived, looking much better than when Dean saw him last.

"Hi, Dean. What do you think? Pretty impressive property, huh?"

"Sure is. Any idea what the land and property cost?"

"Not as much as you might think. I believe around twenty mill."

"A bargain," Dean said. And he actually meant it. "You really can't put a price tag on this view. This is the view I imagine from heaven."

"I agree. But the twenty mill buys you the view only for your time on Earth. And I bet the owner is here only a few weeks a year."

Hayden entered a code into a keypad to get in the front door, and then opened a closet just inside and disarmed the burglar alarm. "I have a few things I should check on, so you wander around by yourself. I don't want to know anything, and you were never here, right?"

"Right, I was never here." Dean held up his hands as he put on gloves.

Although the house was big, it actually didn't have that many rooms, but the size of each room created an echo as he walked across the wood and stone floors. He systematically wandered through each room of the house, opening closets, going through drawers. He was looking for something, really anything that would link Charles Kidwell to Rosati. Or maybe to Birkov, for that matter. He entered the master bedroom —hand-carved, king-sized bed, and matching wooden Western nightstands and chests. He noticed both male and female clothes in the drawers and closets, but the feminine wear was lots of lingerie, thongs, and nightgowns. Not much in the way of daytime wear for the lady, he thought.

He entered the office and laughed. He thought of the poor elk with the rhino antler in the sheriff's office. Here was a mounted moose head, carved of wood, and painted in psychedelic colors. Now that's a flamboyant moose, he thought. He walked over to the large redwood desk that had some papers neatly stacked on it. He saw nothing of interest in the papers on the desk, but there was a stand in the corner with a fax machine on it, and there was a document on the fax machine. Dean thought it made sense for Charles to have access to work when he was at his vacation residence, but he thought fax machines went out of date some time ago, but maybe not out here. He'd noticed a fax machine in Sheriff Dani's office and another in the real estate office. The top sheet was a standard distribution list to the Board of Directors of Prairie Bankcorp. The second sheet contained the bombshell that left Dean numb.

> *To: Board of Directors, Prairie Bankcorp*
> *From: Charles Kidwell, Chairman and CEO*
> *Re: Mario Rosati Jr.*
>
> *As you all know, I am in the process of writing a book about the growth of Prairie Bankcorp, and how our business model could be a new paradigm for a national banking system. I would like to introduce you to Mario Rosati Jr., a talented young financial executive and the newest member of our team. He will be working for me on special projects, and one of his duties is to help with research for my book. He will be attending Board and management meetings to help document our Company's decision-making processes. Please make yourself available as needed to assist on this project.*

Maybe this is what he was meeting with Mario about in Chicago. He photographed the memo with his smart phone and went through the other papers, though he found nothing else of interest.

As he wandered through the rest of the house, he thought about the meaning of Junior's hire. Either Charles and Mario Sr. were close friends, in business together, or Mario had some kind of leverage over Charles. Any of these scenarios could result in Charles's being complicit in any of Mario's criminal activities. Almost certainly money laundering was involved, which is what the original investigation of Mario was about. But what would be in it for Charles, besides greed, of course, which you couldn't discount. He had seen many rich men throw away everything to make a few thousand more. And what would Hayden have to do with any of this? He was mulling all of this over when he reached the front door where Hayden was waiting.

"Done?"

"I think so. Is Charles married or living with someone?"

"Not married. The only woman I've seen around here is the redhead that day with the senator, but otherwise I wouldn't know. I know my crew has seen only Charles here, and sometimes the senator."

"How did you get Charles as a client?"

"His builder recommended me. I've met him only a couple of times, actually, and of course some phone calls."

"Can you let me know when you expect him back?"

"As a matter of fact, he'll be back in town to-morrow. I was just making a list of things for my crew to do to get it ready later today."

Chapter 30

Robbie Benz was not only the Mayor of Alpine, he also owned The Grandest Tetons, which, as he liked to remind the town council, was the largest contributor of any municipal business to the property and sales tax revenues. He also was known to refer to the girls who worked in his business as "his stable," and treated them as such. Some of the girls didn't really mind, for when they were summoned to his office for a "private dance" it would usually be accompanied by a tip much greater than the tips from the cowboys, laborers, and ne'er do wells so lacking in success, looks, or self-confidence that they needed to avail themselves of the girls' services. But those boys were much preferable to Amber than Robbie. For the most part, they treated her with respect and gratitude, and she got the feeling that women hadn't been so nice to them out in the real world. Robbie, however, treated the girls like his property, and he displayed the attitude that they should be grateful they were chosen to service him. She had so far managed to avoid him, but she knew it was only a matter of time. When he came to the girls' dressing room as she was getting ready to go home one night, she knew her time had come. She was naked with her back to the door when she heard it open and boots scuff on the wooden floor. His wheezy breathing gave his identity away, and her stomach tightened.

"Whew, Amber, girl. You've got the booty of a black girl. Maybe not Beyoncé black, but maybe Kardashian black."

"Hi, Robbie. I'm just getting ready to go home," she said as he howled at his own joke. "Well, just put on a robe and come up to my office. No need to get dressed."

"OK." She put on her street clothes anyway and, with resignation, walked up the stairs to his office, which was arranged so that he could look down on the entire restaurant, bar, and dance floor. She entered his office without knocking. He was seated on the brown leather couch, waiting for her. She stood in front of him and asked, "Would you like a dance?"

"Amber, I thought I told you to come on up in your robe. Here you're all dressed. How are you gonna dance like that? Take off some clothes, girl."

"Should I put on some music?" She glanced at the boom box on his shelf.

"No, you don't need music. Just take off your clothes."

When she was dancing on the stage with music playing, she felt somehow removed from the men watching her—she was a performer. When she was giving a private dance, the men often seemed shy and so she could take charge of the situation, controlling what she did and how she did it. Here, with Robbie, she felt out of control. Like what? She wasn't sure, so she stood in front of her boss, unbuttoned her blouse, and removed it.

"Slow. Do it slow."

Slowly she removed her shorts.

"Leave the shoes on."

She removed her bra and slid her panties down her legs.

"Now walk to the middle of the room. We're going to need some space for this."

She walked to the center of the room with her arms to her sides, feeling so self-consciously bare as he stared at her that she closed her eyes, and braced for his touch.

Something grabbed her arm and pinched.

"Ouch!" She opened her eyes and looked down. Robbie was holding some type of metal tweezer thingy and pinching a fold of her arm in it. "Robbie, what are you doing with that thing?"

"Amber, this is what's called a body-fat percent caliper and I'm going to start measuring the body fat in you girls. A boy that comes in here works in a gym up in Jackson and he told me that some of you girls are startin' to look a little on the hefty side. He told me how he measures the body fat of all the members of the gym up there and it sounded like a good idea to me."

He pinched folds of skin and took measurements in several locations on her body. Then he took out a calculator and put some numbers in and shook his head. The head shaking made Amber nervous. "What?"

"Well, it says here that your body fat is off the charts. A lot higher than it should be, even with those boobs of yours adding a couple of percentage points. The fitness guy from Jackson says you girls are starting to have an urban look, and that's not what we're going for here."

Robbie looked up and thought for a minute. "You know what? I was thinking about maybe fining you girls based on your body fat, but I think I just came up with a better idea. I'll post a chart in the dressing room with each girl's percentage on it. Sort of let you girls police each other. What do you think about that idea?"

Amber said nothing, but the blood rushed to her face and she felt the entire upper part of her body turning red. She hurriedly put on her clothes and ran out to her car, thinking how much worse this was than what she thought was going to happen when he called her into his office.

When she got home that night, she took a long shower, trying to wash off the feeling of Robbie's treatment of her. She wondered why this felt worse than giving Robbie a lap dance. At least the boys she danced for saw her as something more, a performer, an object of their desire, someone who would understand and accept their sexual desires, someone who wouldn't reject them. Some people thought what she was doing was demeaning but, although she would prefer not to do it, she liked the attention, and in certain ways, the boys she danced for made her feel better about herself. But Robbie had treated her like he was inspecting one of his farm animals.

As she crawled into bed, Daryl woke up and turned over. "How was work?"

"Honey, how long do I have to do this? When do you think we can get out of here?"

He pulled her close and put his arms around her. "I think about that every day, baby. Just hold on a little longer for me. I'll get you out of that place. I promise."

And she believed him.

Chapter 31

Boris got off the phone and turned to a young Russian man. "Tatiana ran away."

"Who is Tatiana?"

"The short little dark-haired girl we took to Rawlins last week. She got the news her father died and took off. Someone saw her getting into an orange Jeep." Boris paused. "I know that fucking ugly orange Jeep. It belongs to that Chicago cop. Here's what I want you to do. I see that orange Jeep parked at the Starbucks every morning around seven. Follow him until he goes home. When he leaves, go through his house. If the girl is there, take her."

"If she isn't there, should I wait for him and question him?"

"No, we don't want any more heat from the cops. The cops down in Rawlins are very understanding, and the sheriff here has fired the Chicago boy, but if any harm comes to him then it will be very difficult for us. I don't want to create any more trouble than I have to."

Dean came into the house and looked at Tatiana. She was sitting on the couch and Cheney had his head in her lap, looking very content as she stroked him. She had seemed traumatized when he brought her in last night. He told her that she was now safe, that he would protect her, but he could see she wasn't sure if she could trust him. This was going to take a while. "Cheney's a great dog. You like him?"

She nodded and nearly smiled.

"Tatiana, you said you saw three Russian men at the warehouse in Chicago. I have some pictures on my phone that I want to show you. See if you recognize any of these men." Dean took a seat on the sofa—not quite next to the girl, keeping his distance out of respect for her wariness—and pulled up the pictures that Mark had sent him of the guys from Mario's crew in Chicago. There were about a dozen shots. Tatiana kept stroking Cheney as she carefully looked through them, first quickly and, then, a more thorough second look. "None of these men were there."

"Are you sure?"

"I'm sure. Two of the men were very fat and ugly. The third was young and good looking. None of the men are the men in these pictures."

"Can you tell me anything else about the men?"

Tatiana thought. "The three of them would come in together late at night. They would be drunk, and they would try to get the girls to party with them. You know, some of these girls they are not used to drinking, and they would get very drunk, and the men would take them back to a private room."

"They would force themselves on the girls?"

"Well"—she shrugged—"the girls would not resist. These guys were very scary. The good looking one, he punched one of the girls, and the main guy, the guy who drives the van, yelled at him that Boris would be angry if any of the girls had marks on them."

Dean looked at her, and asked quietly. "Did any of them bother you?"

"No, but I think it was going to happen soon. The young one, I saw how he looked at me the night before they drove me to Wyoming."

"I am so sorry this happened to you. But you're safe now. No one knows where you are. And my boss in Chicago can help you get a visa or send you back to Russia, whichever you want, as soon as Boris is arrested." She seemed satisfied—as satisfied as she was going to get for the time being, and so he added, "I'm going to go to the market down the road now to get us something to eat. I won't be gone long. I'm taking Cheney with me. He hasn't been out for a while. Remember, keep the blinds closed and don't answer the door."

A young Russian man watched the orange Jeep roll down the long gravel driveway and drive up Highway 89. As soon as the Jeep was out of sight, he pulled his car into the same driveway.

Tatiana heard the gravel. Dean must have forgotten something, she thought, and peered through the blinds. She saw a dark-colored pickup truck slowly pulling up, and she recognized the face in the truck as a face she had seen at the house in Rawlins. Fear and panic competed for control of her body. She looked around for a place to hide. There was nowhere, the closets were too small, and he would find her there, and the same with under either of the beds in the bedroom. The cabin was just too small. She could hear the door of the truck slam and shoes on the gravel. Her eyes landed on the stove. The oven was her favorite hiding place for a game with her cousins back in Russia. *I hope I'm still small enough*, she thought and opened the oven door, slid out the rack and placed it on the bottom of the oven, carefully folded her small body inside, and pulled up the door. From inside the oven she could hear a metallic picking at the lock on the front door.

It took the Russian about a minute to pick the lock. He wasn't that good at it, but the lock wasn't up to even his poor burglary skills. He popped it and stepped into the small cabin. "Tatiana? Please come out. I won't hurt you. Boris is not angry with you. He wants me to take you to the airport so that he can send you back to Russia to your family. Please come out."

He walked through the house. If she were here, he thought, he would find her. There was just no place to hide. He looked in the closets, under the beds. He saw there was only one door to the cabin so he knew she could not have run out the back door. He looked to see if he could find any evidence of her in the cabin, clothes or shoes, and saw nothing. The cop must not be keeping her here, he thought. He turned around and walked out, got back in the truck and went back to report to Boris.

Tatiana waited a minute and pushed on the oven door. It didn't move. She pushed again. Again it didn't move. It was latched. She waited in the dark claustrophobic oven, not knowing how much time had passed. And then she heard the Russian return. The front door opened and she heard him walk across the floor and into the kitchen. He paused, looking at the stove, reached over and turned the knob. Tatiana heard the hiss of gas then the puff of the ignition of the gas flame. For a moment, she considered letting herself burn instead of turning herself over to the Russian. But the thought of her burning flesh was just too much for her and she kicked at the door and screamed, "Help, let me out!"

The oven door opened, and two hands grabbed her, pulling her out, sputtering, singed and scared, depositing her on the kitchen floor.

"Tatiana, what are you doing in there?" Dean looked at her with fear and confusion.

When Tatiana explained to him what had happened, it was clear that somehow the Russians knew where he lived—and they suspected that Tatiana was with him. He needed to get her out of his place. A motel probably wouldn't be safe either. If either of them checked in, they might be identified—Boris had a lot of contacts in the area—but he had another idea.

"Tatiana, I'm so sorry. I didn't think they had any idea you were here. I'm going to move you some place safer right now." She looked up at him, and he couldn't imagine what must be going through her mind. He wondered if he would trust himself if he were in her position. Realistically, however, she didn't have a choice.

Forty-five minutes later Dean pulled into the driveway of a neatly kept little home. A pretty blonde came to the door, a smiling young man was behind her. "Hi, Dean, what's up?"

"Hi, guys. I have a favor to ask of you. Can a friend of mine stay with you for a few days?"

After he'd deposited Tatiana with Amber and Daryl, Dean made the exhausting trek back from Alpine. He figured Boris had sent someone to follow him, in order to find out where he lived, and he had been careful on the drive to Alpine to make sure it wouldn't happen again. He was conscious of being followed now. He had enough experience in Chicago, being on the other side of tailing suspects, and that knowledge made it easy enough to lose someone if he wanted to.

When he arrived at home, he rigged his front door to create a racket if someone tried to open it, and slept with a loaded gun on the nightstand and a knife underneath the bed. Part of him wanted them to try to enter his house when he was home, but he doubted it would happen.

Two months ago when he came out here, he had put his gun down and managed to turn off the Chicago-cop node in his brain. It had been partially turned back on when he started this case, but he still hadn't felt the foreboding sense of danger he felt nearly every day on the streets of Chicago. Now that switch was fully flipped. He knew the time had come to start carrying his gun on him at all times.

He slept fitfully, finally inviting the dog to spoon with him, but at one point in the night he awoke with a start. There was someone in the pitch-black room. He slowly reached for his gun, and flipped on the lamp at the same time.

"Whoa, cowboy." Sara stood in the middle of the room, and relief at her image replaced the adrenalin of fear with a different kind of fear. "Are you OK?"

He put down the gun and reached for her. "I thought you were a Russian assassin. I almost killed you."

"Don't you remember, honey? I'm already dead."

Chapter 32

HAYDEN lay on his back, naked, sweaty, out of breath, but full of endorphins. He loved make-up sex, and Eliza had definitely made it up to him. She walked into the room, naked and swigging a bottle of water. Without offering him a sip she crawled on top of him, pinning his arms to his sides. "Ready for round two?"

"Don't you mean round three? Sweetheart, a man of my age is going to need a little recovery period. Can't we cuddle for a bit?"

She rolled off of him and threw her bare leg over him, running her hands up and down his chest. "I know I'm being a little aggressive. But usually it's the other way around and I thought you'd like it if I changed things up. Besides, I really missed you. And I was really worried about you. I know it's selfish, but I don't want to raise this child by myself. When you left, I didn't know if something happened to you, or if you were just pissed off that I was pregnant."

"Eliza, I just was shocked. I needed time to process the whole thing. To clear my head. I'm sorry I took off, but it was good that I did." He put his arms around her and pulled her close, lifting her chin so he could look right into her dark eyes. "I'm thrilled that I'm going to be a father. And that you're going to be the mother of my child."

"Me, too."

"But I'm worried about how Matt is going to take this. After all, you're still married to him."

"Well, I'm a little worried, too. I didn't want to tell him until the divorce was final. He's been really good about everything, but every man has his limits."

"I know I wouldn't take it very well if I were in his shoes."

"Well, he's been stonewalling signing the divorce papers. Telling him is going to be hard, but maybe it's what's needed to get him to sign the damn papers right away. Since there aren't any financial considerations, signing shouldn't ever have been a problem."

Her caresses continued, down his body with her incredibly soft fingers, and then she added her lips.

"Eliza, what are you doing?"

"Just trying to accelerate your recovery time." Then she did something with her teeth, which added a little pain to the pleasure.

"Oh, my God."

Chapter 33

MARIO answered the phone, and the thick Russian voice on the other end sounded upset. "One of our girls ran off. We can't find her. I think it's possible that she has gone to the cops."

"So? I thought you have the cops handled."

"I do. But she didn't go to the cops in Rawlins. Someone saw her get into a Jeep that could be the car of the Chicago cop that's out here. His name's Dean Wister and I sent a guy into his house, but I don't think he's hiding her there. Maybe he turned her over to the FBI or immigration or something. If he did, we're fucked."

"What would Wister be doing in Rawlins? Isn't that a long way from Jackson? And how would he even know about your girls? There are a million Jeeps—"

"Well, the Jeep was orange. There aren't a million orange Jeeps. He came out to my house a couple of weeks ago to talk to me about you, and about Fletcher Barns, and that asshole Hayden Smith. I don't think there's any way that he could know about the girls, unless he was following me—and I would know if he was following me, but—"

"I think you're just being paranoid. She probably got into the truck of some horny cowboy."

"Maybe. But do you have a problem if this Chicago cop has an accident?"

"Don't do anything right now. If anything happens to him his boss is going to think I'm behind it. They're trying to pin this Jordy Smith murder on me as it is, but they've got nothing. I don't want to overreact to some Russian whore running away."

"OK, but you know it could be a lot more trouble if they can track the girls back to Chicago."

"I know, but they can't do that, right?"

There was only a slight pause before Boris answered. "Right."

Dean cruised through Jackson, hoping to get lucky. He had spotted Boris's black X-5 with the BMAN license plate frequently parked at various nightspots, but not tonight. He turned his Jeep around and made the fifteen-minute drive to the ski village, the other primary nightspot in the area. He cruised the ski village parking lot and bingo, there was the SUV. It was better he found him here than downtown anyway—less chance of someone noticing him out here. Within seconds he had placed the GPS tracking device on the underside of the car.

He left the Village and made a call to Mark in Chicago to activate the device. The GPS wouldn't help track him if he used one of his henchman to do his dirty work, and the device was illegal without a warrant, but Dean had used it in the past to track a suspect and then removed the device, leaving the suspect none the wiser.

He had very high hopes for the efficient little piece of technology in this case.

Chapter 34

DEAN sat in his car outside the home of Charles Kidwell. Though he was quite familiar with the interior from his unauthorized self-tour, he had to remember to act suitably unfamiliar with the place if Charles offered him an authorized one. Hayden had called to tell him when Charles was picked up at the airport, and Dean hoped the element of surprise would make it easier to get Charles to talk.

A tall, handsome man decked out in Patagonia climbing gear answered the door. He didn't have the build or complexion of the hikers and climbers out here—he was pale, his thin limbs nearly devoid of muscle definition. He looked like a miscast male model. "Charles Kidwell?" Dean asked.

"Yes, how can I help you?"

"I'm Federal Agent Dean Wister, Mr. Kidwell, and I'm working on a case that I hope you can help me with." Dean flashed his badge. "May I come in?"

Dean smiled at Charles's look of surprise, as Charles stammered, "Of course, Mr. Wister, come in."

Charles led him to the study—the same study where Dean had found the document with Mario Jr.'s name on it the day before.

"Please, sit down. What is this about?"

"Mr. Kidwell, I'm working a murder investigation of a man named Jordy Smith, who was murdered in Jackson. Did you know Jordy?"

At the mention of Jordy's name, Charles's face turned pale, and for a moment, he seemed unable to speak. Finally, he said softly, "No, I read about the murder, but I never met Jordy."

"Do you know his cousin, Hayden Smith?"

"Yes, Hayden is my property manager."

"I have reason to believe that a Mario Rosati, a resident of Chicago, may be somehow involved in this. Do you know Mr. Rosati?"

Charles seemed to have regained his composure, but still spoke deliberately. "I know him, but not well. His company is a customer of my bank, Prairie Bankcorp."

"Mr. Rosati is suspected of being involved in certain criminal activities in Chicago. Are you aware of that?"

"I have no knowledge of any criminal activities of Mr. Rosati. If I did, he wouldn't be a customer of my bank."

"But you've heard rumors."

"Mr. Wister, I'm a banker. A businessman. If I rejected all my big customers based on rumors I have heard about them, well, I wouldn't be able to run my business." Charles smiled

the smile you smile when you are saying something to someone that you both know isn't entirely true.

"Has Mario Rosati ever asked you to do anything inappropriate, maybe not illegal, but
something that would be considered out of
the ordinary?"

"Never."

"Did he ask you to hire his son?"

Charles looked stunned. And suddenly realized that the agent knew more than he was
letting on. "Yes, he did. His son would like to
get some banking experience, and he is qualified, so I put him on a sort of internship assign-
ment."

Dean quickly decided to shift gears. "Do you
live here alone, Mr. Kidwell?"

"I do. I'm not married. Why is that relevant?"

Dean ignored the question. "Senator Thomas
McGraw is a personal friend of yours?"

"Yes, he is. Why?"

"Well, a short time ago, Senator McGraw
was observed having sex with a woman in this
very room. Do you know the identity of that
woman?"

"Mr. Wister, I don't think this is any of your
business, really. I don't see how this has anything to do with your investigation."

Dean smiled at Charles, the kind of smile
that you smile when you want the person to
know that you have them by the balls, and
you're getting ready to squeeze. "Mr. Kidwell,
you're a smart man, so I'm not going to bullshit

you. You and I both know that Mario Rosati is a Chicago gangster. And we both know that his last bank cut him loose because he was laundering money through his businesses. And now he turns up doing business with you. And his son is hired by you. And you are a well-known major supporter of a Presidential candidate. Bill O'Malley says you're his closest political advisor and are funding his campaign, in fact. I don't believe a smart man would take on a gangster customer, knowing that it would expose his good friend who's running for President to this kind of scandal..."—Dean paused and stopped smiling—"unless he had no choice. Now, I'm sensitive to the situation that you and the senator find yourselves in, and I don't want any of this to be leaked to the press. I'm investigating a murder, and I'm investigating Mario Rosati. I assume that you and the senator have nothing to do with either the murder or any of Mr. Rosati's shenanigans. So, if you want me to use my best efforts to keep all of this out of the public eye, you need to be honest and forthcoming with me. I'm sure you understand what I'm saying to you."

Dean paused and let that sink in. "Charles, who is the woman with Senator McGraw?"

The wan, nauseated look returned to Charles's face and he didn't speak for a few seconds. When he did, it was softly. "The woman is my sister Charlotte. She lives in Chicago. The senator is married, so this cannot come out. I assure you that his wife knows nothing about any of this. I beg you to leave her out of this."

Dean nodded. "I'll do my best to make that happen. But I need something from you. I need you to have your internal audit team look through your records and give us any suspicious data that might indicate money laundering or any other illegal activities by Mr. Rosati. If you come to me with that information voluntarily, and this is the important part, if you can rack your brain and come up with an incident where Mr. Rosati has asked you or any of your staff to disregard any Federal currency reporting requirements, then I can easily get a warrant to examine the financial records of his company. If you can do that, you can come out of this an innocent banker who, at worst, became a victim of Mr. Rosati's activities."

Charles got up and walked to the window. It appeared to Dean that he was doing some kind of mental calculation. "Let me think about it."

"Mr. Kidwell, I want to get a team in to look at Rosati's records as soon as possible. I need your answer in twenty-four hours."

"Are you saying if I cooperate, you can keep the senator's name, and Charlotte's, out of this?"

"I'm saying I will do my best. I just want Rosati and his associates."

"Let me give this some thought. I'll call you tomorrow."

Dean handed him his card, and walked out the front door. As he drove back to town, something about the conversation came to him and he had to pull off the road. He had told Charles that he was investigating Jordy's murder. Then he had told him that Rosati was somehow involved. But Charles hadn't asked a single question about how those two things were connected, or what it had to do with him. Maybe that was because he already knew the answers.

Dean picked up his phone and left a voicemail for Mark in Chicago. "Mark, can you get me everything that you can find on Charles Kidwell's sister Charlotte?"

Charles watched Dean drive away with a sick feeling in the pit of his stomach. The agent obviously knew he had taken on Rosati's business because of blackmail, and he was on the right track to finding out what the blackmail was about. It was also possible that he may suspect that the Jordy Smith murder may have been Rosati's attempt to silence Hayden, and it had gone wrong. "Fucking, Hayden," he thought. He had talked to the Feds, which was almost as bad as talking to the press. Charles decided he wasn't going to tell Tom about this—a presidential candidate didn't need this kind of distraction. If Wister was on the up and up, the real target was Rosati's money-laundering business, not connecting him or the senator to the murder of Jordy. He, himself, still thought it was a long shot that there *was* a connection.

If he could give them Rosati, maybe everything else would go away. And giving him Rosati would be easy. He'd been ignoring the internal auditors' red-flag reports on Rosati's account since he'd become a client.

Chapter 35

Eliza was dreading the conversation with Matt. He had been so nice about everything with regard to her relationship with Hayden. Unbelievably nice, actually. But being pregnant with Hayden's baby while still married to Matt, well, that would be tough for any man, no matter how laid back and open minded. She had invited Matt to lunch. She didn't want to wound Matt any more than necessary, but finalizing their divorce had been the only thing about which he hadn't been the perfect gentleman. She believed his endless list of excuses to put off signing the papers could be understood simply as his inability to let go, and if she had to pry him loose, well, so be it.

Eliza welcomed him into her home—a home they'd once shared—with a warm hug, and the warmth of her body against him, the push of her breasts against his chest, filled him with desire. Desire, and something else—loathing. Matt's attitude toward Eliza had gradually changed since their separation, souring more and more as he discovered each new bit of dirt about her true nature. At first he had blamed Hayden for the separation, but he had come to conclude that she was the one to blame. He knew he should just sign the divorce papers and put the whole sorry marriage behind him, but it wasn't that simple for him.

They shared Eliza's delicious homemade soup and bread, and Eliza listened while Matt described his latest business acquisition and his plans to enter a poker tournament in Reno the next month. They talked for quite a while before Eliza worked up the nerve to discuss the subject that was so heavy on her mind.

"Matt, there's something you should know, and there's no easy way to say this. You believe me when I told you that I was faithful to you throughout our marriage, right?"

Matt's jaw tightened. There was a time a few weeks ago that he did believe her. But since then things had happened, he had seen things about her, things that made her story unbelievable. "Of course, Eliza, I know you were faithful."

She smiled that sexy smile that still aroused him, but he pushed his desire down to another place. "Well, I'm afraid that Hayden and I, well, we've had an accident."

"What kind of accident? Is Hayden OK? Was he injured?"

"I'm sorry. Not that kind of an accident. Matt, I'm pregnant."

Matt heard the words, but he couldn't quite believe them. So he sat there and stared at her.

Stared at the tight red top she was wearing with her boobs sitting up as if on a display shelf. He wouldn't let her dress like that when they were married, but she was different since their separation. She dressed like the girls he would use in Vegas, not the respectable wife of a businessman. He realized she had the look of a girl he would ask for from the escort service. The girl who would do things that a wife and mother should never do.

"Matt, did you hear me? I said I'm pregnant."

"Yes, I heard you." He struggled to remain calm and in control.

"It wasn't supposed to happen. It was an accident. I'm so sorry. I didn't want anything like this to happen until our divorce was final, and, now, it has happened and don't you think, under the circumstances, we should try to get those divorce papers signed as soon as possible?"

With every fiber in his body he pushed down his rage. Pushed it down and let the cold numbness wash over him. He would not allow her to see him lose control. "Thank you, Eliza, for telling me. I'll sign the papers and get them back to you this week. I'm afraid I have to go now. I have to prepare for a conference call."

He walked out the door, got in his truck, and drove home. And as he almost always did, he locked away the anger, hurt, and disrespect into a dark vault deep inside.

Chapter 36

THE call Dean got as he was finishing dinner that night was quite a surprise. He had given Charles a twenty-four-hour deadline and he didn't expect to hear from him so soon. He smiled when he realized Charles had decided to take his advice.

"Mr. Wister, I have just reviewed some reports from our internal audit department, and there are some alarming signs that may indicate illegal activities in Mr. Rosati's businesses. Also, I have checked our records and Mr. Rosati has been pressuring several of our employees to disregard federal currency report requirements. They're putting the reports together right now and I can get them to you as soon as we agree on the protocol. We would be happy to assist you in your investigation if you can provide a court order."

"That's great. I'm so happy you've decided to help. I'm sure this will work out much better for you than the alternative."

"I hope so. One more thing. Can you provide me with something in writing that you will provide immunity to our bank and bank officers for any of Mr. Rosati's illegal activities, based on our bringing this to your attention?"

"That shouldn't be a problem. I'll get on the immunity arrangements right away. But you'll have to meet my boss Carlos Alvarez in Chicago and go over it with him. How soon can you meet with him?"

"I'm flying back to Chicago first thing in the morning and can meet him any time after noon."

That night, Tom flew in to meet Charlotte in Charles' home in Jackson. It was just one night together but with Tom on the campaign trail, they hadn't been together for a while. Charlotte knew about the meeting with Dean, but she didn't tell Tom. They had so little time together and she didn't want to spoil it. She called their time together "an island of love and pleasure that the outside world should not disturb." They both shared that philosophy, which is what made their romance both possible and sustainable. Other than Charles, no one knew about Charlotte, and Tom knew that it had to remain that way. And Charles and Charlotte knew it too, which is how they had fallen into the trap set by Mario Rosati, when he had used his knowledge, and a video of Charlotte and Tom together, as blackmail.

"How's my girl?" Tom enveloped Charlotte's slender figure in his big arms, squeezing her so tightly in a bear hug that she had to grunt.

Then, as he always did, he kissed her passionately and pulled her into him. "I've missed you so much," he whispered in her ear.

She laughed. "I can tell. It feels like you're going to poke a hole right through me. Didn't you ever hear of hotel porn?"

"Can't use it. TL says that hotel employees could monitor the movies on my TV and leak it to the media. Besides, I like saving it up for you."

"Well, let's go to the bedroom and take care of your problem. I have the same problem myself," she laughed, and led him like a puppy dog to the king-sized bed in the master bedroom.

Afterwards, they talked about the campaign, as they always did. "You know when I started this, I said I was going to be myself and let the chips fall where they may, but I'm not sure I really believed I could do that. I didn't know if my skin was thick enough to withstand all of the haters. But now, I'm totally comfortable with whatever happens. I'm presenting myself, warts and all, to the public, and if they don't want me, that's OK."

Charlotte lay in his arms and ran her fingernails through the soft hair on his untrimmed chest. Tom was just so...manly. "But you are awfully competitive. Wouldn't it kill you to lose to some of those assholes?"

"Oh, I know. I hate to lose. But I know that in many ways, my life will change so drastically, be so much more difficult if I win, that I'm all right with letting destiny figure it out. You know, I couldn't do this without you."

Charlotte bit her lip, working up the courage to say what she had been thinking for the last several weeks. "You know we will have to stop this."

"What are you talking about? Plenty of presidents have had affairs."

"But, Tom, it's different with us."

"You sound like some of those assholes in my party. We aren't different at all. Love is love. And stop talking like this. If you tell me again that I have to give you up, then I will drop out of the race."

Charlotte looked at him and thought, *Damn. I think he actually means it.* She prayed she would, when the time came, have the courage to give him up, for his own good, and for the good of the country.

Chapter 37

DEAN picked up his phone and could tell that the man on the other end was out of breath.

"Dean, are you sitting down?"

"Mark, take it easy. Is everything OK?"

"Everything is fine. But I have some information about Charlotte Kidwell. And you are not going to believe it."

Tom left the next morning after having breakfast with Charles and briefing him on the campaign. After Charles left Tom at the airport, Charles's mobile phone rang, and he saw that it was Dean Wister. "Good morning, Dean. I'm getting ready to fly to Chicago now. How soon do you think you'll be getting your people in?"

"Charles, we have a problem and I am reconsidering the entire immunity agreement. You've been lying to me."

"What? I have not. What do you think I've been lying about?"

"Your sister Charlotte. She's not the person that Senator McGraw is having an affair with. As you know, she's been in a nursing home for the last twenty years, since an auto accident left her with severe brain damage. Look, Charles, I know your involvement with Mario is a lot more serious than you're letting on. I don't give a shit about some sex scandal involving the senator, but I need to know the truth. If you're not going to be honest with me, I can't help you."

Charles said nothing. And neither did Dean. One of Dean's questioning strategies was to use the uncomfortable silence as a technique to get the suspect to talk. It was especially effective after revealing to the suspect that he had been caught in a lie. This time the silence went on so long that Dean had to check his phone to see that they were still connected.

Thirty seconds had ticked by, but the phone still showed the call was active. Finally, Charles spoke. "You're right. There is a little more to it than I told you. But it has nothing to do with any crimes. Can you meet me at my house in about an hour? I'll explain everything to you."

"See you then. But, Charles, no more games."

"No more games."

Charles went back to his house to prepare for Dean's arrival. He thought about how he should tell him, and he wondered if Dean would understand. Most men wouldn't. He knew that. He also knew he didn't have any choice. He could hope only that this federal agent was the understanding type. He was young enough. Younger people had more tolerance for this sort of thing. He sat and thought about it for a long time. Finally, he thought, *I can't really tell him; I have to show him.*

When Dean arrived at Charles's front door there was a note. "Come in and make yourself at home. I'll join you in a few minutes." The note was signed with a large cursive C, and Dean followed the instructions and took a seat in the large living room with full views of the Tetons. He wondered if you looked at that view every day whether it would lose its impact. Like being married to a beautiful woman, would breathtaking beauty become so commonplace that you would pass it without a second look? Would it become as tiresome as a trophy wife in a too-long marriage? Maybe for some people it would, he thought, but he could not imagine he would be one of those.

Behind him, he could hear heels clicking on the floor, and he turned around. "Mr. Wister." A tall thin redhead stood across the room from him. She wore a short black dress that clung to her figure, the kind of dress you would expect to see on a twenty-something girl at a late night Chicago nightclub, not the kind that you would expect to see on a middle-aged woman in Wyoming in the middle of the day.

"Yes," Dean answered, looking confused.

"Please, have a seat. I understand you wanted to meet me."

Dean sat and continued to stare at the woman. There was something about her that was a little off. Maybe the dress that looked like she had just gotten back from a night of big city clubbing, or maybe something about her face. She looked so much like the conservative pundit Ann Coulter that for a moment he thought it might actually be her. But then she spoke again, and he could tell it wasn't.

"I'm the person that Hayden saw Tom with. I understand you wanted to meet me."

"And you are?"

"Dean, I'm Charlotte," she said, and laughed.

"But you aren't Charles's sister. Charles said that Tom was with his sister Charlotte."

"That's right, Dean, I'm not Charles's sister."

And then she said nothing, and they sat, staring awkwardly at each other.

"Dean, maybe I've misjudged your, shall we say, sophistication. Or maybe I've overestimated my own powers of, shall we say, transformation. Look at me a little more carefully, Dean."

Dean stared at her eyes. The insight came suddenly—and made him feel so stupid. "Holy shit, Charles."

"Like I said, I go by Charlotte. I took her name. Tom calls me that."

"So, you are... trans...I'm sorry, I don't know the right word."

Charlotte laughed. "Oh, don't be sorry. I'm not sure of what the right word is myself. Our whole world is evolving. And we're finding out that there are so many different variations of gender and sexuality, and we don't even have labels yet for all of them. But I'm not into labels myself. Human sexuality is so much more complicated than that. Let's just say I'm a gay man with a very strong feminine side. But I have no desire to change my body parts. I am very happy with them. Humans have an infinite capacity for sexual expression, and all these terms are just artificial ways to label people, which is really unnecessary if you ask me."

Dean nodded, not quite absently. "And you're having an affair with the senator?"

"Affair sounds so tawdry, Dean. Tom and I are soul mates. But that sounds like a cliché, doesn't it? It's actually more than that. It's a little hard to explain. When I am Charles, Tom is my best friend. The closest friend I have ever had. A non-sexual best friend. We watch football, go fly fishing, plot political strategies, do everything that male best friends do. And when I am Charlotte, we are the most intimate and passionate lovers you could ever imagine. I can give Tom something that no single other person can give him: masculine and feminine companionship. No, that's not right, masculine and feminine love in the same person."

"Mario Rosati somehow found out about this —and he could use it to destroy the careers of the both of you." Dean said this as a fact, not question, and Charlotte did not dispute it.

"But this is only partly about our careers. Dean, have you ever loved someone so much that the thought of losing that person truly makes it unimaginable to even think how you could continue living?"

Dean swallowed, but he didn't answer.

"Well, I feel that way—and for me, since I am obviously so different than the rest of the population, well, it's truly a miracle to find someone who not only accepts both sides of me, but actually loves me because there are these two sides. I didn't think it was possible. I damn well know it's a once-in-a-lifetime thing to find someone who is so extraordinary, to love you in this extraordinary way—well, to lose that... to lose that, is unthinkable. Can you understand?"

Dean was unable to speak for a moment. He considered what she was saying. He did know the unbelievable agony of losing his soul mate. He faced the unspeakable pain of knowing that no one would ever replace her. That he would never again look into her eyes. He knew the agony of losing that beautiful soul that loved him more completely than anyone had ever loved him. More than he even loved himself. And each day he found himself doubting whether his life was worth living without her. That thought reached inside of him, and it threatened to make him forget what he was here for, so he pushed it away.

"Look Charles, er... Charlotte. I don't really give a shit about your gender confusion, or whatever kinky accommodations you and Senator McGraw have. I do understand that this is a delicate situation and I have no intention of revealing the intimate details of your life or the senator's life. But you have been lying to me, and I am warning you, this is your one and only free pass. If you want my help, you need to be totally straight with me from now on. Am I making myself clear?"

"Yes, very clear. I will cooperate any way I can. My only goal now is to protect the senator's career."

"All right, then, you need to meet with my boss, Carlos, and a federal attorney in Chicago to go over the immunity agreement. Can you meet with them tomorrow?"

"Well, I was going to fly back to Chicago today. But I can change it to tomorrow. Are you coming?"

"Yes, I'll come as well. We can go over the details on the plane. Do you think we can get tickets on the Chicago flight in the morning?"

Charlotte smiled. "Dean, we won't be flying commercial."

As Dean drove back to his house, he mulled over the secret that he had become privy to. He felt that, by rights, he should tell Carlos the whole story. But he was well aware that if he did, in all probability it would be the end of the senator's presidential ambitions—which would be a waste as there was a reasonably good chance McGraw and Charles *were* Rosati's victims. He decided that for the time being, Charlotte would remain his secret. But when he got home he wrote up two different versions of his interview with Charles. He left them both open on his computer and went out for a long walk with Cheney.

When he came back he sat down at the computer and read both versions again. He saved the version with Charlotte to a hidden folder, and saved the other document to his case file. Eventually, he thought, if Rosati gets arrested, he might try to cut a deal to implicate Charles, and if that happened, well, that would be beyond his control. But he would do his best not to make an irrevocable disclosure, a disclosure that could change the course of the history of the country.

Dean was tossing and turning. He wanted to get to sleep because he was hoping for a visit from Sara. When he was confused, stuck in a case, it always helped him to talk it through with her. He used to call her his criminal muse. The first time he'd used that term she was naked and on top of him and she'd said laughing, "Are you calling me a Greek mythological slut?" and then, after, she'd helped him work through some incredibly complex case. He missed their sex life together, but more than that, he missed having the one person in his life who understood him. Who could make him feel like a whole person. The memory made him smile, but it didn't make him sleepy, and he continued his tossing, turning over and over the clues in the case. When he finally did drift off, it was a disturbing sleep and he found himself again trapped in the overturned boat in the river, unable to breathe, with something pulling and grabbing at his legs. He awoke with a gasp and, recognizing the nightmare, looked around the room for her. But Sara wasn't there. He got up and made some coffee and went out on the porch with Cheney, sitting in the cool early morning mountain air, watching the sun rise. When he went inside, she was laying in the bed, looking up at him and patting the spot next to her. He lay in her arms a long time without speaking. Finally, she said, "Charlotte got to you yesterday, didn't she? When she was talking about losing Tom? But you had to play the tough cop with her."

"Well, I have limited sympathy for the senator and his he/she. You know me, I don't care what people do in their bedrooms, but they got themselves into this mess of their own accord. I know how Rosati works. It's the same old story with all the mobsters. They find someone essentially innocent but vulnerable because they need something or they have something to hide, and they exploit what they know. They blackmail them into helping out with their crimes or they steal from them. And you know, it really pisses me off. I'm not going to let him ruin the lives of Charlotte and the senator if I can help it."

"Are you sure that Charlotte, or Charles, or Tom, didn't have anything to do with Jordy?"

"Well, you can never be sure. But the link to Torino seems to be directly through Rosati. And maybe I'm naïve, but I don't think Charles, or Charlotte, or Tom would order the murder of Hayden. In fact, it's hard for me to believe that

Rosati did it either. He would have to believe that Hayden would blab to the press and there was no other way to keep him quiet. I don't think murder would have been his first move."

Sara sighed. "Torino. My first car was a Ford Torino passed down from my grandmother. I keep seeing something about cars in this whole thing."

"Cars? What are you talking about?"

"You know. Ford Torino, the car? My zombie intuition, or whatever you want to call it, keeps telling me it has something to do with cars."

"That's it? I should just free associate from the Ford Torino to the murderer? That's all you got for me?"

Sara smiled wickedly. "No, that's not all I have for you. But no more fooling around until you make some progress in the case. You need to get to work."

Chapter 38

DEAN met Charles's flight attendant Megan at the Teton Aviation hangar at Jackson Airport and she led him aboard the Prairie Bankcorp Gulfstream 450. The private jet was embellished with the bank logo, and the plush interior featured eight leather chairs, two sofas, and a conference table in the back that could double as a dining area. Megan offered Dean a menu with a wide variety of beverages and snacks; he selected a beer and roasted garlic kale chips. Having never traveled on a corporate jet, he wondered if the cabin had been customized by Charles—the dark leather and extensive use of burled wood and custom fabrics gave the interior the appearance of a country club lounge.

Charles entered the cabin after about ten minutes. "Sorry to keep you waiting, Dean. What do you think of my little toy?"

"It's beautiful. Did you design the interior yourself?"

He looked at Dean and laughed. "Pretty extravagant, huh? No, I picked up this baby as you see it. Our bank bought up some bad loans from an Internet company and we were able to recover this from a personal guarantee from one of the owners. Worked out pretty well for us—and, actually, it makes good business sense. It lets me and my exec team be a lot more hands-on in our business. We can even take it to Europe, and we're looking at international expansion in the next year or two."

Charles picked up the intercom and informed the pilot they were ready to leave. They took off to the north, giving them views out one side of the plane of the entire Teton Range. He pointed at the highest of the peaks. "The winds can be really tricky in the mountains. A couple of years ago a glider flew too close to The Grand and a down draft pulled him right into it. Amazingly he survived, but they had to send up climbing rangers to bring him down."

The plane gained altitude and then turned back to the south, passing Sheep Mountain, also known as "Sleeping Indian" because of its resemblance to a giant Native American in full headdress lying on his back. Charles gestured to the mountain as the plane passed over. "Back in ninety-six, a transport plane carrying a bunch of vehicles back from President Clinton's vacation crashed right into that mountain. Everyone on board was killed. They had to send up a team on horseback to recover the bodies. You can still see the scorched scar on the ridge."

"How did that happen? Engine failure?"

"Not at all. Pilot error. They just didn't take into account how long it takes to gain altitude to get across the mountains. The airport sits at over six-thousand feet, and the mountain downdrafts can be powerful." He thought for a moment. "The slightest miscalculation out here can cause you to lose everything."

Dean wondered if he was talking about the plane crash or something else. "Let's talk about what's going to happen when we get to Chicago."

"Yes."

"My boss, Carlos Alvarez, and a federal attorney are going to sit down with you and go over what you know about Rosati's business with your bank. You need to be forthcoming about any evidence you have that might indicate his companies are involved in money laundering or any other type of illegal activities, as well as any statements he has made to you to solicit you to do anything that would violate laws or banking regulations. If they're satisfied with your truthfulness, they'll ask you to sign a formal statement, called a 'proffer' of your information. Let me repeat: only after they're satisfied with your information will they offer you the immunity documents that we've talked about."

"I'm somewhat familiar with the process. I hope you don't mind, but I've talked to my attorney in Chicago and had some discussions with him about the whole situation, and he wants to meet with me before we meet with your people. I think you'll be happy with the information I can provide. Of course, my attorney will need to be present for all these discussions."

"Absolutely, we need to have your attorney there."

Charles hesitated, and then continued. "There's just one more thing that I need to be clear about."

"Sure, what's that?"

"If the senator's name comes up, or if there is any discussion of our affair, then all negotiations will be immediately terminated. I will not be a party in any way to any investigation of the senator."

"Charles, my people don't know about the affair, or that there is any possibility that Rosati could be using it as leverage with you. I haven't told them. And if the information you provide us on Rosati works out, there will be no reason to."

When they landed in Chicago, Charles headed for his attorney's office and Dean called Carlos to discuss the details of the meeting later in the day. With time to kill, Dean directed the taxi to his address in the Lincoln Park area of the city but, when the taxi pulled up to his front gate, he said, "Ah, I've changed my mind. Can you drop me at Delilah's first?"

Delilah's was Dean's neighborhood bar, not a cop bar, more a hipster music hangout, with no particular musical bias. Dean's musical tastes ran the gamut from country, to punk, to metal, to Springsteen. On any given night,

Delilah's juke box or a live band could be fea-turing any of those musical genres. There was another motive for his sidetrack to Delilah's to-day, however. This was the bar in which Sara and Dean had celebrated the purchase of their home in Lincoln Park, and Sara had gotten so drunk on Wild Turkey that Dean had had to literally carry her home. As he walked in the door of the bar, he looked up at the face on the sign that depicted Samson's tormenter, and he found comfort in the bar's mystic darkness in the middle of the day. The bartender brought him a whiskey menu containing over four hun-dred selections, but he didn't even look at it. "Wild Turkey, neat." He sat and sipped his whiskey and thought of dozens of nights that he and Sara had ended up here at the end of the evening, drinking, listening to music, making out as they stood at the bar, and then walking the few blocks home. He dreaded walking into that lonely house but, fortified by the warm spirits, he ambled out of the bar and made the ten-minute stroll to the gate he had passed up before.

It had been more than two months since Dean had been inside the brownstone town-home he had shared with Sara for the last five years. He never would have been able to afford this much space in one of the most expensive areas of the city on his salary, but he loved the completely renovated spacious home and never felt the least amount of guilt that the condo had been purchased with money from Sara's trust fund. It surprised him, then, when he passed through the iron gate to the leaded-glass front door, that he felt for the first time the home didn't really belong to him. It was as if he were walking into someone else's residence when he put the key in the lock and entered the foyer.

During the final stages of Sara's illness, he had vacated the bedroom they had shared together and moved into the guest room. They had moved a hospital bed and various medical devices into the master bedroom and there no longer seemed to be any room for his things. He felt at home in that room only when he would sit by the side of the bed and focus on Sara's face, or when he would crawl into the hospital bed with her late at night and hold her while trying to match each of her labored breaths with one of his own, as if he could somehow breathe his own life into hers. After she died, he never entered that room again, not even when the hospice people came by to pick up their medical equipment.

Now as he stood outside the door, he started to shake. What would happen when he opened the door? Would Sara somehow be there? Would the sick, hollow, emaciated, wasting-away Sara be laying there, instead of the healthy, vivacious, spunky woman he had spent the summer with in Jackson? With great effort, he made himself push open the door, bringing his gaze up from the floor to the place where he feared Sara might be lying. But to his relief, she wasn't there, just the furniture that the decorator had helped them pick out, minus the four-poster bed that had to be moved out to make room for her hospital bed. He stood in the room and closed his eyes, tried to sense her spirit, but he could feel nothing.

He left the room and slowly moved through the rest of the house, pausing as if he were a medium trying to locate a spirit from the world beyond, but nothing came to him. The house was an empty vessel. It no longer contained anything of himself, or Sara's spirit, or their love.

Charles and his attorney gave an impressive presentation of the evidence they could provide on Mario, and then Carlos and the federal attorney spent about two hours trying to pick it apart. But Dean could see that the interrogation was just for show. He knew as soon as the presentation was finished that it was a done deal. Carlos would get to send in his people to examine Rosati's bank records, and Charles would get his immunity.

While the Feds were putting together the paperwork, Dean met with Carlos for a few minutes alone and updated him on the status of the investigation in Wyoming. "I'm heading back to Jackson right now. It looks like you have the Rosati banking investigation under control. I'm following the Birkov thread, and I don't want to lose the momentum."

Carlos seemed distracted. Dean had given him Charles and the banking angle and he wasn't really that interested in Birkov now. "You do that, Dean. Keep me up to date on everything. Call me in the next few days. I want to know when you think you can wrap it all up and come back here. We could really use you right now."

It was late when Dean crawled into bed after flying back by himself on the bank's plane. With Cheney curled up at his feet, he was soon unconscious. In the hour before dawn, he felt her against his back. "I was afraid you would be at our place in Chicago," Dean said. "I know. I'm sorry you thought that. I can't go back there now. But you'll have to decide for yourself if you can. I think maybe you belong there. Your work was always important to you."

"The only place where I belong is with you."

Chapter 39

MARIO Rosati Jr. was in a foul mood as he sat in the office at Prairie Bankcorp that he shared with financial analyst Marina Ogalfsky. He had been angry when he found out he was going to have to share an office, and he would have complained to his father, but then he saw the young, attractive woman sharing his space and decided the complaint could be put off for a while. At least until he had fucked her. He didn't realize he had a thing for Russian girls until he'd discovered the operation that Boris was running, and then he had been hooked, almost obsessed. He would visit the warehouse every time a new shipment of girls arrived, and he found he enjoyed dominating them, enjoyed seeing that they were afraid. In his mind, they were enjoying it as well, even if they pretended otherwise.

He pulled a bottle of vodka and two glasses from his desk drawer. "Hey, Marina. It's six o'clock. Cocktail hour."

She turned around in her chair. "I don't think we should be drinking in the office."

Mario laughed. "You mean you haven't seen the bar in the corner of Kidwell's office? Besides, there's no one else here. Come on, just one."

He poured two glasses, rolled his chair across the room, and handed one to her. "Za ná-shoo dróo-zhboo," he said and raised his glass, swallowing the contents in one gulp.

Marina drank hers down as well and asked, "Where did you learn that toast?"

"I've dated a few Russian girls and I have to say, I really love the way you girls dress. American girls never wear stockings anymore and I've really enjoyed taking a peek at yours the last few days. I love that spot where the top of the stocking meets the soft flesh of your thigh."

Marina looked down and blushed. She saw that her skirt had slipped up in the chair and the top of her stocking was showing. "Stop it."

Mario rolled his chair closer to hers and said, "Marina, lighten up. You want guys to notice, that's why you wear them." He refilled her glass and then ran his hand up her leg to the spot where her thigh joined the stocking. "Right here. This is the spot I'm talking about."

She gripped his wrist in her hand and tried to pry his hand away. "Stop it. I mean it."

"Stop what? What are you going to do if I don't? I just want to see what you have on under here." He squeezed her wrist until she winced in pain and loosened her grip. Then he moved his hand all the way to the top of her leg.

"Oh, no panties. You are a naughty girl. I think you're already wet for me."

Desperately her eyes searched her desk for something, anything. She reached out with her free hand and grabbed a letter opener, turned and thrust the sharp end into his cheek.

Mario screamed as blood gushed from his cheek. He grabbed his face, releasing Marina from his grip. She ran out the door and down the fire exit stairs into the street.

Mario pulled out the blade, grabbed some tissue, and pressed it against his face. "Fucking whore."

Chapter 40

DEAN looked at the number on his mobile phone and wondered when he answered if the person on the other end would be Charles or Charlotte. He wondered how Charles/Charlotte kept it straight when he/she was with Tom. He had seen videos of Charles and Tom together at a press conference and wondered how Charles had revealed his Charlotte side to Tom. How did that work? After a meeting in a hotel room, did Charles call Tom from the other room and when Tom walked in he saw Charlotte on the bed with the red wig, makeup and a lacy teddy? And when had Tom realized that Charles in lingerie got his motor running? He smiled at the scene. It was all very confusing. He finally decided to simply answer with "Hello" and see what happened.

"Dean, this is Charles. Charles Kidwell."

"Good morning, Charles. How's it going?"

"Well, not so good. I have two problems. First, Mario Jr. has been sexually harassing one of our young female execs. She complained to HR and, when I confronted him, he just laughed and said 'all those Russian girls are whores anyway'. I'm not sure what to do, and I also think he's suspicious of the FBI guys that are posing as bank auditors. He's been hanging pretty close to me and I think he may have seen that they're looking at the records of his dad's company."

"Well, see if you can put off the HR thing for a little while. Don't shut it down, just delay. Reassign or promote the female employee or something. Anything to get her as far from Junior as possible. If our guys find something good in the next few days, we can get him out of your hair, but we don't want to rock the boat with his dad if we can help it. If he saw something you'll hear from Senior soon enough. Just stick to the story if he calls you."

"Will do. Just thought you should know."

"Thanks for the update. Have you said anything to the senator about any of this?"

"I have not. He has so much going on... I know this will be a major distraction."

"You're probably right. We'll brief him only when we have to. Don't say anything without talking to me first."

"Got it. Talk to you later, Dean."

Ten minutes after Dean hung up the phone, Charles received another call from a very angry man. The man was shouting so loud that Charles couldn't quite understand all of the words, but he definitely got the message. "You stupid, double-crossing, crossdressing, anorexic, cocksucking motherfucker.

I should slit the throats of you and your fat-assed boyfriend, but I'm going to tell you what I am going to do instead. I'm going to do both of you a giant favor. A favor that neither of you deserve. Now listen to this very carefully. You call Senator Fatass, and you tell him to tell the FBI director to call off the dogs. I know he and the director were roommates in college so they're probably sucking each other's dicks, too. Hope that doesn't make you jealous. Anyway, you have twenty-four hours, and if the FBI isn't pulled off me, then you aren't going to like the headlines, or the pictures that are going to be all over TV. Both of you can kiss your careers goodbye."

Charles felt the panicky bile start to creep up his throat and tried to calm himself. "I had no choice. They had a warrant, and it was a complete ambush. Ah, ah, how did you find out?"

"How do you think I found out, dumbfuck? Mario Jr. isn't just a pretty boy. I put him there for a reason. The FBI is so fucking stupid. They send in a group of guys all dressed alike with white shirts, dark suits and ties. They may as well have sent them in wearing FBI mono-grammed jackets. Also, you need to get HR off Mario's ass about the Russian slut. For her own good, if you understand what I'm saying."

Charles ignored that last part. He would deal with it, maybe promote her or send her to one of the branches. "I'll talk to Tom as soon as I hang up."

"Charles. Listen to me. Maybe I've been too nice to you and you got the wrong impression. That's my fault. If Tom can't get the dogs called off, then both of you are useless to me. I think you don't need to use your imagination to figure out how I deal with useless people."

"I understand."

Mario clicked off without another word. Charles sat and wept. He had ruined not only his life, but the life of the man he loved. As he had always done, since he was a little boy, he allowed himself to feel the pain fully. Then he put the pain back in the closet, pulled himself together, and made the call that he dreaded.

"Tom, I just got off the phone with Mario. We have a serious problem. I know you've been busy, so I've been trying to take care of all the stuff with Mario on my own. I'm sorry, but there's a lot I was trying to keep from you. I was hoping it would go away, but it's gotten beyond the place that I can handle it. Mario is out of control, and I'm afraid of what he might do." He filled Tom in, talking fast, not giving the senator a chance to speak, telling him everything.

Tom didn't say anything for a long time. Finally, he spoke softly: "Charles, you and Charlotte are the best thing that has ever happened to me, and I'm glad it did, even with all of this. I'm not surprised that Mario is trying to compromise me. I've known that it would come to this eventually. I should have taken care of this a while back and not let it get this far. It's been on my mind, and a day hasn't gone by that I haven't dreaded what we would be facing. Call him back. Tell him I need to meet with him this afternoon, face-to-face, in Washington. I have a suite at the W Hotel. I don't care what it takes, but you have got to bring him to my suite. If he hesitates, tell him we can't do this over the phone—and tell him it has to be today, before the investigation goes any farther."

"So, can I ask what you're planning to do?"

"No, Charles, you can't. But I have a plan to get us out of this. And it won't be pleasant, but the less you know, the better. Just trust me."

Tom hung up the phone and sat down. This situation had been haunting him the last few weeks, and he had searched and searched for a better way, but there just wasn't one. He had learned a long time ago that sometimes in politics you had to deal with people who were outright despicable characters. And sometimes you had to do things that were despicable yourself. You had to deal with despicable characters at their own level.

Mario wasn't happy with Tom's summons, but he eventually decided to acquiesce to the senator's request. He personally thought it was a bad idea to meet. What if someone from the press recognized him? The story could be hard for the senator to handle. But he also knew it might be hard for the senator to kill an active investigation, and so he would meet with him and let him know, face-to-face, that his career was over if he wasn't able to call off the Feds.

Chapter 41

DEAN had his eyes closed and was trying to free associate, mainly about cars, specifically Fords. Torino, Thunderbird, Escape. Was that it? Someone is trying to escape? Mustang, well Mustangs are in Wyoming. Ford. Didn't Harrison Ford own a ranch in Jackson?

This is fucking useless, he thought. Sara was just fucking with him, making him the butt of one of her jokes. Eventually, his mind got back to the phone conversation with Charles. What had he said about Mario, Jr. harassing a Russian employee? Junior had said that all Russian girls were whores. Russian whores. Is it possible that Mario Jr. met some of the Russian girls in Chicago? He had shown pictures of Mario's guys to Tatiana but, fuck, Mario Jr. wasn't in those pictures. He texted Mark and asked him to send him a picture of Mario Jr. Even his driver's license picture would do if that was all he could find.

The trip would take forty-five minutes from his home in Jackson to Daryl's place in Alpine, even driving twenty miles over the speed limit, risking being stopped by the highway patrol that cruised the Snake River Canyon. He tried to call Daryl and Amber to tell them he was on his way, but no one picked up. Then his phone dinged and he saw that Mark had sent him Mario Jr.'s license photo, and he knew he wasn't going to delay. His gut roiled with the excitement he always felt when a break in a case was imminent. If Tatiana could ID Mario Jr., they could squeeze him for the address of the warehouse in Chicago, and bust his father, Birkov, and the entire ring.

Boris Birkov's route on his twice-a-week cash pickups in Pinedale, Rock Springs, and Rawlins brought him back through Alpine. Occasionally, he would treat himself at the strip club there. Truth is, he preferred the more emaciated, hollow-cheeked look of his Russian girls, especially the ones to whom he had given the gift of fake titties as a reward for being good earners, to the broad-faced, fleshy daughters of cowboys and Mormon girls that were the entertainment at the Alpine strip bar. The exception was Amber—her American schoolgirl good looks, with a splash of white trash, was a cocktail he couldn't resist. When he got to the bar, they told him Amber wasn't due in for another hour, so he thought he would drop by the house she shared with Daryl. If Daryl was there, he could discuss some EV matters; if Amber was there alone, well then, who knew.

Amber and Daryl were at the Save-A-Lot grocery when Boris's X-5 pulled into the drive, and Tatiana thought she would help bring in the groceries when she heard the crunch of gravel on the driveway. At first, Boris was confused when the petite dark-haired girl came bounding out the door, but when she looked up, first in surprise, then in stone-cold fear, Boris smiled. "Tatiana, sweetheart, I have been so worried about you. I've come to take you home."

There were a lot of luxury cars in Teton County, so the chances of Dean's recognizing the SUV as it passed him going north as he was going south weren't high. But Dean was on the lookout for the dark-colored SUVs operated by the Wyoming highway patrol, and when the BMW X-5 approached, he slowed and spotted Boris Birkov in the driver's seat, Tatiana sitting beside him. He didn't turn around until the next bend, and then he made a fishtailing U-turn, flooring his Jeep to catch the BMW before it turned off. He didn't spot the taillights again until he saw the SUV make a left on Fall Creek Road, south of town.

He called Mark in Chicago but got his voicemail. "I'm following Boris and he has Tatiana in his car. I'll call you back when he stops and give you a location."

Dean slowed his Jeep, allowing a considerable amount of space to avoid being spotted. Several miles up Fall Creek the SUV turned off, and Dean stopped and got out of his car. Crawling up a low ridge he could see the SUV pull up to a metal building that resembled a machine shed. He watched as Boris got out and pulled the young girl over the console and out the driver's side with him, gripping her arm and leading her to the shed.

Dean crept slowly through the scrub grass but, without much cover, he felt exposed, and it seemed to take forever to crawl to the building. When he got to the edge of the steel building, he made his way around the side and peeked into the window. The figure sitting on a metal chair in the middle of the dirt floor looked like a tiny little girl, Boris towering over her. Tatiana was crying, and Boris was talking to her, all the while waving a large knife in front of her face. She said something and Boris slapped her hard across the face. She flew backwards, hitting her head on the floor. Dean pulled his gun from his holster and moved toward the front door.

And then, everything went black.

Chapter 42

CHARLES met Mario Rosati at the back entrance of the W Hotel, amidst the trucks delivering food, liquor, and the myriad other items required to supply the lobbyists, quasi-government officials, and other guests of the roadhouse closest to the country's seat of power. The objective of avoiding the roving eyes of reporters fulfilled, Charles led Mario to the freight elevator, to Tom's suite on the eighth floor. This whole meeting was making Charles uneasy. There was a steely resolve in Tom's voice that Charles had never heard before as he gave Charles the instructions on how the meeting needed to go. And the instructions were strange, even disturbing. Tom had told him to stand by the door to the suite while Mario and Tom were meeting—he was not to leave his post under any circumstances, and if anyone came in, he was to position himself between the person and Tom and Mario, blocking their view. Tom's demeanor did not invite discussion, and since Charles felt responsible for the fix they found themselves in with Mario, he allowed Tom to call the shots. He didn't want to know Tom's plan, and was afraid to hazard a guess.

The two retired Wyoming highway patrolmen—Tom didn't yet qualify for Secret Service protection—standing by the door to the suite nodded at Charles, and Charles used his key card to get in. The patrolmen knew Charles better even than they knew the members of the senator's campaign. When Charles and Mario walked through the door, Tom was standing in the middle of the room, dressed in a suit and tie. Charles knew that he had just come from a legislative committee meeting, and he would be flying out of town in a couple of hours.

"Good to see you again, Mario. I'm glad you could make it on such short notice. Please sit down."

Charles took his position just as instructed near the door and, carefully, latched the dead bolt. Both men took seats in two Queen Anne overstuffed chairs facing each other, with a small table in between. "Can I get you something to drink, Mario? Water or a soft drink?" Tom asked.

"No, I'm fine. Let's just get straight to the topic of this meeting. We have a serious problem—and I do mean *we*—and you are going to have to do something about it. I assume Charles has filled you in."

"He has. But why don't you tell me the situation as you see it."

"Well, as I see it, you, me, and Charles—we're partners. Well, not in the sense that you and Charles are partners. Business partners. Charles is my banker, and I am giving him some very profitable business. Now, the FBI is in the bank looking at my accounts. Charles accepted my business with his eyes wide open, and his bank and his employees have assisted me in all the transactions that I have executed, so if there's anything illegal about any of those transactions, well, Charles is as guilty as I am, but he has done nothing to protect me from the FBI. He should have fought the warrant to look at my accounts, but he didn't. You know what that makes me think?"

Tom believed the question was rhetorical so he didn't respond.

"I said, do you know what that makes me think?"

"No, Mario, what does that make you think?"

"That makes me think that Charles has cut a deal with the Feds."

Tom didn't say anything.

"Well, has he?"

"Has he what?"

"Cut a deal with the Feds."

"Look, Mario," Tom replied, the voice of reason, "your business has been on the federal radar for a long time. It would make no sense for Charles to accept your business based on certain information you might have and then turn around and cut a deal with the Feds. Does that make any sense?"

"It doesn't. But I'm beginning to think that the two of you are a lot dumber than I figured when I got into this. I'm in a pickle here and guess what? If I'm in a pickle then that means the two of you are in the pickle barrel with me. You need to find a way for me to get out of it."

"What is it exactly that you expect me to do?"

"You know how this works. The FBI Director and you go way back. I know you were fraternity brothers. Use your influence to persuade him to call off the dogs."

"Mario, I think you greatly overstate my influence with the director. As I understand it, they're examining the bank records pursuant to a court order. There's no way he's going to kill an active investigation as a favor to me."

"Well, you and your boyfriend, or should I say girlfriend, had better hope he will. Otherwise both of your careers are over."

"I do agree with one of the things you said, however, Mario. It was dumb of both of us to do business with you. Charles took you on as a client only to protect me. That wasn't the right decision."

"Oh, I think it was the right decision. Unless being President isn't that important to you."

"We both find ourselves in very, very difficult positions here, but I've been considering our predicament and what to do about it for some time. I've been doing some reading, to see what other historical figures would advise. Have you ever read this book?" He pointed to a black hardcover on the small table between them: *The Art of War*.

Mario was annoyed now. "Senator, I don't get my advice from books. It comes from real-world experience, not like you high-born SOBs."

"I'm sure that's true, but if you'll just humor me for a moment, I think you'll find that I might have a solution to our problem." Tom picked up the book and handed it to him. "There's a passage underlined on page one-sixty-three. Would you read it for me?"

Mario, even more annoyed now at the senator's games, but curious at the same time, leafed through the pages, looking for and finding the passage, then reading aloud in his Chicago mobster accent: "They may say that if you know yourself and know your enemy, you will gain victory a hundred times out of a hundred. If you know yourself but do not know your enemy you will meet one defeat for every victory. If you know neither yourself nor your enemy, you will never be victorious." He heard the click and looked up. "What the fuck—"

As Mario had been looking for the paragraph, the senator had reached in his jacket pocket, pulled out a pistol and pointed it directly at the man in front of him. Mario sputtered in surprise just as the senator pulled the trigger twice. Shocked by the gun blast, Charles fell back against the hotel door.

The Chicago gangster slumped to the floor, two neat bullet holes in the top of his forehead, a red dot over each eye. The senator, expecting more blood, and thankful that it was a much neater situation than he'd imagined, placed his gun on the chair behind him, reached inside his other jacket pocket, pulled out a loaded baby Glock wrapped in a white handkerchief, and placed it in the dead man's right palm, wrapping his lifeless fingers around the gun.

In the hallway, the security detail, hearing what sounded like gunshots, scrambled into action. One man pulled his weapon, the other put his key card in the door, realized the deadbolt was latched, and kicked the door once, twice, three times. The door gave way, and they entered the room. They found Charles standing to the side in shock and the senator kneeling over a man on the floor. Both patrolmen advanced with guns drawn. "Senator, are you OK?"

"Yes. But I think he's dead."

Mario was lying on the floor, face up, glassy-eyed in death, a look of surprise on his face, his body twisted into an L shape. In his hand was the small nine-millimeter pistol.

"What the hell happened here?" one of the patrolmen asked. The other one appeared to be hyperventilating.

"He drew on me. And I shot him. I think you better get FBI Director Vorhies over here. I know he's in town, and I want him to handle this, so there are no questions."

Chapter 43

Boris had picked up his cell phone as soon as the orange Jeep passed him in the canyon. It was that fucking Chicago cop again. He wasn't sure the cop had recognized him, or the girl sitting beside him, but he couldn't take any chances. He dialed a number. "Alexi, I've got the girl that ran away. I'm taking her to the building off Fall Creek Road. I think that Chicago cop may be following me. Can you cover me from behind? Yes, I'll be there in about fifteen minutes. No, don't kill him. Just make sure he can't interfere. I'll have to figure out what to do with him later."

As he turned off onto Fall Creek Road, he didn't see the Jeep behind him. Maybe he'd lost him, or maybe the cop hadn't recognized his car. Either one of those scenarios would be fine with him—he didn't want the heat he would get from killing a cop, but if the stupid cop had followed, he wouldn't have much of a choice.

He parked the car in front of the metal building and pulled the girl through the door. She was sobbing, "Please don't hurt me. I didn't tell him anything, I swear. I'll go back to Rawlins. I can make you a lot of money, you'll see."

Boris didn't respond, just took her into the metal building and sat her down in a chair in the middle of the room. He went over to a cabinet and pulled out a large knife, the kind you use to fillet a much larger fish than the trout you find in the rivers and streams of Teton County. Then he took another chair and sat in front of her. He turned the knife over in his hand and said, "Tatiana, stop crying. I am not angry with you. I know why you ran away. You are young and afraid. Look at me."

The force of his voice, and the shock of the brutal looking knife in front of her face seemed to jolt her into focus, and she stopped crying for a moment. "But—"

"Shut up and listen to me. This knife. This knife is used to fillet fish. On occasion it has been used to fillet people as well, people who make me angry. Right now I am not angry. But if you insist on lying to me, well, that will make me angry, and then you will be of no use to me. So, I need to know what you told the cop from Chicago. Start from the time he picked you up. Tell me everything, and I might be able to forgive you."

Tatiana said nothing for a moment. Then she started to cry again. "But I didn't tell him anything."

That response seemed to trigger the fury in Boris and he jumped from his chair, punching her so hard in the face that she flew backwards off the chair, her skull saved only by the marginal softening of the impact by the dirt floor. Tatiana, still conscious but in pain, moaned.

The squeak of the door opening caused Boris to turn, and he was greeted by Alexi dragging the limp and unconscious cop through the door.

"Shit, you didn't kill him did you?"

"No, just hit him in the head."

"Well, there's some tape on the bench over there, tie him up." Boris turned and picked up the slight, moaning girl and sat her on the chair. "Tatiana, I'm still not angry. But I'm definitely getting there." He picked the knife up off the floor, and drew a line down her arm, drawing blood and causing her to shriek in pain. "Now that will cause a scar, but not a bad one. Not like the chess board I'm going to draw on your face. Now, talk to me."

Tatiana told him everything. When she was done, Boris went to Dean and stood over him for a moment, silently. Then he turned to Alexi. "Kill both of them. Wrap their bodies in garbage bags and dump them after dark in one of the dumpsters at the big construction site in Pinedale."

Alexi took out his gun, walked over to Tatiana, and stood behind her. He paused for a moment, as if trying to get up the nerve to kill the little girl.

"What are you waiting for? Just do it."

Alexi still didn't move and Boris grabbed the gun out of his hands and pushed him away. Tatiana was sobbing softly now, her little body heaving. "It's going to be OK." He laughed as he brought the gun to her head and clicked the trigger back. "You'll be with your daddy in a minute."

The explosion that followed sent Tatiana flying off the chair and back onto the floor of the shed, as Boris and Alexi reeled away from her. The front door of the shed shattered inward and three men and one woman stormed into the room pointing shotguns, the woman shouting, "Down, now! On the floor! Police! You're under arrest."

Chapter 44

Senator Thomas McGraw sat in the bedroom of his suite at the Hotel W while the FBI evidence technicians worked the living room area where the shooting had occurred. Charles had gone to a room next door to be questioned by the FBI.

FBI Director Jake Vorhies entered the suite and was briefed by the agents that had gotten to the hotel before him. He took charge of the scene and personally interviewed Charles. Charles was smart enough, or maybe in shock enough, to plead ignorance. He had been standing in the room while the two men talked, not really watching them, when he heard a shot and saw Mario fall. The next thing he knew, the door was kicked open and the security detail burst into the room. And that was about all he could say, other than the meeting had been arranged by him at the request of Mario Rosati, because Mario had discovered that he was under investigation. He was still in a state of shock. The only people in the room had been Mario and Tom and himself, and then Mario had ended up on the floor with two bullets in his head. Intellectually, he knew that Tom had shot him, but he still couldn't process it.

Jacob Vorhies was the physical opposite of Thomas McGraw. Tall, thin, balding, and not particularly attractive, he took pride in his physical fitness. He was a near world-class triathlete, and wore tight European-cut suits that, even in FBI gray, couldn't help but display his physique. He was a close friend of Tom's going back to their days together as Kappa Sig pledges. His initial reaction was amazement at how calm Tom appeared when he walked into the bedroom. His heart had been racing since he got the call, and he knew immediately the significance of the case—to Tom, the country, and to his own career. "Tom, what happened here?"

"Actually, it's pretty simple. He pulled a gun on me, and I pulled mine and shot him."

"Why were you carrying a gun?"

"I always carry a gun. It's common knowledge in Wyoming. Hell, I can even carry it on the floor at the state house. Apparently, it's not common knowledge in Chicago."

The director just looked at the senator. The scene was surreal. "Tom, I'm trying to wrap my head around what you could be talking about that got so heated he would be so stupid as to pull a gun on a sitting US senator and presidential candidate."

"As you know, Charles Kidwell, who is a good friend and supporter of mine, is cooperating with your investigation of Mario's company. Mario got wind of it and went ballistic that his banker had turned him in. So I offered to meet with him, tell him the facts of life, try to calm him down. That obviously was a bad idea. He got crazy, said I should lean on the FBI to kill the investigation. When I refused, he got crazier and pulled his gun."

"And you were able to outdraw him?"

"Well, I think he was taken by surprise. As I said, I don't think my concealed-carry ways had gotten back to Chicago."

"You know, of course, that this whole story sounds like bullshit. Most people will think there's something else going on here."

"I swear, Jake, there is nothing else going on here. I obviously made an error in judgment in meeting with him. But I have had no other business dealings with him. It never occurred to me he might pull a gun on me. So really... I think it's pretty straight forward."

"This is going to kill your candidacy."

"Maybe. But I don't think so. I think the American people will like a guy who can take care of himself. This may be a bigger problem for you. A lot of people are going to say that you're covering up for an old friend."

"I don't have a choice. If I recuse myself, Deputy Director Crane will take over the investigation. He's a fucking Democrat and he wants my job. He'll try to crucify you. Don't worry, I can handle it. As long as I don't find out that you had other business dealings with him."

"Don't worry. You won't. I have never met him before today."

"Are you sure? Because I'm putting myself on the line here."

"I'm sure. It went down just as I told you."

"I'll have someone take your statement. We're getting Charles's statement right now. If it's consistent with yours, then we'll be good."

"Thanks, Jake. I won't forget this."

"Neither will I," said Jake.

Chapter 45

IT was a beautiful summer day as Dean drove up the rutted forest service road to reach the well-hidden hiking trail that led to Sara's Meadow. It wasn't really a hiking trail, more of an animal trail that led from the high country down to a creek. The access road was hidden and difficult to locate, so the trail didn't get much use by humans. He and Sara had discovered it by luck really. They had spent much of the summer researching and exploring the more remote trails they could find in guidebooks; then one day they had come across an entry in one of the journals of Owen Wister, a very distant cousin to Dean, best known for inventing the genre of the Western when he wrote *The Virginian* based on his summer vacations in the Tetons. They were trying to follow the vague instructions for the route contained in the journal when they reached this trail. From the trailhead, a relatively easy five-mile hike would put him at Sara's Meadow.

He felt at peace—maybe for the first time in a year. Carlos had been right; coming back to the mountains was what he'd needed to do. He needed closure, and everything that had happened in the last two months since he had arrived in Jackson brought him closer to this day. As he walked up the trail, he felt more alive than he had in years. His senses were somehow turbo-charged—the fresh cool pine-scented air tingled as it flowed over the hairs on his arms, the bright sunlight seared a red sphere into his eyes, the loose gravel crunched under his trail shoes, the chipmunks chattered as they followed him. All of it washed over him, and the beautiful mix of flavors, perfumes, and sensations filled him with joy. *Today*, he thought, *I am coming home.*

A hundred or so yards away he saw the large cottonwood tree that dominated the center of the meadow. It was out of place—the altitude too high for most trees to grow—and it seemed to Dean that the tree had been placed there just for the two of them, a monument to Dean and Sara. He lowered his pack against the tree and then lay down flat on his back, looking at the Teton Range over him. Yes, he thought, this is home. He lay there for a few minutes enjoying the smells and the breeze and the clear dark blue sky. Then he stood, reached into his pack and lifted out his gun. He held it in his hand, his fingers hypersensitive to the cold hard steel. Aloud, he said, "I'll be with you soon, Sara." He brought the barrel of the gun up under his chin, closed his eyes, and placed his finger on the trigger. From behind, her arms gripped him in a bear hug. "Stop, Dean, no! Don't do this! Please!"

"Sara, it's OK. I want to do this. I've had enough. I've tried. You know that's true. I really have. But I can't bear to live without you. I need to be with you."

"Oh, Dean, don't you understand? It doesn't work that way. The only way that I can continue to live is if you live. You keep me alive."

Dean was silent. And then Sara said, "Dean, look up. What do you see?"

His eyes filling with tears, it was hard to speak. "It's The Grand."

"Right. The Grand. That's what we used to say each other about our lives. I used to tell you our romance was 'The Grand'. I still want you to have a Grand life. I love watching you live. I need you to carry me with you through the rest of your life. You have to. Promise me."

Dean closed his eyes and felt her arms around him, and the warmth of the sun, and the breeze through his hair. And a burden lifted.

"I promise. But you have to promise never to leave me. To be with me always."

"Of course I will. I couldn't do it any other way. Come, lay down with me. Under our tree."

They lay together, and Dean fell asleep.

When Dean awoke, he was in a hospital room. He was confused for a moment, and then he remembered—Boris, and Tatiana, and the machine shed. He reached over beside the bed and rang the buzzer for the nurse. In a few seconds a nurse rushed into the room, took a surprised look at him and said, "He's awake."

"Yes, he is." Dean said. "How does a man get a beer around here?"

Chapter 46

THE neurologist came in and put Dean through a brief series of questions to evaluate his short- and long-term memory, his orientation to time and place, and his ability to reason. When he was finished, Dean asked, "Did I pass?"

"With flying colors. You took a pretty severe blow to the head. You had some brain bleeding and you've been in and out of consciousness the last three days. We weren't sure how you would be when you woke up, but it looks like you came out of it pretty well—amazingly well, actually. You're just going to have to take it easy for a while."

"Three days? Can you tell me what happened after you brought me in? I remember pulling my gun and trying to save a girl who was being held in a shed, then everything went black."

"I can probably help you out with that." Sheriff Dani walked into the room.

The nurse shrugged, sheepish. "I called her when you woke up."

"We were pretty worried about you," Dani said. "All of us. Joanie said to be sure to send you her love."

"You're not pissed that I was working Birkov behind your back?"

"Dean, I'm glad you were. I owe you a big apology. I let personal feelings get in the way of professional judgment. I didn't think Birkov was a bad guy, but I should have known better. I was flat out wrong, but I didn't have the power to do anything anyway. Remember, I did tell you to use your Federal friends if you really needed to pursue it."

"Yes, you did, Sheriff," Dean laughed. "Tell me how it turned out at the warehouse."

"Right, you missed all the action. Well, I guess that didn't come out right. A lot has happened, all good. Mark from your office called and told me what was going on and gave me the location of your cell phone. He'd received the voicemail you left for him, but you lost voice service in the canyon. His call wouldn't go through, but he could follow your cell phone GPS. I got a couple of my guys and we tracked you down—didn't get there a minute too soon either. Birkov and his boy were fixin' to kill you and the girl, but we put a stop to that. Tatiana is OK, she's back with Amber and Daryl. Birkov is under arrest along with three of his cohorts. The FBI raided the places in Pinedale, Rock Springs, and Rawlins. They picked up a couple dozen girls, all illegal. Your boss says Birkov will be charged with kidnapping, human trafficking, and a few other federal crimes. Oh, and they also raided a warehouse in Chicago where Birkov had some other girls stashed."

"How did they get the address of the Chicago warehouse? I was working on that."

"Oh, there's lots more. Like I said, a ton of stuff has happened since you were out. Let's see. Tatiana was able to ID that guy you thought she might recognize, Mario Jr.? They squeezed him and he gave up the warehouse address in Chicago."

"Great. I was afraid that Mario Jr. would get lawyered up by his dad and wouldn't talk."

"Well, I think it helped that his dad is dead."

"Mario Rosati is dead?"

"Killed in a shootout by Senator Tom Mc-Graw. Seems they had a meeting in McGraw's hotel suite in Washington. McGraw says Rosati pulled a gun, and McGraw shot him twice right between the eyes. I can't believe I actually said that."

Dean sat stunned. His head hurt. "And I missed all of that? Fuck. So are you still going to arrest Hayden?"

"Well, from what I see now, I think maybe your leads were right all alone. I figure it was Fletcher or Boris that hired Torino. As you know Fletcher was a crazy son of a bitch, and he and Boris lost a lot of money because of Hayden. You all along thought Hayden was the real target, and Jordy's bad luck was to look like a younger version of his cousin. We know Boris had a connection to Chicago through Rosati, so maybe Rosati referred Boris to Torino. Of course, it could be Hayden, but I just don't have enough to pin it on him."

"Now look, Dean, don't be so down. You broke this whole thing open by yourself. If you had listened to me, well, all I can say is, I'm sorry. Oh, and one other thing. I know you love it out here, and if you're ready to give up the big city, well, I would be honored to have you in my department. I know you have some recuperation to do, but will you at least think about it?"

"Thanks, Sheriff. I will definitely think about it."

After the sheriff left, Dean thought about all the pieces of the case, about how it all related to Jordy's death. Most likely, Hayden had been the target, not Jordy, but would Fletcher or Boris hire Torino because of the bad real estate deal? Maybe, but Fletcher hadn't tried to hide his hatred for Hayden, and it seemed to Dean that he would be unlikely to kill him for it and, if he needed to, he'd be the type to do it himself. Or had Mario hired him to silence Hayden about Charles and Tom? That too, seemed unlikely. Hayden hadn't threatened to reveal the secret, so why would he need to be killed? With Fletcher and Mario dead, and Boris facing the rest of his life in prison, he figured justice had been done in its own way even though Jordy's murder was not definitively solved. That bothered him. The one constant through all of this had been that everyone he'd talked to said what a great guy Jordy was. His flaw was a weakness for strippers and the naïve notion that one could fall in love with him—but his fatal flaw, as far as Dean could tell, was that he looked too much like his cousin.

Tatiana was safe, Mario was dead, his son and Boris were in jail. Somehow things had worked out. That was about as much justice as he was used to seeing in his career. Now he could focus on what he came to Jackson for in the first place—what to do with the rest of his life. He lay there thinking of Sara's words to him in the meadow, and the warmth of Sara's meadow came back to him as he drifted off.

Forty-eight hours later, Dean was released from the hospital, with strict instructions to avoid strenuous physical activity for a month, but the missing piece of this whole adventure, the solution to Jordy's murder was still bothering him. He went through all the clues again. He thought about what they'd found in Torino's wrecked car.

His cell buzzed and he picked it up. "Hey, Mark."

"Hi, Dean. How are you feeling? I called the hospital and they said you were discharged."

"Not bad, considering. I'm still having headaches, but the docs say those should go away in time. I'm supposed to rest, but I'm already climbing the walls here. I'm going through the case again. I still believe strongly that Hayden was the target, and in my gut, I don't think it was over a real estate investment. Sheriff Dani said the Jackson billionaires like investing in real estate because it's their way of giving back to the community. What is it that the Chicago mob likes to invest in?"

"Well, Mario had all the currency exchanges, but that's a bit unusual. Mainly drugs, hookers, strip clubs, I guess."

Dean thought about the Starbutts key chain that was with Torino's effects. "Can you do something for me, Mark? Can you do a little digging and find out everything you can about a strip club called Starbutts in Vegas? We found one of their key chains in Torino's stuff."

"Sure thing. Give me a couple of days. When you're feeling better, I'm coming out there. I've heard so much about that place I have to see it."

"That would be fun. I can't wait to show you around. Get back to me as soon as you have something on Starbutts."

Dean sat and thought some more, going through the Big Four motivators that Sheriff Dani liked to promote, but hadn't Sara given him a couple more? Where the fuck was she? She hadn't appeared since his head injury, and that made him worried that he might be "cured." From her. She'd said it was more complicated that the four. She'd added control, betrayal, mental illness. That made him think of Matt Nelson. He'd been preternaturally calm about his wife's affair with Hayden. It was possible, of course, that he was a preternaturally well-adjusted man, but Dean hadn't met a man yet that wasn't susceptible to strong emotion from jealously and betrayal. And he knew that Matt was an avid poker player. Could there be a Vegas connection between Matt Nelson and Rosati or Torino? Maybe Mark would come up with something.

Twenty-four hours after that he had incurable cabin fever. He couldn't bear to watch daytime television and was spending his time experimenting with the gift bag of new EV products Daryl had dropped off. He really liked the moisturizing body wash—his skin had become a flaky mess from the desert-dry Wyoming summer—and the vitamin supplements had the exact same formula as the more expensive brand he had purchased from the health food store. He looked at the "Nature's Viagra" bottle and smiled. In spite of the joke he had played on Daryl before his polygraph test, he didn't expect to be experimenting with that product anytime soon.

A nostalgic raft trip down the Snake had been on his agenda since he'd come into town, but the Jordy murder case had sidetracked it. So he invited Hayden, and Hayden offered to get the raft and the equipment together. They decided to make a day of it, stop on the river for a picnic along the way, and pretty soon the party had expanded to include Eliza, Daryl, Amber and Tatiana.

The morning of the trip, Dean still hadn't heard from Mark and decided he'd put a little pressure on Matt. He drove over to his house. The Teton Village ski villa was huge, and just as he remembered it. He could never get used to the extravagance of the super wealthy. It wasn't that they were elegantly designed, but they had to be a super-sized, almost a monument to capitalism. Dean wondered if someday a future race of beings would view these as the ruins of ancient Rome, the last remainders of a society dedicated to greed. There was a landscaper planting flowers next to the door when Dean walked up. He looked up and said, "He's not home."

"Do you know if he's in town?"

"I don't think so. I know he's been out of town for a while. I don't know if he's back yet."

Dean made a mental note to check in with Mark as soon as he got back from the trip.

Chapter 47

MATT Nelson had wanted Hayden Smith dead from the moment he'd found out that he was dating his wife—and the original plan had been that only Hayden was to die. Then he had downloaded a video from Eliza's computer while she was gone. She was so fucking stupid —she still kept the key to her house in the same hiding place outside, hadn't changed the password on the alarm or on her Mac. So, whenever she was away from home, he would go through her things, and that's how he found out the truth about her. Even after watching the video he still may have let her live, but then she told him she was pregnant. What a fucking slut. She couldn't even wait until their divorce was final to get knocked up. When he'd met her he thought Eliza was going to be the perfect wife and the mother of his children—she reminded him so much of his mother, the dark Middle Eastern beauty, and he had treated her like that, like a lady, just as his mother had taught him—but Eliza had ended up having none of his mother's old-world manners, modesty, or morals.

He had once overheard Hayden at the next booth at a restaurant in town—a reference to Eliza's husband as a little Caspar Milquetoast kind of guy, and that had infuriated him. He wondered if Hayden would think he was so Caspar Milquetoast if he knew he had the phone number of a hit man in the top drawer of his desk. He'd met Torino at Starbutts, the strip club he frequented when he was in Vegas for his poker tournaments. That's also where he'd met Mario Rosati, and that little investment hadn't been much, it made a nice cash return, but more importantly it insured he had girls that knew how to treat him right when he was in Vegas. He'd spent the better part of an evening with Torino over a year ago at the club, and Matt bragged about his auto parts empire. When Matt asked, "And what do you do," Torino had given him a grin that made him believe every word of his reply, "I hurt people for money. Hurt them as bad as you want. You ever need anybody hurt, you call this number." He wrote a phone number on the match cover of the strip club and slipped it into Matt's coat pocket.

And so he had called that number—and the great professional hit man from Chicago had ended up being a monumental fuck up. He had killed the wrong guy, couldn't even drive back to the airport without killing himself, and the upshot was that the detective out here from Chicago had started sniffing around. Luckily, the Chicago cop seemed as big a fuck up as Torino. Was everyone from Chicago incompetent? Seemed that way.

He pressed the computer key and ran the video again. He tried not to watch it too often because every time he did, he wanted to go to her house at night, take the hidden key and slit her throat in her own bed. It would be so satisfying to watch her gurgle on her own blood and die, but he knew he had to throttle himself. He had to kill her in a way that couldn't lead back to him. So he tried to stay away from the video. But he couldn't.

In the video, Eliza was on the bed in her bedroom—the same bedroom she'd shared with Matt when they were together, and now it was about to be defiled. She was naked on the bed, and spread eagled, her arms and legs tied to the bed posts. She was blindfolded but not gagged, and she was saying the filthiest things to Hayden, who was off camera. She was taunting him, asking him if he was man enough take her, to make her his slut. Evidently, the taunting only served to get Hayden worked up, because when he entered the picture, he had the largest erection that Matt had ever seen, even in porn, and he was holding an industrial-sized vibrator. He started working on Eliza with it, pressing its humming knob on her until she was moaning, then backing off. She would swear at him, demanding that he finish her off, and he laughed and came to her with the vibrator again, and backed off again. Finally, after repeating this several times, he pushed it into her, penetrating her vagina, and she screamed in orgasm. As soon as it was apparent she was finished, Hayden grabbed her head, stuffing his engorged organ into her mouth, and humped violently, both hands holding her head. She would gag, so he would stop, and then start humping again. After about five minutes of this, he pulled out and sprayed what seemed like a gallon of his disgusting juice on her face. When he was finished, he took the camera off the tripod and zoomed in on Eliza's face showing the full degree of their depravity. He pulled the blindfold off her, and Eliza looked up at him. "That was so fucking hot," she said. "Next time I'm tying you up."

As the video ended, Matt tried to calm himself. He was unbelievably aroused, but also unbelievably disgusted and unbelievably enraged. It was time, he thought. It was time to pay them both back for what they had done to him.

He took a breath and dialed her number, "Hey Eliza, just checking in. Wanted to see how your pregnancy is going," he said in his sweetest, gentlest voice, the voice he used for women, the one his mother had taught him.

"I'm feeling really good... the doctor says everything is going fine. How are you?"

"You know, busy with work, traveling a lot. I wondered if you might want to get together for lunch on Saturday."

"Oh, I'd love to, but you know that cop from Chicago, Dean Wister? He's taking Hayden and me on a raft trip on the Snake on Saturday. I guess he used to be a river guide a few years back. We're going to stop for a picnic on the river at that little beach area—you know the one I'm talking about? You and I were there once. How about we get together some time next week?"

"I'll check my schedule and get back to you. Enjoy your raft trip. It should be fun. Talk soon."

He hung up the phone and thought for a minute. And then he replayed the video again and again. Glaring at Eliza's face on the screen, he finally let go of every emotion he had swallowed over the last two years, allowing his volcano of rage to erupt, and spit out the words he had been suppressing with every ounce of his psyche, "Let the blood flow."

Chapter 48

IT was a beautiful day on the Snake, warm enough not to need wet suits, but not so hot as to fry them if they were on the river for several hours. Hayden pulled the raft on a trailer behind his truck and picked up Eliza. Dean and Cheney drove separately, and Daryl, Amber, and Tatiana met them at the boat launch where they loaded the picnic coolers onto the raft. Hayden and Daryl sat in the front, the girls and Cheney in the middle, and Dean sat on the back end of the raft to guide and steer.

"I hope I'm not too rusty," Dean said. "It's been over a decade since I ran this river. I got a briefing from one of the guides yesterday, though, and not much has changed. Actually the river is quite a bit lower. It should be fun but not too scary."

Amber looked up with her big blue eyes and said, "Too bad. I like scary."

The guys were dressed in t-shirts and board shorts, the girls in swimsuits. It was an unusually warm day, and icy cold Snake River water splashing over them through the rapids would be a welcome cool off. Eliza's suit showed off her pronounced baby bump, and Dean wondered when she was due. As they launched the raft and started down the calm part of the river, Dean had a great view of the women who sat below him. "I have to say, I don't know which view is better, the view outside the boat, or the beautiful view inside the boat." The women pretended to blush, the men laughed and the raft slid down the calm waters.

The Snake in the upper part of the Canyon, before the rapids, is calm and scenic. The party observed a pair of bald eagles dive-bombing the river for fish and returning to the nest to feed the chicks. A moose and her calf waded in the weedy shallows, munching on vegetation. Dean thought about the group he was with today. He had always been a loner, until he met Sara, but the people who were in this boat with him now seemed like family to him. In many ways, they were his family now. Eliza had that pregnant glow, and Hayden had recently confided how truly happy he was to be a father. They were such a good looking couple—they looked as though they belonged on the cover of an outdoor adventure magazine. Amber had quit dancing. Daryl needed more hands in his business after taking over all of Boris's downline, and Tatiana was helping out as translator /language instructor. Dean looked at Tatiana, who sat quiet and contemplative. Her physical wounds had healed, but Dean was thankful that Daryl and Amber had adopted her into their family. From the outside it would seem they should have nothing in common, but they had managed to find a special bond with each other.

After an hour, they came to a sandy beach—not a beach, really, but a postage-stamp-sized level section of sand that led up into thick pine forest. They stopped, unloaded their coolers, lay down the blankets, and ate, drank, and celebrated the end of summer.

Mark Jeffrey looked at the information that had just come in from the FBI's Washington bureau. He'd discovered quickly that the Starbutts strip club was owned by two different LLCs, one in Nevada that was owned by a company to which he was able to trace to Mario Rosati, the other by a different company located in the Caymans. The Caymans have laws protecting the anonymity of corporate records, but recently those laws had been loosened a bit, and after a few days he'd been able to get some relevant information via the Washington office. The report he just received had listed the corporate agent as an attorney in Jackson, Wyoming. He'd searched that attorney's filings in the state and discovered the attorney was also the agent for the auto parts conglomerate owned by Matt Nelson. He picked up the phone and dialed Dean, but the line call went to his voice mail. "Dean, good work. I got the info on Starbutts and guess who is a part owner of the club along with Rosati? Matt Nelson.

So, we've got the Rosati connection. He has to be the one. Call me and let's discuss getting his phone records, search warrants, etc. Great job!"

Matt Nelson sat in his truck just off the road at Hoback Junction. There was only one route into the Snake River Canyon, and he knew the party would need to pass by. He didn't know the exact time they'd pass, however, so he had been sitting there all morning, fueling his fury with Red Bull, black coffee, and the video he had downloaded onto his phone. He thought his plan provided him with a reasonable get-away strategy but, in the end, it was OK with him however it ended. He didn't want to live any longer with the public humiliation Hayden and his estranged wife had bestowed upon him. He still could not understand how she'd fooled him, how the slut could have disguised her true nature for so long, but today she would pay for her tricks. Both of them—all of them, if necessary, would pay in blood for their sins.

He had been in his truck at Hoback Junction for over three hours, working himself into a frenzy of arousal and hateful vengeance, when Hayden's truck drove by. Matt pulled out and followed, making sure to keep a reasonable distance. When the truck turned off at the boat launch, Matt continued several miles down the road, to the spot he had picked out the day before, with a clear view of the picnic area.

Parking was restricted on the road, and he couldn't risk his truck getting ticketed today, so he had to park at one of the legal turnoffs and walk nearly two miles through the thick forest to his sniper's nest. He took his gun and a small backpack and started off. Since the raft would move faster than his hiking pace through the woods, he couldn't linger. He kept up a brisk pace and, even with the bushwhacking he'd had to do on his scouting mission the day before, he was winded when he got to his sniper's nest, the one with a near perfect view of his target. He was exhausted and sweaty from running up the trail, jittery from the Red Bull and quart of coffee, but also exhilarated as he thought about the enormity of the act he was about to perform. He calmed as he looked at the log gun rest he had assembled the day before, and as he went about the chore of setting up his shooter's seat, he reminded himself of the righteousness of his vengeance.

Kneeling now, he took aim at the beach area about a hundred yards down the slope where his targets would be. He raised his gun and looked through the scope, and— Damn. Even though the rifle was steadied by the gun rest, the image in his scope was a little shaky. All that caffeine and Red Bull, he figured. He put down the gun and stood up, thinking. He walked around in a circle, took out the water bottle and gulped it down. He took a few deep breaths. That was better. He just needed to relax.

He closed his eyes and visualized the group sitting at the beach, talking, smiling, unaware of what was about to happen. He imagined Hayden and Eliza laying bloody and dead, and Dean looking around in panic. He smiled, took another breath, and returned to his perch.

Dean was throwing a stick into the river which Cheney was having a great time fetching. Dean would fake throw the stick, but Cheney would not fall for any of the feints and was barking loudly. Hayden was sitting on a cooler his back leaning against a pine tree, laughing at their game, when the first bullet hit. It wasn't a bad shot, actually, from a 30.06 at a hundred yards, down a steep slope, from the sun into the shade, by a shooter whose hands were jittery thanks to a nervous system overwhelmed with stimulants and the anxiety that would come naturally to someone attempting his first murder. One or more of those factors caused that first bullet to hit exactly one inch above Hayden's skull and splinter the trunk of the pine above his head. The second and third shots were not nearly as close, not with the party scrambling and screaming, the targets heeding Dean's instructions to move back into the woods, out of site of the unknown sniper. Dean had no idea where that first bullet had come from. But the second and third bullets had permitted him to gauge the general direction of the shooter.

"All of you stay put. Get on your cell, Hayden, and call nine-eleven. I'm going after him."

Dean grabbed his gun and headed up the slope. He was amazed that details were coming back to him from his guiding more than a decade ago. The picnic beach was not new to him—one of his frequent trips had featured that exact stop. They didn't carry the picnic supplies on their rafts then—back in his day, the picnics were set up by river guide wannabes who would bring the food and drink down from the closest parking space up on the road. He remembered the short-cut path that led straight to that parking space from the beach.

Three shots, then nothing. He figured the shooter was headed back to his car—there was no other way for him to escape—and Dean needed to beat him there. There was a dull ache in his head, mostly deadened by adrenalin, as he ran up the path. He figured it was about a mile to the road and he hoped his stamina had recovered sufficiently to make it. By the time he broke through the forest into the clearing of the parking area, the pain in his head had become like a hot poker jabbing over and over again into his brain, and his lungs were on fire. Just before he came out of the woods into the clearing, he bent over and gulped a few breaths, his head hurting so badly now that he thought he might pass out. His vision was not exactly blurred, but he was seeing two of everything. He pulled out his gun, walked out of the clearing, and—Shit. There were two Matt Nelsons approaching the car. He raised his gun, and yelled, "Hey, Matt."

Matt turned around but didn't speak. Instead he raised his weapon. Dean shot six times, alternating between the Matt Nelson on the left and the one on the right, and landed two bullets in the middle of Matt's chest and one in his neck. He was dead before Dean could walk the ten yards to the car.

The evening of the ambush, after Dean had filed his report, he and Sheriff Dani shared a drink at Rendezvous Bistro in Jackson. "I understand his motivation. But how did an auto parts executive from Wyoming hook up with a hit man from Chicago?" Dani asked.

Dean just smiled, "Starbutts."

Dani looked confused. "He met him at Starbucks?"

"No, Starbutts. Butts, not bucks. It's a strip club in Vegas. If you look through Torino's effects, there's a Starbutts key chain. Did Matt go to Vegas much?"

"Quite often—he was a pro Texas Hold'em player."

"And also a fan of strip clubs, apparently. Dani, do you remember you told me that the billionaire investors in Jackson Hole think of investing in real estate as giving back to the community? Well, Chicago gangsters are much more self-aware. They like to invest in cash businesses, and strip clubs in particular. It seems that our Matt Nelson was an investor in Starbutts along with Mario Rosati. Maybe Matt thought investing in strip clubs was his way of giving back to women."

Dean thought of all the details that went into solving a crime. All the what if's that determined whether justice was done, or the criminal lived on, free to victimize someone else. Sometimes you solved a crime because of a mistake by a stupid criminal, and sometimes through damned good police work alone. But there was something else, too—the unexplained coincidences in life that lead us to where we end up, that led him to Jackson Hole, that led him to Sara, and eventually had led to this moment.

"If Torino hadn't hit that deer, who knows if we would ever have solved any of this. And Boris would still be running his girls." Then Dean thought of Sara. "There's the car thing, too." He hadn't actually intended to say it aloud.

"The car thing?"

"Yeah, you know. Matt was in the auto parts business. So naturally he hired a hit man named Torino."

Sheriff Dani wasn't sure if that was joke or not but decided that it had to be. "So, Dean, since you're well enough to get in gun fights again, when are you coming to work for me?"

Dean chuckled. "I'm thinking about it. But I need to go back to Chicago next week to take care of some things. I'll make a decision soon, and I really appreciate the offer."

"Take all the time you need. I'm grateful you were here this summer."

"I am too, Sheriff. You really don't know how grateful I am." He patted Dani on the back as he walked out the door and got into his Jeep.

At Matt's house, they found the video on his computer. It was right on the screen, no digging required. On the same desk was the match cover with the Chicago phone number belonging to Torino's brother's business in Chicago. Eventually, they'd found that Matt's phone records showed a call to that number the week before Jordy's murder. The night of Jordy's murder, there was a call to Matt from a throwaway phone with a Chicago area code.

Epilogue

SENATOR Tom McGraw and Charlotte lay together in the master bedroom at the house
on Granite Wayy. Tom looked at Charlotte. She
was so perfect for him. He had tried to deny
this part of himself for so long. He had first ad-
mitted to himself that he liked men during his
student days at the University of Wyoming, and
actually had his first guilt-filled affair with one
of his fraternity brothers. Then he met Lydia
and tried to put it behind him, struggling with
his desires for years. But he finally realized he
couldn't suppress his sexual desire for men—
it was just part of how he was wired. The hard-
est part was that he didn't feel his desires were
normal. That changed the first time he had sex
with a transgender man. The illusion was com-
forting to him. He could pretend in a certain
way that the object of his desire was female,
and he didn't fully understand why, but it sort
of worked for him. And Charlotte, well, she was
the grand illusion, in every way that he could
think of.

"So the FBI is releasing a report tomorrow

clearing me and justifying the shooting as self-defense," Tom said.

"I told you Mario didn't have anything to do with the Jordy Smith murder. So now is your conscience relieved?"

"A little. But it was still stupid for me to let us be blackmailed to begin with. I'm never going to let that happen again. Even if it means the end of my career."

"Hopefully that will never happen. We're more careful now." She knew discovery was a real danger as long as they were together, however, and it was going to get more dangerous in the coming months. "You know this isn't the end of it. The other candidates aren't going to let it go. It's going to follow you throughout the campaign. They're already calling you 'Quick Draw McGraw' in the *NY Post*."

"That might be good. My polling numbers are way up since the shooting. It seems people like the idea of a tough guy as their president. It's like when Reagan was threatening to build Star Wars, and it got the Russians in a panic. But I think they'll try to make something of your link to Mario and your contributions to my campaign."

"I've got you covered on that. I made contributions to both parties and every potential presidential candidate. Remember, we aren't going to up my contribution to your campaign anyway until we really need the money."

"And now with the gun manufacturers stepping all over each other to get on board, I may not even need your money. What's even funnier, I think I can speak my mind for reasonable gun regulation. No one can challenge me 'cuz of my street cred." They both howled at that. Tom grabbed Charlotte and pulled her close. "How are you going to like being the First Mister-Ess?"

Dean and Cheney met Hayden at the Sinclair mini-mart at Hoback Junction. Hayden had been cryptic, but had insisted he see Dean before he left for Chicago. He said he had something urgent to show him.

"So, Hayden, you aren't involved in any more crimes or being chased by any more jealous husbands, are you? 'Cause if you are, I can't deal with it. I've had enough for the summer."

"No, no, nothing like that. It's all good, just need to show you something before you go back. It's pretty important."

They got into Hayden's Land Rover and turned onto a dirt road behind the mini-mart.

"This is a forest service road. It's not plowed in the winter, so the only way in or out during about six months of the year is snowmobile. There's a log cabin about two and a half miles up the road here. I bought it from the bank a couple of years ago as a foreclosure, but it's pretty much unsellable because of the access. I know you're considering taking a job with the sheriff. And I thought of you."

Dean was non-committal. Even if he did decide to move out here, he didn't think he would be interested in a piece of shit log cabin you could only get to by snowshoe or snowmobile.

The road wound up the ridge from the river through a thicket of aspens. When they pulled through the aspens, however, what he saw left him stunned. The "log cabin" was a huge house made from rough logs and stone, with a wrap-around porch and panoramic windows looking down the ridge at the Snake River below.

"This is an in-holding," Hayden said. "That means it's private property surrounded by national forest. No other houses will build around you. It sits on five acres, and there's river access."

Dean was speechless. He walked up to the porch and sat down, amazed and silenced by the breathtaking view.

"Now, I know that you couldn't afford this property on law enforcement salary, but if you want it, I'll do whatever it takes to make it affordable for you. You saved my life. You saved Eliza's life. And I would love to have you as my friend and neighbor."

Dean still didn't speak. He just sat, drinking in the air, the landscape, imagining himself spending the rest of his life waking up to this each day.

Finally, Hayden said. "Well, what do you think?"

Dean looked down at Cheney. "What do you think, buddy?" He looked at Hayden and smiled. "We both think it's grand. It's really grand."

The trip to Sara's Meadow was exactly the way it had been when Dean was laying in the hospital. The same blue sky, the mountain breeze, the fragrance of the pine, the chattering of the chipmunks. But he was different this time. He still ached for Sara. He still thought of her every day. But now, when he woke up in the morning, his first thought wasn't the dread of another day without her. He wanted to live. Not just for her, but for himself as well. Even though so many bad things had happened over the last three months, he couldn't help but think somehow the summer had been a gift from the universe that he didn't fully comprehend. Even so, even without understanding it, he was able to gratefully embrace and accept it.

Sitting underneath their cottonwood, he closed his eyes and said a prayer, meditating in the warm sun. Finally, he pulled a spade from his backpack and dug a hole, and poured in the ashes from the box he had carried with him from Chicago. He looked up at the Grand, and whispered, "Oh, Sara. My sweet, sweet Sara."

THE GRAND PRIZE, the second installment of the Dean Wister Series is coming soon from Dennis D. Wilson. Sign up for our newsletter and be the first to know when it is released.

mailchi.mp/waterstreetpressbooks.com/ waterstreetcrimemailinglist

Get the Water Street Crime Starter Library
FOR FREE

Get four, full-length ebooks—***BLOODY PARADISE***, ***FROM ICE TO ASHES***, ***TROPICAL ICE***, and ***SING FOR THE DEAD***—plus two introductory short stories by the author of **THE GRAND** and lots more exclusive content, all for free!

Building a relationship with our readers is the very best thing about publishing.
We occasionally send newsletters with details on new releases, special offers and other bits of news relating to Water Street Press.

And if you sign up to the mailing list we'll send you all this free stuff:

1.   A free ebook edition of the exotic thriller ***BLOODY PARADISE***—"...a spicy thriller..."

2.   A free ebook edition of the crime thriller ***FROM ICE TO ASHES***—"designed to shoot the ice down your spine..."

3. A free ebook edition of the eco-thriller ***TROPICAL ICE***—"...well-spun, tautly written..."

4. A free ebook edition of the delightfully noir-ish mystery ***SING FOR THE DEAD***—Foreword Reviews' Gold Medal winner

5. A free copy of two introductory short stores from the author of **THE GRAND**—stories that will take you on a thrill ride into the life of your favorite characters from the novel

4. Advance notice about the release of the next novel in the Dean Wister Series, **THE GRAND PRIZE**.

You can get all this and more,
for free, just by signing up at

**mailchi.mp/waterstreetpressbooks.com/
waterstreetcrimemailinglist**

Did you enjoy this book? You can make a big difference for our amazing Water Street Crime authors.

Reviews are the most powerful tools in our arsenal when it comes getting attention for our books. Much as we'd like to, we don't have the financial muscle of a New York publisher. We can't take out full-page ads in the newspaper or put posters on the subway.

(Not yet, anyway).

But we do have something much more powerful and effective than that, and it's something that those publishers would kill to get their hands on.

A committed and loyal bunch of readers.

Honest reviews of our books help bring them to the attention of other readers.

If you've enjoyed this book we would be very grateful if you could spend just five minutes on Amazon or the online vendor of your choice leaving a review (it can be as short as you like).

Here's your direct link to Amazon: **amzn.to/2kfo7vX**

Thank you very much.

About the Author

AFTER a career working in an international consulting firm and as a financial executive with two public companies, Dennis D. Wilson returns to the roots he established as a high school literature and writing teacher. For his debut novel, he draws upon his experiences from his hometown of Chicago; his years of living, working, hiking, and climbing in Jackson Hole; and secrets gleaned from time spent in corporate boardrooms, to craft a political crime thriller straight from today's headlines. Dennis lives in suburban Chicago with his wife and Black Lab Jenny, but spends as much time as he can looking for adventure in the mountains and on his motorcycle. Keep up with him at dennisdwilson.com.

The Grand Prize

ENJOY THIS EXCERPT FROM THE GRAND PRIZE, THE SECOND BOOK IN THE DEAN WISTER SERIES BY DENNIS D. WILSON.

DEAN Wister was more curious than concerned as he waited in Conference Room 1 of the FBI Field Office in Chicago. The listing on the directory indicated a conference room, but that was really just a euphemism that fooled no one, especially the unfortunate individuals, most of whom were in some serious shit, who were invited into the oversized closet for a "conference." Dean looked at the three FBI agents from the Washington, DC office who had just taken a seat and thought if he had to write a description, the kind of physical profile that he was often required to prepare as part of his job on the task force that surveilled the complex and wide-ranging crime syndicate in the Midwest, it would be identical for all three—Race:

cadaver white; Height and Weight: average; Hair: short but not cut in any way faintly resembling stylish; Facial Features: nondescript; Age: mid- to late-thirties; Sense of Humor: none. In more than twelve years of law enforcement he had yet to hear an FBI agent laugh. Although Dean's agency, the Midwest Organized Crime Task Force, was separate from the bureau, as a sister organization, it answered to the FBI, often interfaced with the Chicago FBI office, and had access to the FBI database and other resources. But Dean had never met any of these men. Within the bureau there is little distinction of rank below the very senior levels, and they were all introduced to him as Special Agents, but the silver flecks in the haircut of the one sitting in the middle—Special Agent Gary Eckles—revealed him as the leader of this team, based more on seniority than merit.

"So, Agent Wister, do you know why we're here?"

"To plan my medal ceremony, right?"

The three men looked confused by Dean's attempt to lighten the mood, so he tried again. "Well, my Supervisor said you wanted to interview me about the Rosati case. But I thought that case was closed."

"Technically, it is. But as you know, we have a new Director. And Director Fanning decided to take another look at the Mario Rosati shooting when he took over for Director Vorhies, just to make sure that all the loose ends are tied up. And since you were the lead investigator on this case, we decided it would be helpful if you could walk us through your involvement step-by-step. You can learn only so much from the files, which we've spent the last week or so reviewing. Oh, and we need to inform you that this interview is being recorded, but of course you already understand that."

Dean nodded, but didn't say anything as he looked up at the video camera hovering above the agent's head that was focused on his face like a robotic metal owl. He knew there was an identical camera behind him that would record the face of the agents interrogating him. The room had no windows, and everything in it was some version of gray: the walls, desk, chairs, even the ceiling. Dean called this color, which was, for some reason that escaped him, now so popular with toney decorators in the gold coast of Chicago, FBI gray. When his wife Sara had wanted to use gray as the color scheme in their Lincoln Park townhome, Dean had joked that there could be *no f'ing gray* in his house. Although the only color seemingly permitted in the bureau was gray, the bureau had acquiesced to their outside decorator's demands and allowed three shades to be prescribed in the written office manual that governed everything from coffee cups to mechanical pencils.

"Agent Wister, I see that you nodded, but could you verbally affirm that you understand this interview is being recorded?"

"Yes, of course, I understand."

"Great, then let's get right to it. We'll just start from the beginning, and you can lead us through how the case came to you in the first place. I understand you became involved when you were in Wyoming? Your jurisdiction is the Midwest Region. What were you doing out there?"

"Well, I was on vacation in Jackson Hole last summer when I was contacted by the Teton County Sheriff. Eddie Torino had been found dead in a car wreck in the Snake River. I knew of Torino from my work with the Task Force in Chicago, and was called in to consult on the case. They thought maybe I could figure out what a mobster was doing out there."

"And you initially thought Torino might be involved in the murder of a local citizen?"

"Yes, Jordy Smith, a real estate office manager, had been murdered late the previous night, and it looked like it could've been a hit. That fit Torino's background, so that made it suspicious to the local Sheriff, and they tracked me down to take a look at it."

"What made you suspect that Torino might be working for Mario Rosati in Chicago?"

"We suspected that Rosati had hired Torino for hits in the past. Rosati was a pretty notorious figure in Chicago, and as I am sure you know, he's been the subject of many investigations by our Task Force and even the bureau over the years. Well, as it turned out, Rosati didn't have anything to do with the murder. We found out later that Torino had been killed for a much different reason. But during the course of the murder investigation, we discovered that Rosati's gang was involved in other crimes in Teton County. Rosati was in the prostitution and human-trafficking business with another Jackson Hole resident, a Russian national, Boris Birkov."

"But that wasn't the only Jackson Hole resident that Rosati was involved with, was it, Agent Wister?"

"No, it turned out that he was also laundering money through a Chicago bank, and their CEO, Charles Kidwell, has a home in Jackson Hole."

"And you arranged for Mr. Kidwell to obtain immunity for his testimony against Mr. Rosati, is that right?"

"Well, I was involved in the negotiations, but the actual decision to grant immunity is above my pay grade, as I am sure you know."

"We want to ask you a few things about your involvement with Mr. Kidwell, because there isn't a lot of information in the files concerning that. Can you tell us what you know about the relationship between Mr. Kidwell and Senator Thomas McGraw?"

Dean frowned, and he could tell that his grimace was noticed by the agents. The inability to maintain a poker face when he was upset was one of his weaknesses; he had about as much control over his facial expressions as an infant tasting spinach for the first time. Kidwell and McGraw? So that was what this was about. Former Director Vorhies had been an old friend of Senator McGraw, who was presently leading the field for the Republican nomination for President. But Vorhies had just left the bureau to take a high-paying job in the private sector, and Assistant Director Fanning, a Democratic Party insider, had taken over. "I don't really have any first-hand knowledge of their relationship."

"Well, didn't the Senator kill Rosati in a shoot-out in the Senator's hotel room in DC?"

"All I really know about it is the report issued by the bureau that ruled the shooting was justified self-defense. As you know from the files, I was unconscious in a hospital in Jackson Hole when that occurred. One of Boris Birkov's men had given me a pretty good blow to the head when I was trying to rescue one of the girls they had kidnapped into prostitution."

"And wasn't Mr. Kidwell present at the DC shoot-out?"

"From the reports I've read, I understand that to be true. But again, I wasn't there. And I don't know why you think I would have any more information about it than you do."

"Agent Wister, do you have any reports or other information about Charles Kidwell or Senator McGraw that you have not included in your official reports?"

Dean stopped breathing for a moment. What could this be about? Where would they get the idea that he might have withheld information about the pair? He could feel the adrenalin start to flow; he was not used to being on this side of the interrogation table, and he took a deep breath. "Ah, no, I do not."

"Have you ever accepted any gifts or other consideration from either Charles Kidwell or Senator McGraw?"

What the fuck? Dean could feel his face getting warm as the blood was diverted to his brain, and he knew it was starting to take on a shiny crimson, the biological facial tell that he was angry. *Gifts? Do they mean gifts as in bribes?* "No, of course not." He instantly regretted letting his irritation show on his face and in his voice.

"Have you ever ridden on the private jet owned by Mr. Kidwell?"

An inner voice came to him now. It was the one that sometimes came to his rescue when he was stressed, when his reptilian brain was trying to take over his body, urging him to fight or flee. He hadn't called on that voice for several months, but he reached out for it now. *Calm yourself. Stay in control. Keep your voice in a monotone. Don't let them see that they're getting to you.* Dean took a deep breath. "I accompanied him on his private jet when he flew from Jackson to Chicago for his immunity conference."

"But that isn't the only time that you flew on the jet, is it?"

"Well, it was a round trip. I returned to Jackson Hole on his jet after the conference."

"Did Mr. Kidwell or any other government officials accompany you on that flight?"

"No, Mr. Kidwell had other business in Chicago, so I came back by myself."

"So, you accepted a flight on Mr. Kidwell's private jet to return to your Jackson Hole vacation?"

"Well, it wasn't like that. I was still working on the Jordy Smith murder case."

"But hadn't your supervisor told you that your work on the case was finished? And didn't he inform you you should turn it over to the local officials since it was no longer FBI business?"

"No, I don't believe that's true."

"Agent Wister, our records show otherwise. But let's talk about something else. During the course of this case, did you kill a man when you were in Jackson?"

"As I'm sure you already know, that's how the murder case was solved. I killed the man who ambushed a group that I was with in Jackson."

"Of course, I'm aware of that shooting. I apologize. I should have been clearer. It seems you had quite an eventful summer, Agent Wister. I'm talking about the other man that you killed … the one you killed with your bare hands in a bar fight."

They were really trying to get to him now, and despite his best efforts, they were succeeding. His temper was now completely ignoring his calming inner voice. He should never have been so naïve. This interview wasn't to clear up any loose ends from the case file. It was intended to paint him as some kind of scapegoat.

Or maybe it was something else. "It wasn't a bar fight. He attacked me from behind while I was walking to my car, and I broke his arm. He died when a bone fragment went to his lung."

"This other man you killed, which you say was not a bar fight, but it was just outside the bar you both had been drinking in. This deceased man, Fletcher Barns—wasn't he a suspect in the Jordy Smith case when this happened?"

"I wouldn't call him a suspect."

"Agent Wister, we have in your reports that he was on your list as a 'person of interest' and there is a memo in the file summarizing your interrogation of him. Was there ever a formal inquiry into the altercation that led to the death of Fletcher Barns?"

"It was reviewed by the County Attorney in Wyoming."

"But there wasn't a formal inquest, isn't that correct?"

"I'm sure the County Attorney followed the appropriate procedures, and I was cleared of any misconduct."

"Agent Wister, you say you were on vacation in Wyoming when you became involved in this case, but that isn't true is it? Wasn't it really a leave of absence?"

"I think it was called a leave, yes."

"And why were you granted a leave of absence?"

"Well, I'd been working a lot of hours. I had booked a lot of overtime, and vacation time."

Agent Eckles paused. And then he opened a manila file folder from the pile in front of him, studied it for a long moment, and looked Dean straight in the eye. "But you didn't request the leave, isn't that correct? Isn't it true that your supervisor requested it on your behalf, because he was alarmed by your mental state after your wife died?"

Dean glared at Eckles and did not answer the question.

Eckles closed the folder, folded his hands, and then leaned forward and spoke very slowly and deliberately. "Dean, isn't it true that you believe you see your deceased wife, that she actually appears to you in the flesh, and that you still have conversations with her?"

Dean gulped, and tried to speak but couldn't. How could they possibly know anything about these hallucinations of his wife Sara? The only person he'd told about this was his psychologist. They must have gotten to his therapist in some way. And if they were talking to his therapist, then that must mean that they were trying very hard to target him. All this was bubbling from his unconscious to his conscious mind, threatening to boil over, and as those thoughts came churning to the top of his consciousness, it took every bit of his well-trained emotional suppression techniques to prevent him from acting on one dominant compulsion: to jump across the table, grab Agent Eckles by the throat, squeeze until his tongue stuck straight out from his mouth, watch his blood-red face drain to cadaver pale, and then feel the utmost satisfaction as the life flickered out of his FBI gray eyes. But instead, he stared right into the FBI agent's hound-dog face, and said in the coldest voice that he could muster, "Agent Eckles, kiss my hillbilly ass. This interview is over."